Dead or Alive

Jane Blythe

Bear Spots Publications
Melbourne Australia

bearspotspublications@gmail.com

ISBN: 099241802X
ISBN-13: 978-0-9924180-2-1

Cover designed by QDesigns

PROLOGUE
TWENTY-ONE YEARS AGO
MAY 6TH

Safe for another day.

Safe forever now.

Fingering the gun that felt so heavy in her tiny hands.

She was sitting on the front stoop, alone in the warm night, gazing up at the stars in the sky above. Not that she really liked the nighttime. It wasn't that the days were much better but at least things didn't get quite as bad as they did once the sun went down. Taking a little comfort in the fact that she wasn't the only one who suffered here. She pondered, as best as a child could, whether that made her a bad person.

This was by far the worst foster home she had ever lived in. Not that she could remember all of them, but of the ones she could recall she had reasonably pleasant memories. Most of her foster parents had been somewhat cold and distant, but they had always made sure she had clothes to wear and food to eat, and usually there weren't too many other kids there either.

Here however, she was one of probably twenty children. Most came and went rather quickly, some, like herself, had been here for what felt like forever. Here she never had enough to eat, any clothes she did get were usually fourth or fifth hand, like the pajamas she wore now. They were a couple of sizes too small and even though they were the ones she had been given the first night she came to live here, eighteen months ago, they were still her only pair. They were too tight and revealed too much of her body, although she had to admit they were an improvement on what she had been wearing an hour ago.

Some of the kids she met here were nice, some were not, all were terrified of their foster parents and the couple's creepy son. The boy loved to torture his younger foster brothers and sisters, burn them with cigarettes, break their arms, put a straightjacket on them and lock them in a closet. When he finished with his evil games he would leave them in the huge shared bedroom, used by most of the kids living here, and there they would be found by one of their foster parents. They never helped the children though. They'd find them injured and in pain, take them to the hospital if needed, then deliver them right back here so their son could hurt them all over again.

They never helped because they'd rather hurt.

What her foster parents did was so much worse than what their son did.

In the early evening, after the children had been sent to bed, her foster parents would sneak quietly into the room to choose one of their small charges to play with that night. Sometimes it would just be the three of them, but other times her foster parents invited one of their friends over. Those nights were the worst.

Tonight she had made a decision. She was done. She wasn't going to do it anymore. She was out of here.

That's why she was sitting here on the front stoop. She was trying to build up enough courage to do it, to leave. Every time she thought she was ready, she'd stand and take a couple of steps down the stairs, but then she'd get scared and scurry back up to the top.

She was scared to stay and scared to go.

It was the woods, she convinced herself, they were scary at night. The thick trees blocked out the light of the moon. When the wind blew the branches scraped together like the sound of approaching footsteps. All the nighttime creatures scuttled about, making creepy noises of their own. But it was her own thumping heart that made the scariest noise of all.

Wishing that the house wasn't so far away from everything else, that the road was just nearby, that she wasn't all alone in the deep dark woods. But then again if it were right near the road that would mean she couldn't use her excuse. It wasn't really the creepy woods that were keeping her from running it was also the fact that she had no money, no food, no clothes, and nowhere to go.

Convincing herself that anything out there had to be at least a hundred times better than living in this house of horrors. Without another thought, she jumped up, held her breath and hurried down the stairs. Letting the air whoosh out of her lungs, she looked back up at the door, and decided that wasn't so bad.

She was just about to start down the long, winding dirt track that served as a driveway when suddenly she was caught in the headlights of an approaching car. She froze, her hand tightening around the gun. She wasn't going to let another person lay their hands on her body.

Screeching to a stop just feet from her, a man bounded from the car, he had a kind face but she'd been fooled before and had learnt never to judge a book by its cover.

Catching sight of the gun she clutched, pointed in his direction, the man slowed and held up his hands. "It's okay," he told her, his voice was sweet and deep.

He took a step towards her.

She raised the gun.

"It's okay," he said again, pausing, "I'm here to help you."

She'd heard those words before, so many times before, from more men than she could count. As this man took another step towards her, his face blurred and morphed into that of her foster dad, then continued to spin and change from one face to another, each of the men who had hurt her.

No longer able to hear the words the man was saying as he came towards her, she heard a scream escape from her own throat and then a deafening bang ripped through the universe, stealing her sense of hearing altogether.

The man in front of her looked surprised, his mouth open in a wide O, his hands pressed to his chest and came away bloody, then he looked at her, his brown eyes locking onto hers. They seemed to stay that way forever, joined only by their eyes, and then he dropped and she saw the bright red circle that was quickly taking over his chest.

Bright light flooded out from the house behind her and she turned to see it lit up like a Christmas tree she vaguely remembered from one of her previous foster homes, they never had one here she thought dazedly. Faces appeared in the windows like bizarre ornaments, her foster parents bodies filled the open doorway. Their faces angry, their mouths moving, she knew they were yelling at her but she couldn't hear the words they were speaking.

As she turned back to the man who now lay in the dirt, so close she could reach out and touch him, she finally registered the words he had spoken. He had said he was with child protective services, he was going to take her away from here, he was going to save her.

Realizing what she had done she dropped to her knees beside the man, desperately pressing her tiny hands against the hole in his chest, wanting to stop the blood that poured out like a fire hydrant when it has been hit. She was crying, her tears mixing with his blood as they splashed down onto the man's shirt.

Feeling a hand on her shoulder she looked up into her brother's caramel colored eyes, wide with shock as he took in the scene before him. Then he knelt and gently pulled her hands from the man's chest, he was speaking but the sound was like a dull, distant drone. Then her ability to hear came back with a rush as she heard her brother's words, "he's dead," he whispered as he hugged her tightly. "It'll be okay, Matilda."

JUNE 12TH

2:34 P.M.

"Come on, mommy. Please!" he begged. Then he gave her what they both knew was his most winning smile, "pretty please with cherries on top."

Lila Abbott laughed down at her five-year-old son, laying a hand on his head she tussled his thick mop of red curls. "I'm sorry, honey, but you're not big enough to sit in the front seat. When you're older . . ."

"You always say that," little Joey complained. "What if I never get older, then I won't get to do nothing fun."

"'Anything' fun," Lila corrected automatically.

Changing tracks, Joey tried again, "but Dylan's mom lets him sit in the front seat, and I'm bigger than him."

"No, Joey," Lila repeated more sternly, "and I don't want to hear another word about it."

Joey scowled and ran ahead of her the last few yards to the car. Lila sighed and pushed the shopping cart full of groceries and her two-month-old daughter Molly, a little faster to catch up to Joey.

Reaching the car, she found him leaning against it, his arms crossed, and a sulky look on his normally happy little face. Sighing again, Lila sometimes wondered if being a mother got to be any easier as the children grew older.

Lifting the baby from the cart, she opened the door and put Molly in her car seat. Then glancing at Joey decided she'd leave him to sulk for a moment longer while she put the groceries in the trunk.

As she loaded the heavy bags into the car, her mind wandered again. Older children. Teenage children, she thought, and shuddered. She knew that being a mother would definitely not get any easier the older Joey and Molly got. There would be fights about homework, curfews, parties and dating, maybe even drugs and alcohol, tantrums about where to sit in the car seemed trivial now.

Turning to remind Joey of the surprise they had bought daddy for dinner when she felt something cold press against her head.

She gasped, and a voice rasped behind her, "give me the keys to the car."

Lila tried to turn around but an arm gripped her. "Don't try to move, just throw the keys on the ground over there."

Reaching into her pocket for the keys as she said, "please you can have the car, my wallet, anything, just please let me get the baby from the car first."

"Throw the keys on the ground," a different voice ordered, this voice was higher, a woman's voice.

There's two of them, she thought, fighting to keep her panic under control, she could feel tears pricking the back of her eyes, and she was having trouble drawing in enough air to properly fill her lungs. With shaking hands she threw the keys on the ground. "Please just let me get my daughter."

The man behind her moved to get the keys, and quickly she moved towards the still open back door to grab Molly. Lila felt a hand grab her arm, twisting it painfully so that she gasped. She was yanked away from the car, and as she turned she saw a flash of green and blue. Then she was being thrown, and as if in slow motion she heard the crack of a gun. Turning her head in the other direction she saw Joey falling to the ground, a bright red spot growing bigger and bigger on his tiny little chest.

Her son's amber eyes bored into her, begging his mommy to help him. Lila tried to yell his name, but time suddenly sped up as she reached the hard, cold ground, her head smashing into the concrete, and everything went black.

* * * * *

2:48 P.M.

He hoped he hadn't forgotten anything.

Grocery shopping was no longer as simple as it used to be. Eighteen months ago he just popped into the store to grab a few things whenever he needed to, most of the time he'd eaten take out anyway, so his fridge and cupboards had never been well stocked. Now however, with a teenager in the house, he was quickly learning the importance of the kitchen being fully stocked at all times.

Uttering a mopey groan before he caught himself. It wasn't like him to be so whiney and sulky, but lately he'd been feeling restless. He loved having Tessa's niece, Winter, living with them, and he knew how important it was to Tessa that she had her brother back in her life, but it seemed as though the two of them were never alone anymore. Every time he turned around someone was there and he hardly remembered what it was like to have Tessa all to himself.

Just as he'd loaded the grocery bags into the trunk and was pressing the button to unlock his car, Detective Parker Bell heard the unmistakable sound of a gunshot slicing through the air. Turning quickly he heard doors slam and tyres squeal, then a red sedan came rocketing out of a car space, sending a cart full of groceries careening backwards before the driver gunned the engine sending the speeding car aiming right for him.

Grabbing his gun from under his jacket, he aimed a shot at one of the car's tyres, which exploded, sending the sedan fishtailing across the parking lot, bouncing into several other cars on its way. Unfortunately, the driver turned out to be quite proficient and managed to regain control of the wildly swerving vehicle and sail from the parking lot towards the street.

Calling in the incident before heading in the direction the gunshots had originated from, keeping his gun out in front of him, unsure of what or who could be lying in wait. As he rounded a small white car his breath caught in his throat as he discovered not one but two bodies lying motionless on the ground. One was a woman who appeared to be in her late twenties. She lay on her side, a pool of blood around her head, the effect enhanced by the mass of wavy red hair that fanned out like a pillow. The other body was that of a little boy, no more than five or six, laying on his back, his shirt drenched in blood.

Moving quickly, Parker tucked his gun away then knelt at the woman's side and pressed his fingers against her neck to check for a pulse. Finding one, he checked her head, and saw that she had not been shot but appeared instead to have hit it when she fell. Quickly running his hands up and down her body in search of other injuries, he found that she had dislocated her shoulder, but other than that she seemed okay. Maneuvering her into the recovery position, he then turned his attention to the boy.

Kneeling next to the child, Parker tried to force his shaking hands to still as he checked the boy's pulse, which was already very weak. Ripping his shirt off he held it tight against the child's chest, hoping to stem the flow of blood enough to buy him time to get to the hospital. Unwanted memories of the last time he had dealt with a gunshot wound flashing into his mind. Deliberately he pushed them away.

Running footsteps sounded behind him and he turned, keeping his hand pressed to the boy's chest. A woman in her fifties appeared from around the car, her hand flying to her mouth as she took in the two unconscious bodies and the copious amounts of blood.

Desperate for help, Parker hoped the woman could hold herself together, the last thing he needed was another patient to deal with. "I'm a police officer," he told her in what he hoped was his most calm and assuring voice. "An ambulance is on its way but I need you to keep an eye on the woman. Do you know how to check for a pulse?"

The woman wrenched her eyes away from the horrific sight and fixed her gaze on him, nodding slowly. For a second it seemed like she was going to pull it together but then she paled further. "My goodness, how did this happen?" she asked wringing her hands and looking like she might faint at any moment.

Ignoring her question and hoping desperately that the ambulance would get here soon, gesturing to the unconscious woman, "I need you to check her pulse, can you do that for me?"

The lady sank to her knees and laid her fingers uncertainly against the white skin of the younger woman's neck. "Like this?" she asked, her voice quivering.

Parker nodded, "that's great," he encouraged. "Can you feel anything?"

Her face scrunched in concentration and a moment later she nodded.

Footsteps pounded and the faces of two older men, one bald, one not, peered around at them, initially horrified but both managed to quickly pull themselves together.

"What do you need us to do?" the bald man asked, wrenching his eyes away from the two bodies to look at Parker.

"I need someone to help me keep pressure on the wound, and someone to go and wait for the ambulance, then show it where to come," Parker said, relieved that he finally had some help.

"I did a first aid course a few months ago," the man with hair announced as he came to kneel beside Parker and the deathly white child, deliberately avoiding looking at the little boy's face.

As the bald man ran off to wait for the ambulance Parker took the shirt the other man offered and added it to his own, pressing both tightly against the tiny chest. Beneath his hand the little boy's body felt as fragile as a baby bird's, and Parker had to ponder what kind of person could shoot a child in the chest at point blank range.

"She's . . . she's waking up!" the lady's panicked voice tore into his mind.

Spinning around he saw the young woman's eyes fluttering open, jumping up he ran to her side and knelt down, "ma'am, can you tell me your name?" She was struggling to roll to her back, and Parker carefully eased her over, hoping he wasn't doing more harm than good. Her wide brown eyes stared up at him blankly, so he continued in a voice he hoped came out a lot calmer than he felt, "my name's Parker, I'm a police officer. Everything's going to be fine, an ambulance is going to be here any minute, can you tell me what happened?"

The young woman's eyes started to flutter and he thought she was going to pass out again, but all of a sudden she snapped to attention and he saw panic register in her face. "Joey? Where's Joey?" she asked, her voice weak but loaded with fear.

Joey had to be the little boy.

Hoping to distract her for as long as possible in the hope that help would soon be here, "can you tell me where you're hurt? Is your neck sore? Can you move your finger and toes?" trying to remember everything he could from his first aid training.

She tried to move her head but winced in pain, lifting her hand to touch the wound, he grasped it before she could, he wanted to keep her as still and as calm as he possible.

With labored breathing she struggled to speak, "is Joey okay? I thought they shot him but . . ." trying to cover the concern in his eyes but he was too slow, her face growing panicked again she tried to sit up.

He held her still, "ma'am, I need you to stay still for me, you have a head injury . . ."

"No, where's . . . where's . . . my baby . . .?" she was starting to hyperventilate.

Keeping his voice gentle, he took her face in his hands and held her dazed gaze, "ma'am, you need to calm down for me okay? I need you to try and concentrate on your breathing."

With surprising speed, she wrenched her face free and turned, her eyes grew wide at the sight of her child lying on the ground covered in blood, "Joey . . . no . . . baby."

She tried to move towards the little boy, but she was weak and disorientated, and Parker was able to keep her still, but he could feel his own panic begin to well up, where on earth was the ambulance? The child was going to bleed to death before they got here, and his mother had a serious head injury, they both needed to be in the hospital.

He tried once again to calm down the little boy's mother, the anguish in her eyes making him falter, "ma'am, we're taking care of your son, and the ambulance will be here soon, but I really need you to stay still, can you do that for me?"

"Lila?" a female voice breathed behind him. "Oh my gosh!"

Turning, his hands remaining on the woman's shoulders to keep her still, and blinked when he saw an almost identical young woman also in her late twenties, standing behind him.

"Do you know her?" he asked, thinking they may be sisters but hoping they weren't, an hysterical sister on his hands was the last thing he needed.

The newcomer nodded, her face pale with shock, and for a moment Parker was worried she was going to faint, but she quickly recovered and dropped down beside him. "Yes, she's my best friend. I'm a nurse at the hospital where her husband works," tone clipped with concern. Turning her attention to her injured friend, "Lila? Li, honey, look at me," she turned the woman's face away from the horrible sight.

Lila's eyes were fluttering again, her strength quickly failing. "Savannah?" she whispered, staring up with squinting eyes.

Savannah had tears in her eyes but she kept her voice calm and even, "it's me, sweetie. Everything's going to be fine," she soothed, taking her friend's hand before turning back to Parker and asking, "Joey and Molly?"

Frowning, "I'm guessing that's Joey," pointing to the heavily bleeding child, "but who's Molly?"

Savannah wrenched her eyes away from the little boy to narrow them at him, "Molly's the baby. She's not here?" panic making her voice rise an octave.

With a growing sense of dread as realization sunk in. "She must still be in the car."

"Where is the car?" Savannah asked quickly scanning the parking lot.

"Carjacking," he murmured already running through scenarios in his head.

Savannah looked back down at her friend and saw that her eyes had closed. "Lila" she said sharply, and sighed with relief when Lila forced her eyes open. "Hey, stay with me okay?"

"I don't think he's breathing," a frantic male voice announced behind them.

Parker and Savannah both turned to look then exchanged worried glances. Lila caught them both off guard and managed to push herself into a sitting position. Weak and disoriented from her head injury, her strength almost depleted, she could not keep herself upright and fell backwards.

Parker reacted quickly and caught her before her head hit the concrete, lowering her the rest of the way down. Catching Savannah's concerned glance, "go, I'll stay with her."

Jumping up Savannah ran quickly to Joey's side, and after checking to confirm the little boy was not breathing, she commenced CPR. Parker watched and thought for the first time in his life how truly grateful he was not to be a parent.

"Joey . . . I have to . . . get to him . . . he needs me . . ." Lila whispered, looking up at him with big, desperate eyes, that stood out in her deathly white face.

Shaking his head, "no, honey, you need to rest. Your friend Savannah is taking care of your son. Everything's going to be okay, I promise," regretting the words the second they were out of his mouth. "Trust me, the ambulance is gonna come, it's gonna take you and Joey to the hospital and everything will be fine."

Lila shook her head then winced in pain, "he's my baby," she whispered imploring, struggling beneath his hands, Parker tightened his grip.

The young mother began to sob hysterically, "he's . . . he's going to . . . to die . . . please . . . he's all alone . . . and he's . . . he's scared . . . please, I need to go to him . . . he needs me." Her breathing became more labored as she struggled to suck in air.

Parker felt his own panic beginning to rise but pushed it away, taking Lila's hand and turning her face away from her son's bloody body. "Lila, you need to calm down. Look at me. I want you to concentrate on your breathing, try and slow it down. Breathe with me, in and out," he said taking deep breaths of his own, "in and out, in and out."

Managing to somewhat calm Lila's breathing, he glanced quickly over at where Savannah was still performing CPR on Joey. Where is the ambulance, he thought desperately, the tiny child was promptly running out of time.

Turning back to Lila he saw that her eyes were fluttering closed again, "Lila, sweetheart, look at me. Come on, honey, stay with me," but Lila's eyes closed and her body went limp. "Lila, open your eyes," he commanded, but Lila did not respond.

And then just as his own breathing quickened and terror gripped at his heart he heard the sound they had all been waiting for. The sound that would bring help and hopefully life.

Finally, finally sirens sounded in the distance.

* * * * *

3:07 P.M.

Dr Eric Abbott rode the elevator back downstairs to the ER, he knew it had meant a lot to the man that he had gone up with him to surgery and waited with him until his wife and kids had arrived. Although the man would never admit it out loud, Eric had known that he was scared.

Eric glanced at his watch as he exited the elevator, he hadn't realized he'd been gone almost half an hour, he hoped no one had needed him while he'd been upstairs. It had been a last minute decision to go with the man, so he hadn't told anyone where he was going.

He headed down to the desk to grab a list of patients to check on when Teya, one of the other ER doctors, accosted him. At the sight of her pale and worried face, he felt his stomach flutter.

"Eric, where have you been?" she demanded.

"What's wrong?" he asked immediately, he looked towards the desk and saw that several of the other doctors and nurses were staring at him with the same worried expressions. "What is it?" he repeated, his heart began to thump in his chest.

Before anyone could answer, the ER's door zipped silently opened and a gurney was wheeled in. Moving towards it on instinct to assess the patient, Teya tried to block his path but it was too late, he had already seen who occupied the gurney and his knees almost gave out from under him.

"I'm sorry, Eric, we tried to find you, to warn you," Teya whispered in his ear.

Moving towards the gurney he could hardly breathe. His five-year-old son Joey lay there covered in blood from a gunshot wound to his chest, he was intubated and his tiny body was stiller than he had ever seen it.

"What happened?" he asked, his voice sounding strange to his ears.

"A carjacking," one of the paramedics answered, shooting him a sympathetic glance.

Eric moved forward to help treat his son but Jamie, one of the ER's most experienced doctors and a close friend, held him back. "Eric, I don't think that's a good idea. I'll take care of him."

Opening his mouth to protest he looked at Jamie and knew he

was right, he couldn't risk his son's life by treating him. He watched Jamie disappear with Joey into one of the trauma rooms and wondered why Lila hadn't been in the ambulance with him. Then he felt his heart plummet further as though his chest had somehow turned into a bottomless pit. Turning to face Teya, who was still standing behind him, "where's Lila?" he demanded with more vehemence than he intended.

Teya wouldn't look him in the eye, "we tried to call you," she stammered helplessly, "but we didn't know where you were."

Feeling himself lose control as fear overcame him he grabbed her by the shoulders and shook her, he knew he was being unfair but all he could think about right now was his family. "Where's my wife?" Teya's shocked eyes looked up at him, a couple of the other doctors stepped in to help but Teya waved them away. "Where is she?" this time his words came out as a pitiful plea.

As the ER's door opened again he instantly released his grip on Teya and ran towards the gurney that was being wheeled inside. Lying on it was his beautiful wife. Her eyes were closed, her face an unnatural share of white, she had on an oxygen mask, and a huge, red gash ran across her forehead.

Savannah was with her, she was holding Lila's hand, her clothes splattered with blood, her eyes red, tear tracks down her cheeks, she looked up at him helplessly.

Eric moved towards Lila but Teya gently pushed him back, "I got her, Eric," she said and helped to wheel Lila's gurney towards the other trauma room, listening to the paramedic's run down of her condition.

Savannah moved towards him, tears falling from her eyes, "Eric" she whispered, her voice thick with shock, he took her in his arms and held her tightly, his own body going numb.

After a moment he pulled her back and looked down at her, "what happened? The paramedics said something about a carjacking."

Nodding, "apparently someone tried to take the car. They shot

Joey and threw Lila to the ground, she hit her head, then they drove off in the car . . ."

"Molly!" his eyes opening wide as he realized he hadn't seen his baby daughter.

Refusing to meet his gaze, "there was a police officer there," Savannah began, "he shot at the car, hit the tyres but the carjackers still got away. I found him looking after Lila and Joey, but then Joey stopped . . ."

"Where is she, Savannah?" he demanded his voice had morphed once more, this time into a vicious snarl. "Where is my baby?"

Slowly she raised her brown eyes to meet his own and in them he saw the answer to his question.

"No," he said simply, as if saying it could make it so.

"I'm sorry, Eric," Savannah had started to cry. "I'm so sorry."

"No, no, no," he begun to wail.

"They'll find her, Eric. The police will find Molly. Lila and Joey will get better and everything will be okay," Savannah was babbling through her tears.

Vaguely he was aware of his legs giving out, of his bottom thumping down onto the cold, hard, hospital floor, of Savannah screaming for help. Then he slipped into the beautiful, peaceful, abyss of blackness, where his wife wasn't injured, his son wasn't shot, and his baby daughter was not missing.

* * * * *

3:26 P.M.

"Here you go."

Parker looked up to see his partner, Detective Skylar Wyatt, standing before him, stripy canvas bag in hand.

"Clean shirt?" he asked as he took the bag from Wyatt. Friends for over twenty years, partners for more than five, Parker always thought of Wyatt as more of a brother.

"Isn't that my sole purpose in life? Providing you with a clean wardrobe," Wyatt asked with a grin before growing serious, his bright green eyes clouding over as he saw the huge blood stain on the concrete floor. Wyatt had two kids, ten-year-old Sam and five-year-old Stacey, who was still a month and a half away from her sixth birthday but already busy planning it. "Is the little boy gonna make it?"

Somewhere along the way someone had found him a towel to wash little Joey Abbott's blood from his hands, but he remained bare chested. Not bothering to undo the buttons, he slipped the fresh shirt over his head, delaying answering for as long as possible, for the second time that day glad that he did not have a child. "He lost a lot of blood," Parker said at last. "The paramedics didn't seem to be too hopeful."

Wyatt nodded, looking thoughtful for a moment, no doubt thinking of the tiny white coffin the family would use to bury their small son, and the tiny white coffin that held the remains of his own three-year-old daughter. "So what do we know?" Wyatt asked at last.

Walking through the scene as he summarized for Wyatt the little he knew of the situation so far. "It looks like the carjackers surprised Lila Abbott as she was loading groceries into the trunk of her red sedan. She'd already placed two-month-old Molly in the car, five-year-old Joey remained outside. Most likely surprised her from behind, somehow got the keys, and threw Lila to the ground, knocking her unconscious. Then for some reason decided that they had to shoot a helpless child," fury bubbling up once again as he thought of the callousness it took to attack a little boy, "before taking off in the car."

"That's where you came in, right?" Wyatt asked.

Nodding briskly, "I heard the shots, pulled out my gun, saw the cart go flying backwards as the car ploughed into it. The car came towards me, I fired one shot into one of the tyres, the car swerved, bumped into several others," Parker waved a hand at the crime scene techs who were busy collecting paint samples and tyre treads from the carnage the stolen sedan had left behind. "I don't know why they're bothering to do that," he snapped. "We already know what car left the paint samples, and we have the license plate."

Wyatt said nothing just let his gaze settle on the busy techs, buzzing around like bees, in the parking lot, collecting anything and everything that could be helpful to the case. "Any word on the car yet?" he finally asked.

"None," Parker let out a frustrated and edgy breath. "How does a car just vanish?" Not expecting any answer from Wyatt and getting none.

"Did you see the driver?"

"I was a little busy trying not to get mowed down," he snapped defensively. Wyatt merely raised an eyebrow and waited. "No. I didn't get a look at the driver. Everything happened quickly, I heard the shot, saw the car coming, fired at the tyre, then it left."

"We're working this as a carjacking gone wrong?" Wyatt asked.

"As far as I can tell. We'll talk to Lila Abbott but I can't think what else it would be." For a while they both stood in silence just watching, then Parker began to murmur, "when the car drove off I went to where I thought the shots had come from and found them lying there. There was so much blood," unable to shake the picture of the tiny body, so red, so still, so lifeless, from his mind.

"That must have been hard," Wyatt spoke quietly.

They both knew what he was referring to but Parker didn't take the bait, sometimes it felt like Wyatt wasn't his partner but his shrink. "The little boy stopped breathing just before the ambulance turned up, lucky that friend of theirs, the nurse, was here." Thinking it would be luckier still if carjackers didn't prey on young mothers and their small children. "I promised her," he mumbled aware of the fact that his voice had become distant, that he was saying more than he should, more than was necessary for the investigation.

"Promised who what?" Wyatt asked confused.

"I promised Lila Abbott that everything would be okay," his eyes straying to the two pools of blood on the concrete beside them. "I told her to trust me, that everything would be okay."

"She knows you were just trying to reassure her, Parker," Wyatt consoled.

"The driver managed to maintain control of the car and flee the parking lot," Parker climbed back onto solider ground by refocusing himself on the facts.

"Any witnesses?"

Shrugging, "I think there were a few people who saw the car lurching from the parking lot, but no one saw the actual carjacking." Parker felt a fresh wave of guilt wash over him. "I should have gone after the car. I could have followed it, with a punctured tyre I could have caught them."

Turning to study him carefully, "and then Joey Abbott would be dead," Wyatt stated simply.

"Joey Abbott is probably going to die anyway," he said bitterly, not in the mood to be comforted rather relishing the familiar feeling of guilt.

"At least he has a chance now," Wyatt reminded him.

Running his hands through his thick, black hair, Parker wanted to be out there doing something not stuck here talking about what had happened. "Wyatt, there is a baby missing, out there somewhere, alone with a carjacker," attempting to control his ragged breathing and only barely succeeding, "because of me. Because of the choice *I* made."

* * * * *

4:32 P.M.

"All I need is a dress, everything else is done," fifteen-year-old

Winter Bell announced. Formerly Winter Hamilton, after everything that had happened the previous year she no longer wanted to go by her ex-step-father's name, and since her aunt and legal guardian had gotten married, both Tessa and Winter had adopted Parker's surname.

"We're already three quarters through the mall," Casey Wyatt, her aunt's best friend and Parker's partner's wife, reminded her, "and you still haven't found anything."

"Three quarters of the way through *this* mall," Winter shot back with a giggle. They were busy sorting out the last details of her upcoming sixteenth birthday, now just a couple of weeks away. Winter had been looking forward to the party for months now, ever since she had started at her new school after the Christmas, New Year, break.

Before coming to live with Tessa and Parker she had been an unhappy, lonely girl. She'd had no friends, she'd been picked on at school, where despite being very intelligent she never managed to get good grades. Since she had started at Harlwood Academy however, things had certainly picked up. She was now doing well in school, had a good group of friends, and was happier than she had ever been before. From the hushed arguments between Parker and Tessa she knew that Parker had been a little concerned about her attending the academy. From what she could gather because of something that had happened to Tessa there in the past, but Winter adored her new school.

After her mother's death, almost six months ago, Winter had met the aunt she had never known existed, and the two of them had quickly grown close. After being released from the hospital, Tessa had begun teaching her to horse ride, something that she had been trying to teach Parker, apparently without much success. Winter loved the long rides they took out in the woods on the estate that Tessa had inherited from her grandparents, Winter's great-grandparents. The two of them talked for hours about anything and everything, so long as it wasn't in any way related to

Tessa's past. Winter had learnt quickly that anything to do with Tessa's past was strictly off limits.

"Ooh, look at this one," Casey stopped in front of a boutique as she gently fingered a mauve silk dress, with spaghetti straps, and ruffles around the bottom.

Staring in awe at the beautiful dress, picturing how the color would complement her pale skin and long dark hair. Casting a rueful glance at the price tag, "it's too expensive," Winter said with a wistful sigh.

"Whatever you like you get," Tessa told her.

While they had never gone without when she was growing up Winter and her mom had never had a lot of money. They'd moved around a lot, her mom had been married several times, and most of her husbands had been low-life losers, so Winter was used to going without. Tessa on the other hand had been raised in a very wealthy, albeit highly dysfunctional, family where money was no problem.

"Really, Winter, don't worry about . . ." Tessa broke off as she swayed unsteadily on her feet.

Both Winter and Casey grabbed Tessa's arms, holding her up as her face turned an unnatural shade of grey before breaking out into a sweat.

"Easy," Casey turned immediately into doctor mode, her smooth cocoa brow creasing in worry. "Here you go, sit down slowly." Casey carefully lowered Tessa down to the floor and pressed the back of her hand against Tessa's forehead, then lifted her wrist to take her pulse.

"I'm fine," Tessa protested weakly, making a feeble attempt to stand.

"Uh huh," Casey murmured noncommittally.

"Really," Tessa tried again. "I just felt faint for a second but I feel much better now."

"Actually she hasn't been feeling well for a few days," Winter piped up. Now that she thought about it for the last week or so her aunt had been paler and quieter than usual, plus she's been eating less and sleeping more.

"Traitor," Tessa shot her a half-hearted mutinous glare.

"Maybe we should call an ambulance," one of the people from the small crowd that had gathered around them suggested anxiously.

"No, I'm a doctor, she just needs to rest, and some air," Casey pointedly eyed the crowd who reluctantly moved back, away from the action. "Maybe some water too," Casey said to Winter.

"Sure," Winter bounded to her feet and hurried to ask the boutique's manager for a glass of water. By the time she returned Tessa was standing up, Casey towering over her, she had a good ten inches on Tessa's tiny five foot frame, her hand was gripping Tessa's arm to help steady her. A little of the color had returned to Tessa's cheeks, and the crowd, deciding that no one was about to drop dead, had dispersed. "Here you go," Winter passed the glass to Casey.

"Drink," Casey said, as she in turn passed it to Tessa, who immediately opened her mouth to protest. "Don't make me take you to the hospital," Casey warned.

Tessa rolled her eyes but obediently drank a couple of mouthfuls of icy water. "There, happy?"

"No," Casey raised an eyebrow as she took the glass back, "I don't like it when my best friend collapses. What's going on with you?"

"Nothing," Tessa assured her. "It's probably just the flu or something."

Casey studied Tessa closely with steady inky black eyes then sighed, unconvinced, "okay. Come on, let's get you home."

"What about Winter's dress?" Tessa protested, pulling her arm free from Casey's grip.

"We can come back for that another day," Winter jumped in immediately.

"But it's only two weeks till your party," Tessa reminded her.

"Yeah but it's only a dress and nothing is more important than you," Winter assured her.

"Oh no," Tessa moaned, "I'm surrounded by sappy characters in an after school special."

Offering a small smile, "that's cute, Tess," Casey told her before growing serious, "but I'm taking you home or I'm taking you to the hospital, your choice."

Sighing long-sufferingly, "home," Tessa finally answered, and couldn't quite hide the weariness that flashed through her greeny-blue eyes.

Winter felt a stab of real worry, if there was one thing she had learnt in the six months she'd been living with her aunt it was that Tessa was an expert at hiding her feelings.

"Okay, lets go," Casey said briskly, but from the tender way she reached out to brush a sweat-dampened tendril of Tessa's white-blonde hair from her forehead, Winter knew she too was worried about Tessa.

As Casey began walking Tessa towards the exit Winter fell into step beside them, sliding her hand into her aunt's and squeezing it tightly as though she could will Tessa to get better. Despite the fact that her aunt was only eleven years older than herself, Tessa was the closest thing to a mother that Winter had ever known, and she didn't know how she would cope if anything happened to her. Her mind conjuring every possible reason Tessa could be feeling ill. Then she settled herself, Parker, she thought, he would make Tessa tell him what was wrong. Parker would take care of Tessa, make sure that she was okay. Parker was always there to protect Tessa no matter what, as long as he was around nothing bad could ever happen.

JUNE 13ᵀᴴ

1:07 A.M.

Holding her limp hand in his, Eric Abbott stared forlornly at his unconscious wife. Her head was bandaged, she had a concussion, a couple of cracked ribs, and her dislocated shoulder had been put back into place. Grateful that at least she was stable, and that her CT scan and MRI had shown no signs of severe brain damage.

Joey was still in surgery.

Molly was still missing.

Looking closely at Lila's face, framed by thick, wavy red hair, Eric found himself willing her to wake up. She had not stirred since being brought to the hospital, but Savannah had said that she had been conscious and lucid at the parking lot.

Lifting his hand he gently ran it across Lila's cheek, where bruises were already beginning to mar her white skin with their ugly purple and black mottling. Lifting his hand again he hesitated, then held it above her mouth, relieved to feel her warm breath against his palm. Laying his fingers against her neck he felt her pulse, then moving it to her chest he felt the reassuring thump of her heartbeat. Eric knew she was connected to a dozen machines monitoring her condition, but it was more reassuring to feel the life inside of her with his own hands.

Once again he took her hand and raised it to his lips to press a kiss softly against it, then turned as the door opened, a weak smile forming, "Charlie."

Charlie walked over to him, "hey, little brother, I came as soon as I heard. Someone's covering my shift, so I'm here as long as

25

you need me." Charlie patted his back, then squeezed his shoulder reassuringly, and with a glance at his sister-in-law he asked, "how is she?"

"Concussion, dislocated shoulder, cracked ribs, bruises . . ." his voice faded and he turned to give his brother a terrified glance, his big brother could make everything better just like he had when they were kids. "Charlie, she hasn't regained consciousness yet. She's been here for . . ."

"Eric," Charlie interrupted, "she's been through a major trauma, physically and emotionally, her body needs time to regain some strength. She'll be okay," Charlie reassured in a soothing voice that Eric recognized was just like the one he used himself when comforting a patient's family.

He laughed softly.

"What?" Charlie asked confused.

"You just used your doctor voice on me," Eric explained.

Charlie smiled back. "Hey I'm a psychiatrist, not a doctor, that's what . . ." he broke off as the door opened once again, this time to reveal Jamie.

And Eric knew.

Before Jamie ever spoke the words. He knew.

"Eric, can I talk to you outside for a moment?" Jamie asked.

Eric glanced at Charlie, who nodded, "I'll stay with her."

Giving his wife's limp hand another kiss, he gently laid it down on the bed before following Jamie out the door, casting a last glance back to see Charlie sit at Lila's bedside and take her hand.

Entering the hall he softly closed the door, then wearily rested his forehead against it. "Joey's dead isn't he?" he asked at last.

Jamie sighed, Eric could feel him squirming uncomfortably. "I'm sorry, Eric. They did everything they could, but there was too much damage and he had lost too much blood . . ."

Hearing the words numbed his body with shock even though he had been expecting them. A technicolour display of images ran through his mind. The day he found out Lila was pregnant. The day Joey was born. The day they brought him home from the hospital. The first time Joey had smiled at him, the first time he uttered a gurgley little giggle. His first steps, his first word, his first day of preschool. Then the images turned dark as he thought of everything Joey would never get to do. His first day at school, his prom, college, girlfriends, marriage, children.

"No, no, no," Eric heard the desperate, keening wail. Wondered briefly where it was coming from before realizing it was him. And for the second time in less than twenty-four hours he came close to passing out.

"Eric . . ." Jamie begun.

Cutting him off and pulling himself together. "I'm okay." Taking several long, deep breaths.

Glancing at Lila's door Jamie asked, "how is she? Has she woken up yet?"

Eric shook his head. How was he going to tell his wife that their son was gone? That he was never coming back. The thought of telling Lila made him feel physically sick, and for a second it felt like someone was vacuuming out the air from his lungs leaving them tight and empty. Looking up at Jamie with forlorn eyes, "how am I going to tell her?"

"You want me to do it?" Jamie asked kindly.

Forcing air into his tight chest, willing his heart to slow it's frantic pumping, "no. But thanks. It should come from me." Eric wished desperately that Jamie could tell Lila, he dreaded seeing the devastation in her eyes when she learned her son was dead, but he knew he had to be the one to do it.

"Any word on Molly?"

"No." He honestly didn't know if he or Lila could survive if they lost Molly too. For the moment he couldn't think about it, right now he had to focus on Joey.

Turning back to the door, he felt Jamie's hand on his shoulder. "He's in room 104 when you're ready."

* * * * *

2:42 A.M.

She was so tired.

Her whole body ached.

Each breath felt like her chest was being squeezed in a vice, her head throbbed like her brain was trying to break through her skull, her shoulder burned like fire.

Something pressed against her neck and then her chest and she winced in pain.

"Charlie, I think she's waking up."

That was Eric's voice. But it sounded different. Tired and scared.

Feeling another wave of overwhelming exhaustion wash over her, Lila was about to let it pull her under but a distant memory kept poking at her mind, like a nightmare upon waking. Something bad had happened.

"Lila? Honey, can you hear me?"

Eric again.

She wanted to answer but it took too much energy.

"Lila, open your eyes."

Hearing the desperation in her husband's voice, she tried with all her might to do as he was asking, but her eyes were so heavy and she was so tired.

"Come on, baby, open your eyes for me, please."

This time she focused all her energy and managed to force her eyes open.

Eric was standing at her side, his large brown eyes peering down at her worriedly. When he saw she was awake, he pasted a reassuring smile on his face. A face that looked haggard and older, framed by a wild mess of thick brown hair, he needs a haircut she thought absently. Eric widened his smile but it didn't fool her, something was wrong, she could see it in his eyes.

She looked around, this wasn't their bedroom. Turning her eyes back to her husband's, her throat was as dry as the desert sand, but she managed to murmur, "where am I?"

Her husband cast a worried glance to the other side of the bed, and Lila turned her head, wincing once again in pain, and saw her brother-in-law Charlie standing beside her. Seeing the fear in their eyes she started to panic, she felt her heart thumping, and was surprised to hear a beeping sound behind her.

Eric took her hand and she looked back at her husband as he spoke in what she recognized as the voice he used when speaking to patients and their families and her panic grew. "It's okay, honey, calm down, you're in the hospital," he told her.

Attempting to do as he said, Lila tried to take a deep breath but her chest hurt, ignoring the pain, she whispered, confused, "the hospital?"

"Yeah, you don't remember?" he stroked her cheek. His tired eyes looked down at her, concerned, loving, but also scared, he was afraid of her, afraid to tell her something.

Closing her eyes and trying to concentrate, Lila knew there was something important she was missing, but she couldn't remember what is was, and the tiredness was lapping at her mind again. "I don't know," she said at last because she knew he expected some sort of answer.

Feeling Eric squeeze her hand she opened her eyes to look at him, he was still smiling down at her. "It's okay, it's gonna be okay," he soothed, but she knew it wasn't. "Try to get some rest, I'm right here."

Lila closed her eyes and all of a sudden something came rushing back to her. Something cold on her head, a flash of green and blue, a loud sound and red. She knew it was important, but she couldn't make sense of the jumbled thoughts. Then all of a sudden it clicked. The loud sound was a gunshot, and the red was . . .

Her eyes flew open and she stared at Eric in shock, hoping

desperately that he would not confirm what his eyes had already told her was true. "Joey! They shot him! Where is he?"

Eric didn't answer, and she looked from him to Charlie, her panic deepening. She pushed herself off the pillows, ignoring the protesting shot of pain that flared in her shoulder. "No!" she screamed. It couldn't be true. Not her baby. He was only five years old.

Her head was spinning, her heart was thumping, she was vaguely aware of a symphony of loud beeps behind her. She felt Eric gently lay her back down. She heard the door opening and voices jabbering.

Closing her eyes she concentrated on forcing the swirling in her head to stop. Joey needed her. Focusing on her breathing she managed to slow it down. Opening her eyes, she saw Eric and Charlie were still hovering over her, they had been joined by some of the other doctors from the hospital, she recognized Jamie and Teya.

"Take me to him!" she demanded. Joey quite simply could not be dead. She refused to believe it.

Pain shot through Eric's eyes and he shook his head.

"Eric, please, I want to see him," Lila begged, trying to keep the desperation out of her voice, she knew he would never let her see Joey if he thought she couldn't handle it.

"Lila, listen to me, you need to rest, you have a concussion, cracked ribs, you dislocated your shoulder, you need to calm down and take it easy." Jamie spoke in that overly calm doctor tone that only served to further annoy her.

"Joey is not dead. I don't believe it," she told them, sticking her chin out defiantly.

They all looked at one another, then Eric took a deep breath, caught her hand in his, and looked at her with his warm brown eyes in a gaze she couldn't force herself to break. "Joey was shot in the chest, he lost a lot of blood, he wasn't breathing on his own, they did everything they could but . . . his brain scan showed no brain activity, they're keeping him on life support so we can say goodbye."

Lila could feel the tears streaming down her cheeks, she wanted to yell at her husband that it was lies, her son was fine, but she saw the devastated faces of everyone in the room, and knew that it was the truth.

"Take me to him," she commanded, trying to make her voice as strong as she could.

Eric glanced at Jamie who shook his head. "Lila . . ." he began.

Cutting him off, "take me to my son," her high-pitched hysterical voice sounded even louder in the quiet room.

"Lila, honey, we will, but right now you need to . . ." Teya started.

Voice growing more out of control by the second, "I don't care what I need, my baby needs me, I want to go to him." No one moved. Fine, she decided, if they wouldn't take her to her son then she would simply find him herself. With a frustrated yelp she began to rip at the IV and the other tubes that ran from her body. As she did so every pair of hands in the room grabbed at her. "I want to see my son!" she screamed.

"Okay," Eric's voice soothed. "Okay. I'll take you to him."

"Eric," Jamie's voice warned.

Eric turned to face him, "she's going to go whether we let her or not," he countered. He gently started disconnecting the tubes and wires, and turned to Teya, "can you grab a wheelchair?"

The second Eric had removed the last tube, Lila dragged herself to her feet, but found herself unprepared for the overwhelming nausea and dizziness that rocketed through her body. Her sight went black, her legs could not support her body and she felt herself falling. But Eric was right beside her, catching her in his strong arms and holding her tight against his body before lowering her carefully into the wheelchair and kneeling in front of her, stroking her hair, "you okay?"

The dizziness slowly subsiding, she managed to nod her head.

Jamie pushed her out the door, in the hallway she noticed that every one of the doctors and nurses were looking at her with a mixture of concern and sympathy. Reaching one of the rooms Jamie stopped, and once again Eric knelt in front of her, taking her hands in his, "are you sure you're up to this?"

Not sure that she was but certain that her little boy needed her, Lila gave a shaky nod and was rewarded with a stab of pain at her temples. Eric pressed a gentle kiss against her mouth then stood and nodded to Jamie.

Slowly they entered the room.

Joey was lying on a bed, eyes closed, long lashes fanned out on his pale cheeks. If it hadn't been for the tube that ran from his mouth to the respirator that stood next to the bed he would have looked like he was sleeping.

Pushing herself up, she felt Eric's steadying arms wrap quickly around her, and she was grateful to have him to lean against until the crippling waves of dizziness stopped rolling over her. When she was ready, Lila slowly made her way towards the bed, Eric right behind her. She stood beside it for a moment, then reached out and took Joey's hand, holding it to her cheek, she felt tears tumble from her eyes.

Her little boy felt so alive, he was breathing, he was warm, maybe if they just left him alone he would wake up and everything would be okay.

"If we leave him like this he might wake up on his own," she whispered, turning to Eric and the others, moving her hopeful eyes from doctor to doctor. She couldn't understand why they looked at her like there was no hope. Her baby was still alive.

Eric turned her to face him, "I'm sorry, Lila," his devastated eyes bored into hers. Then he turned to Jamie and nodded. Jamie walked over to the respirator and flicked a switch. Lila felt panic begin to well up, chest tightening, heart hammering, they were killing her son.

She turned to Joey then back to Eric, her voice desperate,

begging, pleading, "you can't let them kill him. Eric, he's our baby, our little boy, don't let them do this, please."

Tears were falling from his eyes now too, he tried to pull her towards him but she pushed him away. "No!" she screamed and beat her fists against his chest. "How can you let them do this? You're letting them kill Joey," she looked at Eric's eyes and saw that they were full of patient understanding and she hated him for it. How could he stand there *understanding* why her child was dying, *understanding* why she was so upset. He had no right. He should be screaming right along with her. He was her husband, Joey's father, and yet he was standing by and letting them kill her child, their child.

As the beeping turned to a drone, she turned frantically, grabbing Joey's hand. This can't be happening she thought to herself. I cannot be standing here as my five-year-old son's life slips away.

Eric moved towards Joey and reached for his hand and Lila let her anger take over. It was Eric's fault. He had let them kill Joey. He was a doctor, therefore it was his job to save people, so why hadn't he saved her baby. Pushing him away, "don't touch him," she screamed, teetering right on the edge of insanity but beyond caring. "It's your fault he's dead, you let them kill him!"

"Lila," Eric pleaded, his voice as stricken as his eyes.

Turning to her son, lying her head down on his chest, anger giving way to grief, she began to sob. Sobbed for all the things that Joey would never get to do. He would never finish school and go to college, he would never have a job, he would never get married or have children of his own. And she would never get to hold him in her arms again, she would never get to rock him to sleep, or wipe away his tears, she would never hear his sweet little voice call her mommy.

Eric's hands were on her shoulders, and as quickly as it had gone her anger returned. Head shooting up, ignoring the pain throbbing at her temple, and glaring at him. "Stay away from us, and don't you dare touch my son!"

"Lila," Eric whispered, "he's gone." He pulled her away from Joey and held her against him.

For a moment she fought wildly, swinging her fists at him, but then she was overwhelmed with tiredness. Her whole body was aching and her anger was melting away again, replaced by pure grief. She laid her head against Eric's chest and held on to his shirt, desperate to keep him close and terrified that he too would leave her.

His arms tightened around her, "I love you," he whispered into her hair. "We'll get through this together."

Then something else forced its way into her exhaustion-hazed mind, followed by a stab of guilt. Lifting her weary head and untangling herself from her husband's arms. "Molly?"

The look on her husband's face told her everything she needed to know. Her remaining strength ebbed away, her head started to spin again, and blackness started to tug at her, she tried to tell Eric, but it was too late. And then thankfully, her shocked, grief-stricken, aching, blissfully in denial brain finally did something helpful and pushed her into the quiet, black hole of unconsciousness.

* * * * *

3:04 A.M.

Eric stood, his body numb with shock.

Joey lay dead in front of him.

Molly was missing.

Lila was an hysterical mess.

She blamed him and he couldn't fault her for it.

She was right. It was his fault Joey was gone. He should have been the one to treat him, he should have saved him, he should have protected him.

Lila suddenly swayed, eyes rolling back in her head. Jumping forward Eric caught her as she fell, supporting her head as he carefully laid her down on the floor. Jamie and Teya came running, he had forgotten they were there, and knelt down beside Lila, Jamie reached for her wrist.

"No!" Eric screamed, surprising himself. "Don't touch her!"

They stared at him in shock. "Get away from her," he repeated more forcefully as he pulled Lila's limp form into his arms, cradling her against his chest.

"Eric . . ." Teya started.

He didn't want to hear what they had to say. "Just leave," he pleaded, a sob catching in his throat. He had left Joey in their care and now Joey was dead, he didn't care how irrational he sounded he could not let them touch his wife. He couldn't lose her too.

Standing but not leaving, they looked down at him worriedly, "Eric, I can't even imagine what you're feeling right now. But Joey is gone. I know you don't want anything to happen to Lila, so let me check her out, please." Jamie spoke as a doctor, but Eric knew that he was genuinely concerned about both him and Lila.

Just yesterday everything had been so perfect. He and Lila had taken a shower together, his hands gliding over her body as he washed her hair, then they'd eaten breakfast with Joey who had been yapping away about school, which he would start in the fall. He'd given Molly her bath. Played Twister, Joey's favorite game, with his son and his wife, the baby gurgling in her sleep beside them. Kissed them all goodbye and gone to work. Now Joey was dead, Molly was missing, and Lila was lying unconscious in his lap.

Slowly he stood, gathering Lila's unconscious body into his arms, wanting to give her to Jamie but at the same time unable to bear letting her go. "Jamie," he hesitated, "I can't lose her."

"I know," Jamie nodded. "I won't let anything happen to her. I promise."

Taking a step forwards, he gently placed his wife in Jamie's outstretched arms.

"Everything's going to be okay, Eric," Jamie reassured him, then moving quickly he called to the team waiting outside with the gurney, "bring it in." The door flew open and Jamie carefully put Lila on the gurney, the doctors and nurses immediately began to assess her condition.

Jamie cast a questioning look at him, but Eric shook his head and pointed to his wife, "go with her, Jamie."

Shooting him one last worried glance Jamie departed with Lila.

Now that he was alone Eric walked quietly to the bed that held his son's lifeless body. Slowly he disconnected all the tubes and wires, then lifted his little boy into his arms for the last time.

* * * * *

9:53 A.M.

"It happened so quickly," Lila Abbott paused to gaze listlessly out the window. "And my memory . . . everything's fuzzy."

The two detectives had turned up a little while ago to ask her about the carjacking, about the people who had taken both her babies from her. Eric hadn't wanted her to talk to them, he had been worried that it would be too much for her, that it would push her over the edge again. He needn't have worried, Lila felt numb now. During the night she'd had nightmares, waking screaming, with machines screeching and the room would instantly fill with people. Guns, a bloody Joey, and a man who kept running away from her, Molly in his arms, had haunted her dreams. But now she felt nothing, she was just tired and sore.

Eric squeezed her hand and tried to reassure her. "That's the concussion, honey, your memory might come back."

She nodded, not really hearing his words, and resumed staring out the window, watching a flock of birds flutter past. How did they all know when to turn, she marveled, they never crashed and always knew which way to go. Did they have a leader who chirped out instructions? Could they read each other's minds? Ever since she was a kid, this had baffled her.

Gently tucking her hair behind her ear Eric spoke to her in a soothing, almost condescending, voice that made her feel as though she were three years old. "Honey, I know this is really hard, but you need to try and remember everything you can, okay?"

"Okay," she said softly. "We were shopping, and . . . and Joey wanted . . . he wanted to . . . to sit in the front and I told him . . . I told him no . . . he had to wait till he was bigger." Remembering little Joey's face as he had frowned up at her. Pushing the image away, Joey was gone now, it did no good to think of these things. "I put the baby in the car," she continued tonelessly, "then I felt something cold against my temple," she lifted one hand to point to her head, and was surprised by the tight pinching feeling in the back of her hand. Absently she began to fiddle with the needle, "a voice asked for the keys . . ."

"Stop, Lila," Eric gently pulled her hands apart, the moment he released them they immediately strayed back towards one another, Eric caught hold of one and held it firmly.

"What happened next, Mrs. Abbott?" one of the detectives asked her kindly.

For the first time she really looked at them, a jolt of memory flashed through her mind, she'd seen that face before. Cocking her head, "you were there," she said, studying the Detective with the dark hair.

"Yeah I was," he gave her a small smile, "Parker Bell. Do you remember what happened after that?"

Lila was too busy gazing at his eyes to hear his question. They were an amazing yellowy brown color, kind of gold, just like Joey's eyes.

"Mrs. Abbott," Detective Bell prodded softly, leaning forward in his chair, elbows resting on knees, face patient.

Shaking herself she tried to focus her foggy mind, "I threw the keys on the floor." Scrunching her brow in concentration, "I asked them to just let me get Molly . . ."

"There were two of them?" asked the other Detective, Lila turned to look at him. He had thick strawberry blonde hair, a serious face, a pale blue shirt and matching blue tie that blended in perfectly with his grey pants, and green eyes that seemed to say he knew exactly what she was going through.

Nodding, "there were two," she confirmed.

"Did you see them?" asked Detective Bell.

"I don't think so," Lila answered, but she wasn't sure anymore. Everything had happened so quickly, she had been scared, she hadn't been taking mental notes on all the details. And she was tired now, her mind longed for sleep where maybe she would be lucky enough to dream of her beautiful son.

"After you gave them the keys what did they say?" Detective Bell's voice penetrated her thoughts.

"I don't know," she said again. "I was trying to reach for Molly when an arm wrapped around me," vaguely aware of a wetness on her cheeks. "Then I was falling, and there was a crack, and then Joey was red, he was so red, and then there was blackness. When I woke up you were there," she said to Detective Bell, "and you told me that everything was going to be okay."

He flinched, "I'm sorry." He reached for her hand and squeezed it gently.

"It wasn't your fault," she told him honestly, feeling a tear drop onto her hand. "You were trying to be nice to me, you were trying to save Joey."

"I shouldn't have said it," he said again.

Looking into his eyes once again, Joey's eyes, she saw that he felt genuinely guilty about what he had said, and what he had done. She wondered if Joey would have grown up to be like this man, so full of empathy for another human being, and the next thing she knew she was sobbing uncontrollably. "I told him no,

Eric," she was screeching. "It was only riding in the front seat of the car. What harm could it have done? We were only five minutes from home. But I told him no and he was mad. They shot him and he was mad at me. They killed him and he was mad at me . . ." she broke off, sobs wracking her entire body.

Moving to sit on the bed beside her, her husband pulled her into his arms, holding her tightly, stroking her hair, rubbing her back. "It's okay, it's okay," Eric whispered against her head. "I think that's enough for now," she heard him tell the detectives as she clutched desperately at him, wanting him closer, wanting to meld their bodies together so that he could never be taken from her.

"I'm very sorry for your loss," the blonde Detective said softly.

"We're going to find your daughter," Detective Bell told her, and she felt his warm, steady hand on her back. "I'm not giving up on this case, I'm gonna be right here, every day, and I'm going to bring your daughter home to you."

Then they were gone and she was sobbing harder, thinking of nothing but her precious little boy. Voices buzzed in the room, someone took hold of her arm, fiddled with the IV, and then she felt a familiar feeling tugging at her mind. As she floated away on a cloud of unconsciousness, she had one last thought. Detective Bell had promised to bring Molly home to her, but she didn't want Molly she wanted Joey. She had time to think that she was the world's worst mother before everything vanished away.

* * * * *

12:32 P.M.

"Joey Abbott died from blood loss due to a single gunshot wound to the heart," medical examiner Zak Fenton was announcing to the small group gathered in Lieutenant Jacob Jacobson's office.

Parker could have told them that. From the second he'd first dropped to his knees beside the child he'd known it would take a miracle for him to survive, he was surprised the little boy had made it to the hospital at all.

"So far we don't really have a lot to go on . . ."

Parker cut off his boss, "so far we don't have anything to go on."

J.J. frowned, he did not appreciated being interrupted, but Parker didn't care right now. "Anyway," J.J. resumed with a pointed look Parker's way, "the bullet was recovered from Joey Abbott's body and is currently at the lab waiting to be processed," he raised a questioning eyebrow at crime scene tech Marty Jenkins.

"It's still waiting," Marty supplied.

"Time is of the essence," J.J. reminded him tersely in his usual booming voice, Jacob Jacobson was almost seven foot tall and three hundred pounds.

"Just like every other case," Marty countered, his beady grey eyes narrowed behind thick-rimmed black glasses. Just like the rest of them, the crime scene tech was over worked and under paid.

Ignoring him J.J. ran a hand through his thick brown beard as he continued, "are we anywhere on the car?"

"Nowhere," Wyatt replied. "A couple of people noticed it leaving the lot, with the way it was driving, but no one seemed to pay a lot of attention."

"What is wrong with people?" Parker demanded, thumping a fist into the table and sending the coffee cups jumping.

It had been a long day, after visiting Lila Abbott, where he had repeated his mistake and made more promises to the woman that he couldn't fulfill, they had interviewed the couple of witnesses who reported seeing a car with a busted tyre leave the parking lot. The interviews had yielded nothing that they hadn't already known. A bad day on top of a restless night, Parker estimated he had gotten maybe thirty minutes total in sleep. Most of the night he'd lain awake, listening to Tessa's even breathing, and debated waking her up for sex, anything to get his mind off his guilt. In the end he had let her sleep only because he'd heard from both Wyatt and Winter about her collapsing at the mall.

"Parker," J.J. began placatingly.

But Parker wasn't in the mood to be calmed. "When will people learn that they need to be aware of their surroundings? You see a car driving around with a blown up tyre you take notice of where it goes."

"And we have no ID on the carjackers?" J.J. ploughed on, apparently deciding to let him sulk.

"Some people heard the shots and came running but the car was already gone," Wyatt told him. "Parker was there and even he didn't see anything useful."

Bristling, "what's that supposed to mean?"

His partner frowned at him, "nothing. I was just saying that we don't have any witnesses who can give us a description of the carjackers."

"The car was coming straight for me," Parker defended himself, more for the benefit of his own guilt than anything else. "I didn't have time to stop and take a photo. Would you rather I . . .?"

"Parker," J.J.'s voice was quietly demanding. "No one is saying you didn't do your job."

"Well it feels as if they are," Parker ignored the exchange of worried glances between Wyatt, Zak and Marty. "I should have gone after the car. Then at least there wouldn't be a missing two month old baby involved."

"Where are we on the baby?" J.J. asked as though he'd forgotten all about it. Raising a hopeful eyebrow, "no one dropped off a baby at any hospitals or police stations?"

Wyatt shook his head.

"The baby's dead," Parker insisted dejectedly, two dead

children on your conscience definitely sucked the life right out of a person. "Statistics say that three quarters of abducted children who are murdered are killed within the first three hours, and that's when the kid is the reason for the abduction, this was a carjacking gone wrong, what do you think the odds are that Molly Abbott is still alive? You carjack a car you don't expect to get stuck with a screaming infant. They probably killed her as soon as they got far enough away from the scene. Smothered her, or drowned her, or snapped her neck, maybe they just left her in the abandoned car to starve to . . ."

"That's enough," J.J. was staring at him now with intense brown eyes. "Right now we need to focus on locating the car *and* the baby," he said with a pointed look Parker's way.

"We'll never find her," Parker glared back, daring them to disagree. "They'll put her in a garbage bag, weigh her down with rocks and throw her in a river, or bury her body in a shallow grave, or throw her out in a dumpster."

"You are on my last nerve," J.J. warned him. "We are going to find that car and we are going to find that baby. You are all dismissed, except you, Parker," he snapped as they all stood. "You and I need to have a little chat."

Slumping back down in his chair, Parker crossed his arms sullenly like a teenager waiting for a lecture by the principal.

Once everyone had left J.J. sat opposite him and fixed him a penetrating stare, "what's wrong with you today? I get that you feel responsible for the missing baby. I get that you feel personally involved in this because you are, you were first on the scene. You found the victims, you tried to save them, but you're letting yourself get too caught up in this case. Again," he added.

Finally looking up to meet his boss' eye, J.J. was staring at him kindly, but Parker could see the concern written all over his face.

"This is becoming a pattern for you and one that doesn't always end well. There are ethical guidelines about becoming involved with the victims we come into contact with for a reason," J.J. lectured. "Have you forgotten about Gina O'Hara?"

Of course he hadn't forgotten about Gina. He'd let himself become too involved with her with almost disastrous results.

"And then after that almost blows up in your face, your first case back you get involved with Tessa."

"Tessa was different," Parker insisted immediately.

"Yeah, she was," J.J. agreed. "You love her and that's great. She's great. But, Parker, you're always complaining that Tessa never talks about stuff, that she bottles everything up inside, but you do exactly the same thing. And now you've got the perfect excuse, you're too busy taking care of Tess to worry about yourself." Raising his hands to abort Parker's protestations, "now granted," J.J. continued, "Tessa has an unnatural ability to get herself into trouble. And she has more emotional baggage than any twenty-six year old should have, but you're the one who said you could deal with it."

When he'd met Tessa, eighteen months earlier, Parker had been instantly attracted to her. The infuriatingly stubborn and calm way she had reacted when they'd told her that she was a possible target of a vicious serial killer had sparked something inside him. At the time everyone had warned him about becoming involved with someone like Tessa. Someone who had never had a supportive family, a stable relationship, or people she could trust and depend on. He, however, had insisted that he was ready, willing and able to help her through anything, to prove to her, and himself, that it was okay to be happy.

"If I'm so incompetent and such a liability," he told J.J. tightly, barely able to control his temper, he did not appreciate being treated like some sort of gullible, lovesick puppy. "Then why don't you just fire me?"

"Parker, no one is denying that you're a great cop," J.J. continued undaunted. "You're compassionate and empathetic, and victims and their families trust you, but lately you keep letting things get too personal."

"Are you done?" Parker asked with a frown as he stood, "cos I've got work to do, there's a baby somewhere out there that I promised to return to her mother."

"I'm serious, Parker," J.J. cautioned. "You're already too involved in the Abbott case and I won't hesitate to take you off it if I think it's going to be a problem. I want you to think about taking a break, a holiday . . ."

"I just came back from my honeymoon," he objected.

"And look at you. You didn't come back rested and happy, you came back wound up tighter than I've ever seen you." His boss was back to studying him with eyes that were much too perceptive for Parker's liking. "Six months ago you saw Tessa die right in front of you."

J.J.'s pause allowed time for Parker's mind to conjure up images of the night he had found Tessa lying in a pool of blood from a gunshot wound to her abdomen. He had tried desperately to stop the bleeding, but it was already too late, and he had watched helplessly as Tessa's life ebbed away. Thankfully they had been in a hospital and help had arrived in time. The doctors were able to resuscitate her and she had recovered.

"I know you got her back," J.J. continued, "but did you ever take the time to deal with that. Did you talk to someone, did you really process it, or did you just push it away into the too hard basket."

Parker glared, he didn't want to think about that night. Tessa had survived. That was all there was to it. "If I tell you I'll think about the holiday will you leave me alone?"

"No way," J.J. grinned, then sobered, "you have a wife now Parker, and whether she'll admit it or not, Tessa depends on you to hold it together. Right now, quite simply, you're about ready to implode." J.J. breathed deeply then pushed away from the table and stood. "Alright, I've said all I need to say for now, but remember I'm watching you. Now go. Go find that baby and prove to all of us that sometimes the world isn't a completely awful place."

At the door Parker paused, finding himself too tired to maintain his righteous anger, which scared him more than anything else. Casting a last look back at his boss who had resumed his spot at his family photo covered desk. "I'll think about the break. Really."

Looking up J.J. just nodded.

And all of a sudden Parker really needed some fresh air.

* * * * *

3:16 P.M.

Eric was stretched out on the couch in his brother's office, eyes closed but not asleep.

Jamie had given Lila a sedative after she'd broken down while being interviewed by the police, and he had remained by her side while she slept. When she had finally reawakened she'd been calmer but also more withdrawn. Her eyes had been distant as though she were someplace else, where no one could reach her, and she had insisted that she needed to be alone. Reluctantly he had left her, but only after extracting a promise from Jamie that he would personally check in on her at regular intervals. *Extremely* regular intervals.

Lost, he had wandered around the hospital for a while. But he had no patients to tend to, a home he couldn't bear to face, and a wife who couldn't stand to be in the same room as him. In the end, with nowhere else to go, he had taken refuge here, drawing the blinds, turning off the lights, discarding his shoes, and crashing down on the couch. Exhausted as he was, sleep refused to come.

The door creaked slowly open, and Charlie tiptoed through his office to his desk. Eric watched him rifle quietly through a drawer until he located whatever he was looking for then start his quiet track back towards the door.

"I'm awake you know," Eric announced as Charlie's hand reached for the doorknob.

"I know," Charlie grinned as he flipped on the lights. "I just didn't know if you felt like talking."

Stomach cramping as he sat up, Eric realized that he hadn't eaten since breakfast yesterday. Magically, Charlie produced a fruit salad, and Eric couldn't help grinning. When they were kids fruit was the only thing Eric could eat when he was stressed, or scared, or worried.

"Thanks," Eric began gobbling down the fruit. He hadn't known just how hungry he really was until he started to eat.

"How're you holding up?" Charlie asked when he finally set aside the empty plastic container.

"As well as I can be I guess," Eric answered with a shrug.

"Talk to me Eric, it's best to talk at times like this, tell me how you're feeling," his brother, ever the psychiatrist, pushed gently.

Rubbing his tired eyes, Eric often found it difficult to reconcile the two different sides of his brother. The fun loving guy who had teased him mercilessly when they were kids, with the quiet and sensitive psychiatrist.

"Angry," he admitted at last knowing that his brother wasn't going to stop until he got an answer. "I feel angry."

"Angry at who?"

"I don't know," Eric responded untruthfully as he stood and began to pace the small office restlessly.

Pushing him carefully, Charlie contradicted him, "yes you do."

"The carjackers," he replied deciding half the truth was better than none at all.

"And . . ." Charlie prodded.

Eric stopped his pacing and went to hover by the window, he didn't even know what time of day it was. Pushing aside the blinds he saw the sun shining in a sky painted in the seemingly endless deep blue of summer. Below him, people were busily going about their lives. Some, even from this distance, looked dazed and confused, the ones who had not gotten good news today. Others walked briskly, proudly, joyfully, the ones who had come, hopes not set too high, and left with a heavy burden removed from their shoulders.

He had been a doctor for several years now, all of those spent in the ER, and he thought himself quite adept at handing out bad news. How empathetic and sympathetic and compassionate he was when dealing with families who had just lost a loved one. It wasn't until last night that he came to understand just how little he truly understood the life crushing sorrow, and anger, and helplessness that weighed you down when someone you loved was snatched from you too soon.

"Lila," he whispered at last, then hated himself so deeply he had to turn quickly from the window and cross to the other side of the office in case the temptation to fling himself down to the ground below grew too strong. "I'm so . . . so furious at her," pressing back against the smooth painted wall. Giving in to the desire to make himself hurt physically as he did emotionally, as if he could somehow work out some sort of trade off, he banged the back of his head against the wall a couple of time. "I'm so angry, Charlie."

Part of him blamed Lila for the entire incident. She should have done something to protect their son. She should have done something to protect their daughter. He knew it was irrational and illogical, but he was exhausted and grief-stricken and long past being rational. "I know it's not her fault," he murmured at last, he could feel fatigue starting to take over and knew it was only a matter of time before he crashed. "But I can't help it. Part of me blames her," giving his head one last thump against the wall. "What kind of husband am I? I blame my own wife for the death of our son."

Waiting for Charlie to say something. When he didn't respond Eric finally turned to him, looking into his brother's eyes he saw that Charlie had already known what his answer would be. Then he let nature take it's course and allowed the exhaustion he had been keeping at bay by sheer force of will come crashing over him like a tidal wave. Sliding down the wall till he bumped down onto the rough carpet, crossed his arms over his knees, rested his forehead on his folded hands, and let sleep come.

* * * * *

7:42 P.M.

Striding quickly through the building, Parker was still on edge from his talk with J.J. earlier, when he spotted Tessa lounging in his desk chair. Instead of the usual rush of tenderness he always felt when he saw his wife of just four months, he felt a wave of irritation and even worse of intense claustrophobia. Now on top of everything else, he had to worry about why Tessa was passing out in shopping malls.

As a child, growing up in foster care, he had been tortured mercilessly in his last foster home by his foster parent's biological son. Malcolm's favorite pastime had been tying up the smaller children in a straightjacket and locking them in a closet. Parker had been lucky, he had escaped the foster care system and been adopted by a wonderful family, who had helped him change from an angry, withdrawn child, to a happy, carefree, loving child. His claustrophobia, however, had remained. Until six months ago when he had worn a jacket for the first time in over twenty years. For Tessa he had overcome his greatest fear, and it had ended up helping to save her life. Now however his claustrophobia seemed to be back with a vengeance.

"I heard what happened yesterday," he told her flatly when he reached his desk. "You were asleep when I got home last night and when I got up this morning," he told her and caught the accusing tone in his voice, they both knew she had been faking sleep to avoid a conversation on the topic of her near fainting spell.

"Was I?" Tessa asked, blue eyes wide, blonde curls framing her pale face, she looked like the world's sweetest, most innocent little angel.

Counting to ten to calm himself before he said something he'd later regret. "Are you okay?" he asked gruffly.

"I'm fine." Giving him her usual answer.

Sighing deeply, "if you're spouting that at me again then something is definitely up. What kind of trouble have you gotten yourself into this time?"

Standing up but remaining perfectly, and infuriatingly, calm. "What is that supposed to mean?" she asked evenly.

It means, he thought to himself, that I am so tired of worrying. So tired of sitting next to Tessa as she lay in a hospital bed. So tired of the panic that crushed his spirit after she went off recklessly and alone to face a monster. So tired of being patient as he waited for her to finally open up to him and trust him. So tired of worrying about what trouble she was going to get herself into next, and then coming running to her rescue. He was so tired of feeling guilty.

"It means," he said at last, "that maybe J.J. is right. Maybe I need a break."

A brief flicker of panic lit her eyes but she quickly shoved it away. "You're leaving me?" Being tied up and helpless may be his greatest fear, Tessa's was being alone.

Rather than making him feel remorseful, her comment only fanned the flames of his frustration. Tessa was an expert at making herself a martyr. "Don't do that," he snapped, keeping his voice quiet with an effort so as not to draw the attention of the few remaining detectives. "Don't make me out to be the bad guy."

"Fine," she said frostily then turned on her heel to leave.

"Wait," he said snapping his hand around her wrist. Her thin, tiny, wrist, that reminded him of little Joey Abbott. Then to his horror, he felt tears pricking the backs of his eyes. He was a guy, more he was a police officer, and he did not cry. Pulling Tessa against his chest, "I'm sorry," he murmured against her hair. She remained stiff in his arms, but right now he didn't care, he was overwhelmed by the need to hold her, to feel her heart beating against his chest, her breath whooshing across his shoulders. "I don't know what's wrong with me lately. I'm just . . . I'm just so tired."

Tessa relented, he felt her anger ripple away as she wrapped her arms around his waist and snuggled her head against his chest, wiggling it around until she had her ear over his heart.

"I'm sorry, Tess," he whispered as he stroked her hair, absently twirling one of her curls around his finger.

"It's my fault," she said immediately, and for once he loved her ability to blame herself for anything and everything. "I've been too preoccupied with Winter lately."

Squeezing her tighter, he was about to say something when a familiar face peeped around the door and the bottom dropped out of his world.

JUNE 14TH

5:43 A.M.

His hands wouldn't stop shaking. Parker clutched them firmly in his lap, folding them into fists so tight his fingernails begun to cut into his flesh. The call hadn't come at a good time, but at least it had given him a temporary reprieve from having to deal with the visit. Parker knew it wasn't fair to leave Tessa to handle things, but he was having a hard time caring.

Thirty minutes ago they had received an anonymous call from someone claiming that they had seen a shadowy figure burying a bag in the park near the grocery store. Immediately he and Wyatt had jumped in Wyatt's car to head out to the park. A CSU team had joined them, and was currently combing the park looking for signs of recently disturbed dirt that might indicate a shallow grave.

"Anything yet?" Wyatt asked coming up beside him, returning from the car where he'd been calling his wife.

Parker was standing listlessly on his own by the deserted playground. A children's playground, like a school or a fairground, was an eerie place when it was empty. The swings were swaying backwards and forwards in the gentle breeze, even the teeter-totter was rocking slightly, the wind in the trees sounded like children whispering as though the whole playground were inhabited by ghost children making the most of the quiet before all the real children arrived to play.

Thankfully Wyatt had been at home when his little visitor had shown up and Parker was glad he didn't have to suffer through what would have been Wyatt's interrogation had he known who was back.

"No," he replied at last. The waiting was almost killing him, but at the same time he was dreading hearing the news that they had found what they were looking for.

"It could be anything," Wyatt said absently as he watched the busy crime scene techs.

"Could be," Parker agreed half-heartedly as he too watched the scene, the hustle and bustle seemed incongruous with the calm dawn sky. A puddle of gold was forming in the east as the sun slowly rose, the sky around it tinted with pink and orange and yellow, above their heads it faded to such a pale blue it was almost white then darkened out to a deep purpley grey. The darker color fitted his gloomy mood perfectly. Realizing what he'd just been thinking. Puddle of gold. He never thought about the sunrise like that, never even thought about the sunrise at all. Apparently he was more out of sorts than he'd imagined.

"I never thought I'd be hoping to see a bag full of dead kittens," Wyatt was muttering. It was a sad fact of life that many unwanted puppies and kittens were drowned or killed and buried in bags.

"Uh huh," Parker nodded distractedly. All he could think about was the Abbott's car coming careening towards him in the parking lot and the look in Lila Abbott's eyes as she recounted the events of the carjacking. Events that he could have changed if he'd aimed his shot for the driver, or climbed into his own car to follow.

"It wasn't your fault, Parker," Wyatt's voice broke into his thoughts.

Parker looked up to see his partner studying him carefully. "I know." Already the morning was hot and sticky, hinting at a long hot summer to come, and Wyatt's probing stare was making him squirm even more uncomfortably.

"You had to make a choice," Wyatt continued. "You couldn't have known that there was a baby in that car, you heard the shots, you had to go and check it out."

Before he had a chance to answer one of the CSU techs called out, "got something."

Both he, and Wyatt, and almost everyone else in the assembled gathering, bolted over to a tiny clearing in the wooded section of the park not far from the playground. Reaching the spot Parker could see immediately what had sparked the crime scene tech's attention. Grabbing a shovel he began to dig furiously but carefully, if it was Molly Abbott's body buried in this hole, then they would need whatever evidence they could gather to find the perpetrator.

It didn't take long to find something, quickly shoveling away the last couple of scoops of dirt to uncover the black, plastic garbage bag,

Parker knew the second he saw it what was inside.

Waiting anxiously while someone took a few photos of the bag in the hole, then sliding on a pair of gloves as he crouched down and cautiously slit open the bag. Several apprehensive heads hovered over him as he peeled back the edges to reveal a very tiny, naked body.

Muttered curses sounded from the small crowd at the sight of the infant's body, and Parker scrunched his eyes closed, wondering whether it would ever be possible to erase the image of Lila Abbott's distraught face from his mind. He didn't know how he was going to face her and tell her that they'd found Molly's body after promising her that he would bring her baby home. He didn't know how he was going to face himself with yet another death on his conscious.

"Parker, it's not Molly Abbott," Wyatt announced suddenly.

Eyes snapping back open. "What? How do you know that?"

Pointing, "it's a boy."

* * * * *

9:19 A.M.

Pulling into the driveway Eric felt his breath catch in his throat. It was the first time he had been home since the accident. Lila had been in the hospital for the last two days and he had stayed with her, unable to face the huge empty house on his own.

Lila sat silently beside him. She hadn't spoken a word since they'd left the hospital. She had barely spoken at all since Joey had died and Molly had been taken, spent most of her time simply sitting and staring blindly into space.

Casting her a worried glance, Eric desperately wanted her to talk to him. They needed each other so much. He needed her so much. He needed to assuage his guilt over blaming her for what had happened.

Glancing at her again he stuck a smile on his face. "We're home," he said with as much cheer as he could muster.

Lila didn't move.

Reaching over to gently touch her shoulder. "Honey?"

Gradually she turned to look at him. Her brown eyes, that had once been so bright and sparkling, were now dull and distant. She looked at him vacantly, like she had forgotten he was even there.

"We're home," he repeated, forcing himself to keep the smile on his face, Lila needed him to be strong right now.

Looking at him like he was speaking another language she nodded slowly, then resumed her sightless stare out the window.

Getting out of the car, he walked around to the passenger door and opened it. Kneeling down in front of Lila he turned her face to look at him. "You ready?" he asked.

Looking him in the eye she asked in a small childlike voice, "he's really gone isn't he?" Eyes boring into his, begging him to make this nightmare go away,

"Yeah, he is, honey."

Tears began to trickle down her cheeks, but she seemed not to notice. Leaning forward, Eric gathered her up into his arms, pushed the car door closed and carried her to the front door.

Balancing her carefully in his arms as he opened the front door, where he was instantly met with hundreds of reminders of his son and daughter. Joey's jacket and a pair of his shoes were lying in a pile near the front door. The lounge room was full of Joey's toys and his pajamas were lying in front of the TV where he had dropped them the morning of the incident. The box of Twister was still on the table. The baby blanket lay over by the fireplace. Molly's teddy bear perched on the table in the middle of the room. Joey was going through a phase where he insisted that every stuffed animal hated to be left lying down, they wanted to be part of the action he would say, so the teddy sat, right where Joey had left it.

"Hey," Savannah called softly as she and Charlie came down the hall from the back of the house.

"Hey, princess," Charlie said, giving Lila a kiss on the cheek.

Princess had been Lila's nickname when they were growing up. An only child, very spoiled and used to getting her own way, she had been given the nickname 'Princess' when she was eight. Eric and Charlie, Savannah and her older brothers, and Lila had grown up together, living on the same street, and had played together nearly every day of their lives.

"Hey, little brother," Charlie gave him a gentle slap on the back and a questioning look that asked, 'you doing okay?'.

Eric nodded in response.

"Hi, sweetie," Savannah also gave Lila a kiss on the cheek, but then hung back, unsure of what to say.

Lila looked at them both as if she had never seem them before in her life, she turned to him, panic in her eyes. Eric smiled at her reassuringly and carried her into the lounge room, setting her carefully down on the couch.

"I'll make us some tea," Savannah suggested brightly and hurried from the room. The rest of them sat in uncomfortable silence. Well that wasn't quite true, Eric corrected himself, he and Charlie sat in uneasy silence, Lila was once again staring blankly at the wall like she didn't have a care in the world.

Then Savannah must have banged a cupboard in the kitchen, a loud crack slicing through the oppressive silence, and Lila instantly sprung to life. Letting out a shrill scream as she leapt to her feet, looking wildly around the room for the source of the noise.

Eric moved to grab her shoulders but she lurched away from him. "It was just Savannah in the kitchen," he soothed, his hands hovering uncertainly above her shoulders.

"What happened?" Savannah asked appearing in the doorway.

Lila was still looking around in a panic as though she expected someone to jump out at her, skittering away when he once again tried to touch her. Her gaze flitted around the room, jumping from him to Charlie, to Savannah, to the toys littering the room, then she headed for the stairs. "I think I'll take a shower," she mumbled under her breath as she ran up the stairs as fast as her battered body would allow.

Watching his wife go, Eric found himself wandering over to the pile of pajamas lying on the floor. Kneeling down he picked them up, underneath was Joey's favorite teddy bear, Snuggles. When Eric had left for work the morning of that day, Joey had been in a panic unable to locate his beloved bear. He wondered how Lila had managed to coax him into leaving home without it. Had she promised him that when they got home they would look for the bear together, telling him that Snuggles would enjoy having the house to himself for the day?

Snuggles had been given to Joey by Charlie on the day he was born. Joey had adored the teddy, taken him everywhere, and slept with him every night, as a result the bear was stained and tattered in places. Lila had tried on many occasions to give Snuggles a bath but Joey had insisted that he liked him just the way he was.

Standing with the teddy bear gripped tightly in his hand, "I think we should put Snuggles in Joey's coffin." At the word 'coffin' he felt a tidal wave of sobs about to burst out from inside him. Charlie moved towards him, but Eric shook his head and swallowed back the sob. "I think I'll go check on Lila."

Hurriedly making his escape from the room, taking the stairs two at a time. Heading down the hall and through his and Lila's bedroom he entered the ensuite. It was empty. "Lila?" he called. There was no answer.

Leaving the room, he walked back down the hall, pausing at the door to Molly's room. Fingers tracing the big baby pink love heart with Molly's name embroidered on it in a darker shade of pink. Right now he couldn't think about his baby daughter or he would fall apart. Dealing with the loss of one child was bad enough, for now he had to believe that Molly would come home to them unharmed.

Moving further down the hall he stopped outside Joey's room, remembering the first day they brought Joey home from the hospital. He had been so tiny, so perfect, and both he and Lila had been terrified. They must have checked on him about a hundred times that first night.

Readying himself, Eric took a deep breath. The door was open a crack and slowly he pushed it the rest of the way open, his breath catching in his throat at the sight of the room. Lila lay curled up in a ball on Joey's bed. In her arms she held Joey's favorite sweater, a photo of him on his fifth birthday, and his toy rhino.

Eric stood frozen in the doorway. His mind filled with memories of Joey's birthday party. Although it had been only three months ago, it felt more like a lifetime. They had all been so happy then. It had been an unusually hot early spring day. Lila was eight months pregnant, and they were both looking forward to the birth of their new baby. Joey had been excited about his clown birthday party and the puppy, which had been his present. After the clown had left Eric and Lila had taken Joey and his friends over to Charlie's house and the kids had played in his pool for hours.

That night, back at home, the three of them had sat outside under the stars for hours. Eventually Joey had fallen asleep in his arms, the puppy in Lila's, and the two of them had talked for hours about their plans for their future.

Gazing now around Joey's room, at all the things that he loved, his stuffed toys, his books, his games, his baseball things, Joey had started little league just a few months ago. Eric felt like he was drowning in a sea of grief.

Walking across to the bed, he gently removed the jumper and rhino from his wife's arms.

Registering his presence, she looked up at him, tears cascading down her pale cheeks. When he reached for the photo she tightened her grip on it. "No," she begged.

Feeling tears start to fall down his own cheeks he left the photo in her hands and lifted her up into his arms. She laid her head against his shoulder as he carried her from the room.

* * * * *

11:25 A.M.

"Winter told me what happened at the shopping mall," Daniel announced accusingly, looming over her chair.

It had been a long day. After her argument with Parker, which Tessa was still trying to figure out, and the arrival of Matilda Bell, Parker's twin sister, her husband had told them both he had work to do, he'd talk to them later, then he'd stormed off. They'd waited for a while, making small talk, before it became clear Parker had no intention of returning any time soon. Tessa had brought Mattie back here, to her and Parker's place, around one in the morning, set her up in what had been Matilda's childhood bedroom, then laid awake waiting for Parker to come home. She was still waiting.

"I'm fine," she told her older brother as he pressed the back of his hand to her forehead. Raising a skeptical eyebrow when he reached for her wrist, she snatched it away. "You are not a doctor," she reminded him.

"I know how to take someone's pulse," Daniel countered, as he reached over and managed to grab a hold of her arm.

Pouting, Tessa reluctantly allowed her brother to check her pulse, while she focused on quelling the rolling nausea that seemed to have taken up permanent residence in her stomach. It had only been in the last six months that she and Daniel had reconnected, and things between them were just starting to get back to the way they had been when they were kids. When she looked back up Daniel was frowning at her with genuine concern. "What?"

Sitting on the coffee table in front of the armchair where she was curled up, under a blanket despite the warm morning. "What's wrong?"

"What do you mean?" Tessa asked, keeping her face neutral.

"Tessa, I am your brother, your big brother," he added as though that made a difference. "If there is one person in this world that you cannot fool it's me."

He sat waiting expectantly for her to explain, with an exasperated sigh she was about to comply when Matilda appeared in the doorway.

"Sorry to interrupt," Mattie hovered nervously.

Tessa smiled reassuringly, if there was one thing she had learnt about Parker's twin sister, it was that she was extremely jumpy. "It's not a problem, Mattie, this is my brother Daniel. Daniel, this is Parker's twin sister Matilda."

Daniel shot her a look that clearly said their conversation into her current state of health was not over, then turned to greet Matilda and did a double take. People thought that she and Daniel looked alike, they had the same greeny blue eyes, the same pale skin and smattering of freckles, the same curly blonde hair although Daniel's was darker, the only characteristic they didn't share was height, while she was short, only five feet tall, Daniel was over six feet. Parker and Matilda on the other hand, were exact clones of one another. Whoever said that fraternal twins couldn't be identical had obviously never met the Bell twins. Both were tall, both had thick black hair, and both had the exact same amber eyes.

"Hey, Matilda," Daniel went to her and shook her hand.

"She came by last night, she and Parker haven't seen each other in years," Tessa supplied.

Daniel shot Mattie a sympathetic smile. "How are things going?"

Wincing, "I think Parker's pretty mad," Matilda told him. "He's barely said two words to me."

"Join the club," Tessa mumbled under her breath. "Hey that sounds like him now."

But it wasn't Parker who came through the back door, it was Winter, party dress in hand, huge smile on her face, "hey, Tess, I got the dress," she sung, then caught sight of Mattie, "hi, I'm Winter."

"Matilda, Parker's sister," Mattie returned.

Before anyone had a chance to say more they heard a key slide into the lock, and moments later a rumpled and exhausted Parker strode into the living room, surveyed the gathered crowd and scowled.

"I got the dress for my party," Winter announced at last.

Giving her a tight smile, "that's great," Parker nodded. "I'm sure you'll look beautiful."

Winter smiled back then hurried from the tension filled room.

"I'm gonna grab a couple of hours sleep," Parker stated abruptly.

Taking that as a cue that her brother was not in the mood to talk, Mattie scurried from the room, tears in her eyes.

Daniel frowned at Parker, "that was pretty rude."

Parker frowned right back, "I don't think that my relationship with my sister is any of your business."

Rolling his eyes, "but when it was my relationship with Tessa you just had to throw yourself right in the middle of things."

Tessa noted something in her brother's eyes, desire maybe, as he watched the doorway through which Matilda had disappeared, and had to hide a grin, Parker would not like it if Daniel and Matilda got together. Parker and Daniel had had a rocky start to their relationship, but had managed to put their differences aside to save her from the Iceman's clutches. Following that they had gotten along cordially, she had no hopes they were ever going to be best friends, but lately they seemed to have regressed back to how things had been in the beginning.

"That was different," Parker yelled at Daniel's back as he followed Matilda out the back door. "Tessa is my wife."

Alone now Tessa smiled at Parker, hoping to calm him down a little, return him to the sensitive, passionate, sweet guy she'd fallen in love with. Lately he seemed to have morphed into someone else right before her eyes. Now he was moody and sullen, edgy about everything, and avoided contact with her at all costs.

"Speaking of husbands and wives, today is our four month anniversary, so maybe," Tessa murmured as she started to undo the buttons of his shirt, "maybe you might want to take your mind off things." Sliding her hands up his smooth rippling chest, the muscles twitching beneath her feather soft touch. Reaching up on tiptoes to kiss the hollow of his neck as her fingers traced his jaw line through his thick two-day old stubble.

Then all of a sudden his hands clamped around her wrists. "Sex doesn't fix everything, Tessa," he snapped at her.

She recoiled as though he had slapped her. Parker of all people, who knew her past better than anyone else, knew that was a sure fire way to hurt her.

Too late he seemed to realize what he'd said. "I'm sorry, Tess," he mumbled, face pained, eyes dark and stormy.

But the damage had been done. "Parker, let go of me," her

eyes straying to her wrists which Parker was still holding, his grip crushing. The look he gave her sent shivers up her spine and she had to struggle not to let the tears that were building up start to fall. "You're hurting me," she whispered at last.

Releasing his death grip on her wrists he apologized again, "I'm sorry, Tessa." Gaze growing intense he pulled her to him, pressed a fierce kiss to her lips, then eyes turbulent with conflicted emotions, he gave her a last glance and practically ran from the room.

Staring after him, gently rubbing her wrists, where no doubt a bracelet of black and blue would soon begin to form. Tessa didn't know what had just happened, what had changed, what she had done, but something had definitely shifted between them.

Just four months ago today they had been married in a magical wedding ceremony in the snow. A small gathering, Daniel and Winter, her old friends, the Wyatt's, J.J. and his wife, and a couple of Parker's other friends. They'd married out on her estate, which she had inherited from her paternal grandparents, on the site where her cottage used to sit. The cottage had been destroyed eighteen months ago in a fire that had almost claimed her life, but it was the place where she and Parker had first met. It had been sunset, snow thick on the ground, snowflakes swirling through the air, the clouds on the horizon a mass of pink, orange and gold. It had been, without a doubt, the happiest day of her life.

And now everything was falling apart and she didn't understand why. Parker was pulling away from her, now, when she needed him the most. She didn't understand what she had done to make Parker so sad. His caramel colored eyes never glowed anymore, his smile never lit up his face. She'd been the one who had been reluctant to start a relationship with him. She had been the one who'd told him that she didn't know how to trust people and that she didn't know how to be what he needed. But he had promised her. He'd promised her that he would show her how to be happy, he had promised that he would love her no matter what, he had promised her that they would be together forever, that he would never leave her.

And she had believed him.

That had been her mistake.

* * * * *

4:31 P.M.

Staring at the phone in his hand.

He should call her. Apologize. Explain.

He should call.

And yet he didn't.

Parker sat in Wyatt's car, on their way to where an abandoned car matching the description of Lila and Eric Abbott's red sedan had been discovered.

If it was possible, he was feeling even worse than he had earlier today. People were supposed to be made up of approximately eighty percent water, he felt like he was made up of eighty percent guilt. Guilt over Molly Abbott's abduction, guilt over what he'd told Lila Abbott, guilt over how he'd treated his wife, guilt over how he'd treated his sister. Guilt, guilt, guilt, it seemed to be the new mantra of his life.

In the last twenty-four hours he had really made a mess of things.

He had been a jerk, and not at all like his usual self. He was supposed to be Tessa's rock. For all her appearance of calm and composure, inside she was as vulnerable as a child, and while he might be dark, moody, and sometimes pessimistic whenever he was with Tessa he was always in control.

Until today.

Feeling a sharp stab of guilt as he thought of the words he had hurled thoughtlessly at Tessa just hours ago. Remembering the look in her eyes, the pain, the anger, the confusement. Parker knew he had hurt her in the most vicious way possible.

The truth was he had been afraid of hurting her, tried to avoid it, and managed to do it anyway.

A storm had been raging inside him, a desperate need to drag Tessa up the stairs, throw her down on the bed, and plunge inside her again and again until everything else faded away. He had managed to restrain himself, partly because he knew that Tessa couldn't handle that yet, and partly because his desire was so strong he was afraid he might actually hurt her. And so, he had made the infinitely better choice and cut her to shreds with his words. Shaking his head, he was an idiot.

Regretting his words the second they were out of his mouth, he'd hurried from the room, then guilty he'd gone looking for her. He'd found her in the shower, heard her sobbing from the hall, and lost his nerve. What he should have done was climb under the pouring water, kiss Tessa, tell her he loved her, and then try to explain everything that was going on inside his head. Instead, he had crept back to their room, climbed under the covers and fallen into a fitful sleep full of haunting nightmares.

Awakening when Wyatt had called a few hours later, he'd found Tessa asleep on a chair in the living room, apparently she had chosen not to join him in bed. Palms pressed together, pink cheek nestled against them, pale lips forming a small o, whimpering quietly as her own sleep was plagued with bad dreams. Looking down at her he hadn't seen his sleeping wife, but her tied to a chair inside a burning building, covered in blood a gun in her hands, unconscious in the snow, lying dead in his arms drenched in blood from a gunshot wound. And then he'd imagined her lying in a coffin, and the thought of losing her was so overwhelming it literally took his breath away.

Back when he had been convincing her to start dating him, Tessa's biggest fear had been losing him. She had lost every person she'd ever loved and didn't think she could cope if she let herself fall in love with him and then lost him too. He had been the one to comfort her, reassuring her that she would never lose him, that he would never leave her, that they would be together forever. And now . . . now he was fearing the exact same thing he'd promised Tessa would never happen.

Once again Parker had known he should wake her up, offer some sort of explanation, but he'd convinced himself it was better to let her sleep. Or to be more accurate he had chickened out. He should've woken her with a kiss, told her he loved her, then found Mattie and told her he was glad she was back and that he loved her too, he could even have been on a roll and found Daniel telling him despite himself he actually liked Tessa's brother.

Fingering the phone in his hand, he really should call her and make up, so before he could change his mind he dialed speed dial one and held the phone to his ear. Seconds later he was greeted by Tessa's breezy voice telling him she was busy and couldn't come to the phone right now, but to leave a message and she'd get back to you as soon as she could. Parker listened to the beep, then found that his throat had closed up and he couldn't talk. The silence stretched out, and once again the coward, he hung up without a word.

"Well aren't you a little ray of sunshine today," Wyatt said at last, breaking the oppressive silence.

Shooting him a tired glare, "just thinking about what we're gonna find," which wasn't entirely untrue.

"Well then I got bad news for you."

Confused, Parker looked up at him.

"We're here," Wyatt jerked his head towards the passenger side window.

Turning to look out the window.

They were out deep in an old industrial estate, several abandoned warehouses dotted the landscape, piles of discarded junk rose up like small hills. Over in a corner nestled between a small, dilapidated building and the biggest pile of moldy cardboard boxes Parker had ever seen, was the car they had been searching for.

The call had come in just an hour ago. A security guard patrolling the grounds, which had been bought by a developer and were about to be turned into a shopping mall, had found the abandoned car. At first, he hadn't been concerned, he found dozens of dumped cars every week, but upon closer inspection, he saw that the side of the car was splattered in what appeared to be blood.

Immediately the guard had pulled out his cell phone and called the police, who, after checking the license plate, had identified it as the Abbott's car. A call had then gone through to J.J. who in turn had called him and Wyatt, Parker had slept through his boss' call, but woken for Wyatt's.

Reluctantly he followed his partner from the car, not sure that he wanted to get too close to the sedan. The guard had reported that there was no sign of the baby inside the car, but they still had to check out the trunk, and for any signs of foul play inside the vehicle. Marty and his crime scene techs were on their way, but he and Wyatt were the first to arrive.

Reaching the car both he and Wyatt walked a slow circle around it, eyes scanning up and down, side-to-side and horizontally as they looked for anything out of place. Parker found himself stopping in front of the blood spatter that was spread across the passenger side door, like some sort of crazy dot-to-dot picture in a child's coloring book. Images of the blood soaked child lying on the ground flew into his head, and for one horrifying second he thought he was going to pass out, but then the sensation passed and he found himself staring at the empty baby capsule still strapped into the back seat.

"This car's from the carjacking right?" a voice suddenly boomed behind them making both he and Wyatt jump. "Where the little boy was killed?"

Catching his breath as he turned to face the tubby, middle-aged bordering on old age, security guard who had suddenly materialized out of thin air.

"Where did you come from?" Parker barely kept the growl out of his voice.

"I was in my car," the security guard pointed to where it was parked partially obscured behind the cardboard mountain. "Saw you two walk over, thought I'd come see if I could be of any assistance." He was studying them with curious brown eyes, and Parker guessed this was the closest to any real crime he'd ever come in his pseudo police officer life.

"When was the last time you were here?" Wyatt asked in the hopes of nabbing down a time line.

"Well," the security guard drawled, running a hand through the thick stubble on his chin.

Parker raised a hand to his own rough face, and realized with a start he hadn't shaved in days. He was really starting to fall apart.

"I usually come by every third day," the security guard was saying. "Today's the fourteenth so must have been the," counting backwards on his fingers, "the eleventh."

Which was the day before the carjacking and did nothing to help them learn how long the car could have been left here.

"You notice anything else unusual around here?" Parker asked with a sweeping glance across the huge expanse.

"Same old, same old," the guard told them. "Name's Henry by the way."

"Alright, Henry, we're going to have to ask you to go and wait by your car," Parker ordered, there was no use putting it off any longer.

Henry hesitated, but apparently decided it was a done deal and followed the instruction.

Once Henry was safely out of the way, Parker slid on a pair of gloves and with a resigned sigh eased open the driver's door and popped the trunk. Waiting for Wyatt's moan, or groan when he found the tiny little body left all alone in the trunk of a car, like a piece of garbage. When there was no sound from his partner,

Parker straightened and went to join Wyatt, and breathed a sigh of relief. The trunk was empty. Well not empty it was full of grocery bags and the usual junk that lives in the family car, but there was no baby inside.

Giddy with the brief reprieve from his dark mood. "Maybe they did drop her off somewhere and it just hasn't been reported yet. Or maybe they took her with them and are just waiting for things to calm down before they drop her off." Scowling at Wyatt when his partner didn't chime in with a constructive comment of his own. "What?"

"They left the diaper bag," Wyatt said softly as he unzipped the bag to reveal diapers, and bottles, spare clothes and all the other necessities for people with infants.

With that any lingering optimism vanished. "She's dead. I knew it, I told you she would be. What carjackers want to be stuck with a baby?"

The events of this morning firmly embedded in his mind. They had been lucky then, well rather the Abbott's had been lucky, the parents of the tiny male infant had not. Parker hadn't been able to get the image of the small child out of his head, the chubby arms and legs, the round tummy, the button nose, the little curled toes and fingers with dimples at the base, it was like it had been ingrained on his retinas.

Beginning to spin in circles, scanning the ground to look for signs of recently disturbed dirt. Catching sight of the pile of dirty cardboard boxes, a perfect place to conceal a small corpse. Then he was at the pile, carelessly flinging aside box after box. Hating Wyatt for not being in a blind panic, hating the carjackers who could kill two innocent children, hating Lila Abbott for not protecting her own children, hating his own mother for abandoning him and Matilda.

But most of all hating himself.

* * * * *

8:11 P.M.

"You found her?" Lila asked dully, as she walked stiffly into the room, the entire left side of her body was covered in bruises. She wanted to feel scared for her baby, devastated by the loss of her son, terrified by the traumatic event she had been through, but she felt nothing. Just an all-consuming emptiness. Her life had become one giant void.

Detective Bell looked back at her with bloodshot eyes, his black hair a wild mess, his face covered in short, dark, stubble. He looked haunted, and for a second she envied him his ability to feel, to be part of the real world.

"Not yet, I'm sorry," he told her, voice heavy with grief.

Nodding, she sunk down onto the couch beside her husband, a glimmer of something, fear, sorrow, resignation, nipping at her heart, before disappearing into the blackness that had become her existence. Instinctively she leaned into her husband when he wrapped an arm around her shoulders, but she felt like they were oceans apart.

"We *will* find her," Detective Bell told her emphatically, the fire in his eyes almost convinced her to believe his words.

"We did find your car," the other detective, Detective Wyatt she thought, told them.

"And there was no sign," Eric paused to clear his throat, "no sign that they had hurt Molly?"

As her husband talked with the detectives about their discovery, Lila found herself looking around her own living room as though it were a foreign land. Since Eric had brought her home from the hospital earlier this morning, she had spent most of the day in Joey's room. Eric kept finding her in there and taking her out, but as soon as he was gone she kept finding herself back in the room, curled up on her son's bed. She liked to be in there, it made her feel closer to him.

Someone, probably Charlie or Savannah, had cleared the living room of all of Joey's toys and games and books. The family photos hanging from the wall looked a little lopsided, as though someone had taken them down only to hang them back up again. Finding herself looking at one particular picture, a grinning Joey cradling newborn Molly in his lap. He'd lost his first tooth the day Molly was born, and it had been a toss up as to which was the more exciting, a new baby sister, or a tooth falling out. In the photo Joey had made sure his mouth was wide open to show off the gap in his bottom row of teeth, and the baby was nuzzling her little head against her big brother's shoulder.

"Tell me the truth," Eric was demanding, "I need to know. Do you think that Molly is still alive?"

The two detectives exchanged wary glances and Eric was about to repeat his question more insistently, when she interrupted, "Molly is still alive," she announced confidently, positive in her heart that this was true.

"Mrs. Abbott," Detective Bell begun in an understanding voice. "I know that you're Molly's mother and you want to believe that she's coming home to you, but . . ."

Cutting him off, "they wouldn't hurt her," she said more forcefully, a memory dancing frantically in her head. "They wouldn't."

"I know you want to believe that," Detective Wyatt joined in gently.

"They wouldn't hurt her," she repeated adamantly, then more quietly, "they were singing to her."

"Did you remember something?" Eric asked, eyes wide.

"She was crying and they were singing to her," aware that all eyes in the room were staring at her inquisitively. "A lullaby."

The phone begun to chirp insistently and Eric reluctantly stood to answer it.

"Mrs. Abbott, do you remember anything else?" Detective Bell asked softly.

Thinking hard, trying desperately to make the rest of the events of that fateful afternoon return to her, but she couldn't, that was all there was. Just singing.

"Do you remember what the lullaby was?" Detective Wyatt asked.

Chewing on her lip and subconsciously pulling her tattered old purple robe tighter around herself. "It was that one where someone brings the baby gifts, mockingbirds and rings." Frowning, annoyed she couldn't remember the name of the song. Lately she seemed to be having trouble remembering a lot of things.

"Hush Little Baby?" Detective Wyatt asked.

"Yes," she smiled the first smile she had in days. "That was what she was singing to Molly."

"She?" Detective Wyatt repeated. "One of the carjackers was a female?"

Nodding enthusiastically, feeling alive once again. "Yes, one was a woman and the other was a man."

"Do you remember anything else about them? Anything distinctive?"

"No."

"What about height? Were they tall or short?"

"I'm not sure."

"Young or old?"

"I don't know."

"Skin color?"

"White?" She thought this was true but couldn't be sure.

"Anything distinctive about their voices?"

Her momentary invigoration waning. "I don't know. I don't remember anything else, but I know that they wouldn't have hurt Molly. Why would they be singing to her, trying to calm her down, if they were just going to kill her?" Looking up as Eric returned to stand above her, the somber expression on his face ending her fleeting journey back to the land of the living, the emptiness was quickly returning.

"That was the minister," Eric told her, dropping down at her side and taking her hands in his, and she pictured Joey's tiny hands reaching out to her as his life slowly ebbed away. "He wants to talk to us about the funeral."

Snatching her hands back. Funerals were for old people, people who'd lived their lives, not for tiny children who were only at the beginning of life's long journey. It wasn't fair, parents weren't supposed to bury their children. Life just wasn't being fair.

Slowly she became aware of the fact that she was crying. Eric tried to reach for her but she shrunk away from him, the doctor that couldn't even save his own son. And then Detective Bell was kneeling in front of her, one hand on her knee, the other reaching up to brush away her tears. His golden eyes, Joey's eyes, as tormented as she knew her own must be.

"It's going to be okay, Mrs. Abbott," his voice surprisingly reassuring. "I'll be there at the funeral, I promise. We'll get through it together."

And then for some reason she couldn't explain she was sobbing uncontrollably and flinging herself into his arms. The arms of a stranger she'd met just days ago at the scene of her son's bloody murder, and felt a strange sense of peace descend over her.

JUNE 15TH

6:08 A.M.

"Been out all night?"

It was the wrong thing to say. He realized it as soon as the words tumbled out.

Immediately Matilda's eyes clouded over, she crossed her arms tightly across her chest, and pouted at him. "What do you care?"

"I'm sorry," Daniel stifled a yawn. He had barely slept a wink last night. Between worrying about Matilda, a sharp renewal in his dislike towards his brother-in-law, and Tessa who'd been up sick most of the night, he'd got maybe two or three hours sleep. "I just meant I was worried about you."

Arching a perfectly shaped dark eyebrow. "I repeat, what do you care?"

Daniel studied the woman in front of him. Her gaunt frame, the dark circles under eyes that held a haunted gleam, pale skin that hinted at too many hours spent indoors. Matilda Bell was beautiful but seemed to shrink away from it, like the thought that someone might find her attractive terrified her. With the bits and pieces he knew about the Bell's past he was pretty sure he knew why.

"We're related," he ventured.

Giving him a 'nice try' smile.

"Because I like you," Daniel told her honesty.

The answer seemed to catch her by surprise, her mouth dropped open and she stared at him, then recovered, "you don't even know me."

There was nothing he could stay to that. She was right of

course. He'd only met her yesterday, never even spoken to her before now, but there was something about Matilda that had stirred up something inside him, something he hadn't even known existed.

"You hungry?" he asked at last, pointing to the table where he'd made a giant bowl of fruit salad.

Relenting, she gave him a penetrating stare, before taking a seat at the far end of the table. Taking the hint, Daniel sat as far away from Matilda as was possible and for a while the two sat eating in silence.

"Where are Tessa and Winter?" Matilda asked at last, devouring the fruit as if she hadn't eaten in months.

"Winter's still asleep, won't be up for hours, according to teenage time it's about one am," Daniel joked.

Matilda offered up a small smile at his joke, but quickly replaced it with her usual somber expression. "What about Tessa?"

"She's been up sick most of the night, I just got her to sleep before I came down and made breakfast, I'll try to get her to eat when she wakes up next." With a wry smile that he knew couldn't quite hide his worry, "my sister's not big on taking care of herself. Others, yes, herself, never."

Noting the concern in his voice, "you're really worried about her?"

"I'm her big brother, it's my job to worry about her."

Wistful, "it's nice that you're so close."

"We weren't always close. I let something keep me away from her, I wasn't there for her when she needed me. Then when I did come back it was almost too late, she didn't want to see me, and your brother . . . well let's just say that we didn't get off to a great start."

Another wistful smile, "Parker really loves her huh?"

"He's saved her life on more than one occasion and risked his own in the process." Daniel may not be crazy about Parker, but he respected the fact that Parker loved Tessa and she loved him.

"That sounds like my brother, always the protector," Matilda stated, a little sadly.

"He loves you too you know, despite his little tantrum yesterday," he added quietly, sensing Matilda's unspoken fear.

Shaking her head, "he's disappointed in me. For leaving. For not being able to get over what happened to me when we were in foster care. For being weak," tears began to spill from her amber eyes and embarrassed she swiped them away.

Wanting to reach out and comfort her, but not sure she would allow him to. "You were raped?" he asked gently.

Surprised for a second, then resigned, then just plain sad. "Foster father and his friends. Not just me, all the little girls."

"Parker knows?" he asked tightly, there seemed to be a never-ending supply of creeps who preyed on defenseless children.

Nodding, "he blamed himself because he couldn't save me, it got worse after . . ." she broke off to tuck her feet up onto the chair, resting her chin on her knees. "There was an accident. I was going to run away. I had a gun," she continued haltingly, the haunted look back in her eyes was magnified a hundredfold. "I thought he was going to hurt me. I shot him. It was an accident," she said again but sounded as though she were simply parroting back words she'd been told.

"The man died?" he asked gently.

Choking back a sob Matilda nodded.

"You were protecting yourself," he told her softly. "You were a child and you were protecting yourself. Tessa's killed someone in self-defense and so have I. It's a horrible thing to have to do but it's not anything to be ashamed about."

Crying harder now, "but that's just it. I thought I was protecting myself. I thought he was coming to hurt me, but he wasn't. He was a social worker. He was coming to help us," and then she was burying her face in her hands and sobbing.

Wanting to help but not knowing what to say, Daniel reached

across and laid a hand on her heaving shoulder, but Matilda shrunk away from his touch. "But you didn't know that, Matilda. You were a child, a scared child who had been abused, you were trying to protect yourself the only way you thought you could."

Looking up at him as if he was an idiot, tears still streaming down her cheeks, "but I was wrong," she said harshly. "I killed an innocent man. I let myself be raped over and over again and did nothing to stop it. I'm dirty and disgusting and vile and . . ."

"Stop," he commanded with more force than he'd intended. "You are not any of those things," reaching across to brush away strands of her shoulder length black hair that were clinging to her wet cheeks. "You are beautiful, Matilda," leaning in slowly, his lips coming to meet hers.

"Daniel!"

Footsteps on the stairs sent them both springing away. Daniel pushing quickly back from the table as Winter came barreling into the room. "What's wrong?"

"It's Tessa, she's throwing up again," his niece twirled her hair around her finger, as was her custom when she was nervous. "Daniel, she doesn't look good."

Another stab of worry as he pondered just what was wrong with his baby sister. She had insisted she just had the flu but he was starting to think that, once again, Tessa knew more than she was letting on. As Winter hurried back up the stairs, he turned to Matilda, who was rubbing at her red eyes.

"I'll be fine," she told him before he could even ask the question.

Turning to follow his niece down the hall he paused, "Matilda, when she's feeling better you should talk to Tessa."

Confused for a second then understanding dawned.

"Promise me something."

"What?" she asked, instantly wary.

"Promise you won't shut me out, that you'll let me try to help."

"Why would you want to do that, Daniel? You just met me."

"Because you're special," he told her simply and he could hear her break out into a fresh batch of tears as he ran quickly up the stairs.

* * * * *

10:17 A.M.

"So we are now looking at this as an abduction?" J.J. clarified.

"Lila Abbott is positive that the people that attacked her were singing to calm the baby, to me that doesn't sound like carjackers," Parker told him.

"Insights, Beth?"

"Well," Elisabeth Bennett, the psychiatrist who regularly helped them with profiling, began slowly. "According to the profile of the 'typical' infant abductor used by the National Centre of Missing and Exploited Children, the abductor is usually female. Usually between the ages of twelve and fifty-three, and usually cannot have children of her own or has recently lost a baby, lives in the area of the abduction and is able to provide good care for the baby. Given that the baby was not taken from a healthcare facility, the abductor is probably more likely to be single but may claim to have a partner, to have targeted a particular mother and tried to meet the family, and has planned the abduction beforehand. Now the fact that we appear to be dealing with two abductors is a little unusual, is Lila Abbott positive that she was attacked by two people?"

"She seemed very convinced," Parker answered defensively.

"Pretty positive," Wyatt agreed when J.J. shot him a questioning look, and Parker felt a stab of annoyance that his ability to do his job objectively seemed to still be in question.

"So I guess the question is was this a case of being in the wrong place at the wrong time, or were the Abbott's being targeted. We need to talk to them again, see if they remember anyone suspicious, especially any women, popping up in their lives," J.J. mused. "What else can you tell us about our abductors, Beth?"

"She's probably compulsive and a liar, deceiving and manipulating to get what she wants. She's probably approached the Abbott's at their home, possibly by impersonating a healthcare or social services professional. I'm still a little baffled by the fact that there are two of them though," Beth confessed as her hand absently began to rub her belly. Beth had finally married her boyfriend of several years, who had spent most of their relationship battling cancer, several months ago, and had just announced a week ago that they were expecting their first child.

"Did we ID the baby from the park?"

J.J. directed the question at him and Wyatt, but Parker let his partner field it. He was still conflicted about the little boy, whose tiny little body they had dug up the other day. He was infinitely relieved that the baby was not Molly Abbott, but at the same time he was horrified by the callousness of someone who would bury their own child's body in a shallow grave in the park.

"His name was Harrison Kirrle. Only a month old, his mother is just fourteen, a baby herself, father goes to her school, he's fifteen. Girl's parents were raising the child as their own, she was supposed to be babysitting him night of the thirteenth, but her boyfriend came over and the two of them were too busy making out. When they go to check on the baby he's not breathing, they both panic, the dad takes Harrison and buries his body in the park. When her parents arrived home the girl claimed someone stole the baby while she was taking a nap. Her parents didn't believe her and called the police, who notified them when an unidentified infant male was found, did a DNA test, and it confirms the baby from the park is Harrison Kirrle."

"Did the kids do something to him?" J.J. asked.

"It's looking like a possible SIDS death at the moment," Wyatt told him.

"Alright," J.J. nodded, tucking this information away, and returning his attention to the Abbott case. "What about the car, Marty?" he asked as he reached for a bottle of aspirin that balanced on the edge of his family photo strewn desk. J.J. and his wife of thirty-five years had four kids and fourteen grandkids, which made for a lot of photos.

Watching J.J. tip a couple of pills into his massive hand, Parker noticed for the first time just how old his boss was beginning to look.

"The car was dumped with the keys still in the ignition, fingerprints everywhere." Marty's head bobbed backwards and forwards like a bird's, as he spoke in the excited voice he used only when talking about work. As far as anyone knew Marty, a widower most of his adult life, had no interests outside of his job. "We took samples from Eric and Lila Abbott to exclude their fingerprints, so far we have two distinct sets of prints. So far no hits on the prints, but fingers crossed."

As Parker studied the CSU tech, with his hair that was now more grey than black, and his narrow face that was becoming increasingly lined with wrinkles, he wondered when it was that everyone had become so old. It was like in the last couple of weeks they had all aged ten years, himself included.

"Wyatt and I'll go visit the Abbott's again," he announced.

J.J. nodded, "talk to them about doing an appeal to the public for help. I know they said no at first, but maybe this new information will change things. Our priority now is identifying the abductors."

Everyone nodded wearily and pushed back their chairs, trailing out of J.J.'s office. Marty called a quick goodbye over his shoulder as he hurried towards the lift to get back to the lab.

Wyatt too headed for the lift, "pick you up in a couple of hours. At your place," he added with a pointed glance at Parker's rumpled clothes.

Despite the fact that he was pretty sure Wyatt also hadn't

gotten much sleep last night, his partner looked calm, cool and collected. Wyatt's white shirt was crisp and wrinkle free, his strawberry blonde hair in place, his green eyes alert, while Parker knew he looked like he'd just been in an explosion. Sometimes life just wasn't fair.

Sinking down into his uncomfortable desk chair, he became aware that Beth was studying him with her probing psychiatrist stare. He'd gotten to know Beth quite well a couple of years ago after he'd been forced to shoot dead a psychopathic teenager holding a gun on her newborn daughter. As per department requirements he'd gone to see a shrink, positive that the whole thing would turn out to be a complete waste of time, only to find that talking with Beth actually helped him. "What?" he asked her now.

"You look tired," she commented mildly.

Raising an eyebrow at her, "been talking to J.J.?"

"Actually Tessa called me." Beth's dark brown eyes betrayed that this had surprised her too, since Tessa never bothered to hide her distaste for psychiatrists.

"Tessa? Called you?"

Nodding, "she's worried about you."

"Well she shouldn't be," he said crossly.

"Don't like it when the shoe's on the other foot?" Beth asked with a smile.

"I've got your number, if I need you I'll call," gathering his keys and cell phone and heading for the stairs. Aware of Beth's steady gaze on his back he paused, "I'm tired, Beth," he said quietly, "really, really tired." And then he was hurrying down the stairs and out into the warm morning where he drunk in several mouthfuls of fresh air and headed for home.

* * * * *

11:26 A.M.

The house was quiet.

Winter had gone out with some of her friends, after assurances from Daniel that Tessa would be okay.

Daniel had gone to work, after assurances from Matilda that she would keep an eye on Tessa.

Tessa had finally fallen into a restless sleep.

So, Matilda sat in the living room of her brother's house, the house where she had grown up, and wondered whether she had made the biggest mistake of her life by coming back here.

She'd known the day she left that there could be no going back. That leaving Parker and her adopted parents would change things forever. At first she hadn't planned to be gone for so long, but the longer she stayed away the harder it was to think about coming back.

Now she was pondering packing her bags and hightailing it out of here as fast as she could. But every time she took a step towards her old room something, or rather someone, held her back. Matilda hated to admit it but she was finding herself intrigued by Daniel Micah. There was something about his steady blue eyes that prodded at something inside her.

Plus he'd called her special.

She'd been called that before of course. By her brother, their adopted parents, the long line of psychiatrists she'd been taken to see to try to help her get over what had happened to her, to deal with shooting a man, to help her adjust to life with her new family, but she'd never believed it. It had always felt like they were trying to convince her of something they themselves didn't believe, but when Daniel said it . . .

Pushing thoughts of Daniel from her mind, even if she had been capable of having a normal relationship, there was no point in starting something when she would soon be gone.

Wandering aimlessly to the fireplace, the mantle of which still held the same family photos that had been there when she was growing up. Photos of her adopted parents wedding, of their biological son Taylor who had died from cancer at the age of seven, of her and Parker at various stages of adolescence. New ones had been added, Parker and Tessa at their wedding, at the beach, playing in the snow. Her brother looked so happy in the pictures, nothing like the man she had seen two days ago.

Matilda could see why her brother had fallen for Tessa. She was beautiful. Not a word Matilda usually liked, but a word she was used to hearing. From her foster father, from each and every one of his friends, from the boys at school who had wanted to get inside her pants.

Matilda knew she was not beautiful, she was too skinny, too pale, too solemn, but the word definitely fitted Tessa. With her enormous aqua eyes, her white blonde curls that framed a delicate face, she looked like an angel.

Upon closer inspection, Matilda could see the stiff way Tessa held herself, the smile that never fully lit her eyes, and she remembered what Daniel had said to her. Talk to Tessa. She had understood his meaning, Tessa knew what she was going through because she herself had been through it, and she had found happiness with Parker.

Maybe . . . maybe that meant things weren't *completely* hopeless.

Speaking of the devil, she heard a rustle at the front door and moments later Parker filled the doorway. They both stood, staring at one another in silence, taking in each other's bloodshot eyes, pale and haggard faces, and rumpled clothes.

"Looks like I wasn't the only one who stayed out all night," she said hoping to break the tension.

Her brother merely huffed. "Where's Tessa?"

"Upstairs asleep. She's been up sick all night."

Momentarily stricken, "is she alright?"

"She's sleeping now, Daniel was with her."

That seemed to make him angrier.

"Daniel's a nice guy you know, and he really cares about his sister."

His face took on the patiently reproachful look it used to when they were kids and she'd disappointed him. "I care about you, Mattie. Only no matter how many times I told you I loved you, or mom and dad told you they loved you, you never believed it."

In that second, she hated her brother more than she hated anyone else on the planet. His ability to make her feel despicable had not diminished over the years. Parker had always been the good one, life for him at the Bell's had been wonderful. He'd been able to put behind him what had happened to them in foster care and move on. He'd had Luka and Laura and Wyatt. He'd been happy. She on the other hand had always been a disappointment to all of them. She was the one who'd remained quiet and withdrawn. She was the one who hadn't been able to love Luka and Laura like parents. She'd been the one who had fallen for Caterina's lies when their biological mother had come back. She was stupid and naïve and ruined everything she touched.

"I was always a disappointment to you." Matilda felt tears stinging her eyes but bit them back, she would not let him make her cry.

Face softening, "I was never disappointed in you."

"Yes you were," she countered. "Every time I wouldn't talk to you, every time I spent the day in my room alone, every time I made mom cry because I couldn't tell her I loved her."

Matilda remembered the first time that Parker had called Laura mom. The pure joy on the woman's face, the pure love she had for them, she had loved them just as much as she had loved her son Taylor. It was barely a couple of months after they'd moved in but already Parker had changed so much. After he'd said it she remembered everyone looking at her, waiting for her to say it too. And so she had.

"You're the one who left, Matilda," Parker reminded her. "You're the one who bailed on me."

"Because you never forgave me for not being happy," swiping

quickly at her eyes to brush away the tears before they fell. "The Bell's saved you, Parker, but it was already too late for me."

It hadn't been her brother's fault that she had been too damaged to repair, he had loved her, he had spent hours entertaining her when she'd known he'd rather be out playing with his friends. It wasn't her adopted parents fault either. They hadn't just sent her to shrinks to try to help her, they had spent lots of time with her, trying to encourage her interests, trying to build up her self-esteem.

Matilda remembered the night of her senior prom, her senior prom that she had decided not to attend because she'd been afraid about where things would end if she'd taken a date, what the boy would expect from her. Laura had sat with her in her room, trying to get her to talk about her feelings, then burst into tears and asked if Matilda believed that she loved her. Matilda had felt so guilty and so helpless, she hadn't known how to explain the jumble of emotions inside of her, and so she'd told Laura that she knew that she was loved, and allowed the woman to hug her tightly. Then just days later she had packed her bags and left.

Waiting now for Parker to correct her. To tell her that it was never too late. That he loved her, that he was her brother, even though they were twins he'd always been more like her big brother, her protector.

But Parker just stared at her with empty eyes that scared her more than anything else, then sighed, "Wyatt's going to be here soon, I need to take a shower. Can you stay with Tessa?" he asked before trudging up the stairs.

"Sure," Matilda nodded to her brother's retreating back.

Once she heard the sound of pounding water, she wandered over and picked up an old family photo, taken about a year after the Bell's had adopted her and Parker. The photo was of their first family vacation, and in it everyone but herself was grinning widely at the camera. Little Matilda had a smile on her face, but there was no light behind it. She had positioned herself slightly away from the others. The only thing tying her to the rest of her family was Parker who had wrapped his arm around her shoulder. Matilda wondered whether it was too late to fix her relationship with her brother or if things were already beyond repair.

* * * * *

6:45 P.M.

Anger, fear, hurt, guilt.
Rage, terror, pain, shame.
Fury, panic, grief, remorse.
Spinning around and around in his head, driving him half insane.

Glancing down the hallway at the closed bedroom door Eric wondered if he was doing the right thing. It had only been a couple of days since the incident, as they'd begun calling it, but it felt like years. The hospital had said that he could take off as much time as he needed, but he wanted to go back to work, to do something with his time, something to stop him from thinking about his dead son and missing daughter.

He was desperate to escape, he felt like he was suffocating in this house. A house that was so full of memories of Joey and Molly. Everywhere he turned there were photos, or toys, or clothes.

Lila was not getting any better, if anything she was getting worse. Physically she was recovering well but emotionally she was a mess. This morning she'd only gotten out of bed because he made her, and even then, she'd just sat and stared listlessly into space. He had tried talking to her, but half the time she looked at him like she had no idea what he was saying. When she did talk, it was always about Joey, he didn't think he'd heard her mention Molly's name since she was taken. Eric tried to convince himself that his wife was just avoiding thinking about Molly to protect herself. He himself found it hard to think about his baby daughter, the more time that ticked by the less likely it was that Molly would ever be returned to them.

Ashamed at the relief he felt at being able to get out of the house tomorrow and spend some time away from Lila. Looking into his wife's distant, haunted eyes scared him. She seemed so far away that he was beginning to wonder if she was ever going to come back to him.

There had to be something he could do, some way he could reach out to her and yank her back into the land of the living. Right now, though, all he could think about was getting away from this place. This oppressive, stifling, crushing house, if he didn't get out he was going to scream . . . letting out a startled squeak as the doorbell chimed.

Plodding down the stairs to the front door and opening it to reveal the two detectives who were working his family's case. They seemed like nice people, seemed like competent cops, the dark haired one seemed especially involved, and Eric remembered that he had been the one who shot at the car and found Joey and Lila.

"Mr. Abbott, may we come in?" Detective Wyatt asked.

Shrugging, he held the door open and let them follow him to the kitchen. He didn't know why they were here, Lila had already told them everything that she remembered, but he was desperate to get his baby back and whatever the police wanted him and Lila to do they would do.

Fixing drinks, when he brought them to the table where the detectives were waiting, he felt their gaze fall to his battered hands.

Waking late last night from a fitful doze, angrier than he'd ever been before in his life. Lila's pitiful whimpers, emanating from her own fitful doze, egging on his fury. Eric had started to stroke her face to soothe her, only to find his hands dipping to her slender white throat, and afraid of what he might do he quickly left the room, heading for the basement. His old punching bag still hanging from the ceiling, he'd forgone gloves and honed right in on the firm, blue material. With each thump of his bare fists his anger had grown, stronger and stronger, until it built to a crescendo where Eric thought it was going to burst right out of him. And then, like a balloon when you stick it with a pin, it was simply gone, and nothing was left of him but a few broken, useless pieces. Lying on the floor, sweating, shaking, panting, and staring at the grey ceiling his thoughts flitting from one thing to another until Lila's screams had pierced the still night, and he'd dragged himself back to their bedroom.

Giving a half-hearted shrug in answer to their unasked question, that seemed to be sufficient.

"Where's Mrs. Abbott?" Detective Bell asked, scanning the kitchen.

"Upstairs, asleep. I gave her a sleeping pill, she needs to rest." He needed to rest as well but was afraid of what his dreams would contain when he did. It wasn't nightmares he was scared of, but dreams of happier times, when their family was whole, only to have to wake up and realize that it wasn't real. Eric didn't think he could take that.

Detective Bell gave a brisk nod and then began, "we think that the primary aim of the attack on your family was to take Molly."

Feeling the color drain from his face. "You think some abducted Molly on purpose?"

"We think so," Detective Wyatt confirmed.

"Well is that good or bad?"

"It probably means that whoever took your daughter is taking good care of her."

Eric didn't know if that made him feel better or worse. The idea that someone was out there with his baby, taking care of her as though she were their own, that someone was trying to make her a part of their family, was beyond creepy. Suddenly feeling ill, he stood and began to pace the room.

"The focus of our investigation at the moment is figuring out whether the abduction was planned or spur of the moment," Detective Bell continued.

Balancing himself against the counter to keep from crumpling to the ground. "You . . . you think someone was . . . was stalking her?" he stammered. "Stalking a baby?" aware that hysteria was beginning to lace his voice.

"We think that it's a possibility," Detective Wyatt's voice was clam, almost hypnotic, and Eric wondered how many times he had conversations just like this with the family of a victim. Probably the same amount of times that Eric himself had spoken with relatives of a patient at the ER. He wondered if those families felt the same way he did now. Detached, spinning alone in a dark sea where there was nothing in sight but endless black waves, broken with no idea where to begin the process of healing, or even if that was possible.

Calming himself by breathing deeply and slowly counting to ten. "What do you need from us?"

"We need to know whether you remember anyone unusual who came into your lives at some time in the last few months. If the abduction was planned then there is a good chance that the abductor tried to make contact with you at some point. Does anything ring a bell?"

"I'm not home a lot," he began dejectedly. "And when I am it's usually spending time with Lila and the kids," he felt himself choking up and had to remind himself to focus, this could be the key to getting his daughter back alive. "We don't go out a lot, and most of our friends are from the hospital . . ." his words trailing off as a tiny hint of a memory caught in his mind.

The two detectives exchanged promising glances. "You thought of something?" Detective Bell prodded.

"Maybe," Eric frowned. "It was a week or so after Molly had been born," the more he talked the stronger the recollection became. "Lila had brought her to the hospital to introduce her to everyone, there was this woman, at the time I thought she was a patient. She was pregnant, she came over, asked to hold the baby, was entranced by her, we practically had to pull Molly from her arms at the end. She had all these questions, she said she was just nervous about being a first time mom. At the time we had no reason to be suspicious," he finished helplessly. It was a pity hindsight couldn't turn into furturesight. It would save so much trouble.

"Do you remember what she looked like?" Detective Bell asked hopefully. For the first time Eric noticed how similar his eyes were to Joey's, and instantly he understood why Lila had allowed this man to comfort her.

"I see dozens of patients and families every day," Eric told them, frustrated as he tried to recall a face, a detail, anything that might help.

"Was she younger or older, was she white, or black, Hispanic, Asian?" Detective Bell was firing questions at him. "Was she blonde or brunette, tall or short? Anything you can remember could be crucial in locating this woman. Maybe you could check hospital charts for that day, see if it spikes your memory."

The feeling of helplessness and foreboding growing right alongside his anger. "I don't think she was a patient, I think she left right after we did." Panic bubbling he resumed pacing frantically, "she was the one, she followed us out, she's probably been following Lila and Molly for months. She killed my son, she has my baby." The air in the room suddenly seemed to have evaporated and he felt himself starting to hyperventilate, probably would have if a scream hadn't rung out from upstairs.

"Lila!" he gulped as all three of them turned towards the noise.

Sprinting up the stairs, the two detectives on his heels. In their bedroom Lila was sitting up in bed, thrashing wildly against an unseen assailant and sobbing hysterically. Eric ran to her and tried to pull her into his arms, but she fought against him frantically. Taking firm hold of her shoulders he shook her gently. "Lila, wake up!" When she continued to struggle against his grip, he shook her harder. "Come on, Li, wake up!"

Coming to with a start, brown eyes darting around the room in a panic, searching for the enemy from her dreams.

"It's okay," Eric soothed attempting to pull her against him. "It was just a dream."

Skittering away from him, Lila backed off the bed and down into a corner, gaze wild, movements shaky.

Following her, hands held out in front of him in a gesture of submission. "It's okay, Lila, it was only a dream."

"No it wasn't," her voice strange, like everything else about her it had changed. "Joey *is* dead." Back pressed up against the wall she slid down to the floor in slow motion, she was crying quietly but didn't seem to notice.

Once again, Eric moved to comfort his wife, but she shrunk away from him again, her gaze moving to look at something behind him. He turned to see what she was looking at and saw Detective Bell crouch down in front of Lila.

Before Detective Bell had a chance to say a word Lila reached out a trembling hand to trace the skin under his eyes, her face morphing into a ghost of a smile. "Your eyes," she whispered, "they're just like Joey's." Then she jerked away from both of them, lurched to her feet and promptly passed out.

JUNE 16TH

8:29 A.M.

Pulling herself out of bed, Lila felt like she was in a fog. Her brain felt cloudy and slow, her thoughts were jumbled and illogical, but there was one thing she knew, she was glad to be alone.

Eric's constant hovering was killing her. She did not want to eat, to shower, to go on with her life. It was only four days since her son had been murdered, and she wished for nothing more than to spend her time in sleep, where she could be reunited with Joey in her dreams, or at the very least be blissfully unaware of his death.

Bypassing the nursery, she paused at Joey's bedroom door, her hand tracing the wood as though it were her son's cheek. Turning the knob, Lila remembered a day a couple of months ago when Joey had announced that he needed a lock for his bedroom door. Suspicious as to what a four-year-old could be hiding in their bedroom that required a lock to keep his parents out, she had distracted Joey in the kitchen with some cake and searched his room. Hidden under the bed, in an old shoebox, Lila had found a tiny, mewing grey and white kitten that she recognized as belonging to their next-door neighbors. Joey had been devastated when they returned the kitten, which he'd named Sparky, and had yelled at her that she was mean and unfair. The recollection brought tears to her eyes.

Inside Joey's room, Lila bee-lined straight for his bed. Sliding under his Spiderman covers and pulling them over her head, so that she was cocooned inside.

As sleep came trickling back, she began once again to dream. She and Joey running in the park, the sun shining, the sky a brilliant electric blue, the grass the brightest green she'd ever seen, butterflies flitting through the air, birds chirping. She and Joey were laughing and running and rolling in the soft, sweet smelling grass. Then everything faded to black.

"Joey? Joey?" she called. "Where are you, honey?"

The blackness swirled once more, this time it became the parking lot at the grocery store. Spinning wildly around, looking for her son, he appeared before her, holding the baby in his arms.

"Joey?"

Hurrying towards him, scared by the empty look on his sweet, freckle-strewn face. Something cold pressed against her head. The gun. Then the kidnappers were standing beside Joey and Molly. Their faces smooth, blank masks.

"Joey, come to mommy."

Shaking his head, his red curls bouncing. "No. You're not a good mommy."

Then the parking lot exploded with the sound of the gunshot. Joey was on the ground. He was red. The kidnappers were walking away, the baby in their arms. She was kneeling beside Joey, holding him, shaking him, begging him to wake up. Screaming when his eyes popped open.

"You killed me, you killed me, you killed me," he began to chant.

And then she woke in a sweat, struggling to breath, shaking violently, pushing away the covers. As she climbed from the bed Joey's face appeared all over the walls, continuing his chant.

"No!" she sobbed silently, as she backed as quickly as she could from the room, slamming the door behind her she leaned tiredly against the wall. Sinking slowly to the floor Lila let exhaustion sweep over her, too tired to make it to the bedroom she stayed where she was.

Terrified to go to sleep, terrified to stay awake, wanting only to be with her little boy once again. Her happy, carefree child. Thinking of the bottle of sleeping pills on the bedside table in her room, she began to crawl along the hall. Made it to the door, tried to stand to reach for the handle, failed and fell, her head bouncing into the hard wooden floorboards, and the darkness came.

* * * * *

1:56 P.M.

Feeling a little better this afternoon. She was tired but at least her stomach seemed to have taken mercy on her and settled itself down. Now all she cared about was sorting things out with Parker.

Tessa thought that he might have come by their room some time last night, or yesterday afternoon, but she was a bit hazy on the events of the last twenty-four hours. She thought she remembered his cool hands on her burning cheeks, him pressing a cold washcloth to her forehead, and whispering to her that everything would be okay. But then again, she might have dreamt the whole thing, she hadn't actually seen her husband in two days. Or maybe it had been Daniel, her brother had been practically glued to her side while she'd been sick.

"Where did you run off to?"

Spinning around to see Matilda staring back at her with worried indignation, Tessa stifled a chuckle. "I went out."

"I promised Daniel and Parker and Winter that I would keep an eye on you. Then the next thing I know I turn around and you're gone." Matilda gave her the exact same look of reproach that Parker would have.

Taking pity on her sister-in-law. "I went to the doctor."

"Are you okay? You should have told me, I would have gone with you."

Not wanting to get into the details until she'd talked to Parker.

"I'm fine," she answered vaguely.

Matilda raised an eyebrow but didn't push the issue, then grew nervous and began to nibble on her fingernails.

"What's up?" Tessa asked, as she poured herself a glass of water and took a seat at the table.

Intently watching her every move before tentatively joining her. "I don't want to pry."

Catching on to where this was going, "you can ask me anything you want. I don't guarantee I'll give you the answer you want to hear, but you can certainly ask."

"Fair enough," nodding her acceptance of the terms but then lapsing into silence.

Tessa gave Matilda time, not that she was particularly anxious to have this conversation, and wondered who had ratted her out. Since Parker had hardly said two words to his sister, and Winter didn't know the details, she assumed it was Daniel, and wondered just how much he'd spilled.

"You killed a man?" Matilda asked as last, refusing to make eye contact.

"It was an accident, he was a serial killer, he was insane, he wanted the two of us to run off together, he had a gun, he was going to shoot me, we struggled, the gun went off, he died," Tessa summarized briskly, she didn't like thinking about Dylan Riley. The way she preferred to deal with things was to lock them away in box in her brain and pretend that they never happened.

"I killed a man once," Matilda said softly.

"Parker told me."

"I thought he was going to hurt me, turned out he was a social worker coming to help," Matilda trailed off, her eyes distant, reliving the event Tessa suspected. Then she turned and finally made eye contact, "my foster father used to rape me and the other little girls. Liked to make a party out of it, invite his friends. I was going to run away, stole his gun, when I saw the car I thought it was another one of his friends. Next thing I knew there was a loud explosion and the man was falling. He died instantly." When Tessa said nothing Matilda asked, "aren't you going to tell me it wasn't my fault?"

Examining her carefully. "Would it make a difference?"

Solemnly, "no, it wouldn't."

"Part of me knows that killing Dylan was an accident. I was fighting for my life, but he was insane and I deliberately pushed him over the edge. In my head and in my dreams it's my fault," Tessa raised an indifferent shoulder, "I just have to accept that what happened, happened."

Relieved Matilda smiled at her, a real smile that actually reached her eyes, and Tessa guessed this was the first time Matilda had ever felt free to talk about what she had gone through. Then her sister-in-law sobered, "you were raped too, weren't you?"

Fighting the urge to squirm uncomfortably, most of the time Tessa was able to keep her emotions safely under control, but sometimes it was harder than others. "Yes."

"How did you move on? How did you get past it?" Matilda asked desperately, as though Tessa somehow held the key to solving all her problems.

"Who said I did?"

Before either of them had a chance to say more they heard the door closing and seconds later Daniel appeared.

"Hey girls," he grinned at them. "Tessie, you're feeling better?"

"Absolutely," she smiled confidently back at him.

Seemingly too preoccupied to push further. "You want to come out with me and Mattie tonight?"

Surprised, "you two are going out together?"

Matilda blushed but Daniel's grin grew wider, "I'm taking her over to go horse riding at your place, and then we're going out to dinner."

Not only did she not want to intrude, but she also did not want to pay a visit to the house where she had grown up, the house that she had inherited from her grandparents, the house where she had met Parker and she had almost died in a fire. "I think I'm gonna go to bed early, I'm feeling better but I'm still pretty tired." Shooting them a mischievous grin, "you two have fun though."

"I just gotta change," Daniel told Matilda as he dashed up the stairs.

Matilda moved to follow but Tessa grabbed her hand, "you might not move on, Matilda, but you can try to be happy. With every fiber of your being you can try to be happy."

* * * * *

8:29 P.M.

Exhausted but the most invigorated and content he had been since Joey had died, Eric pulled his car into the driveway. Guilty for having a place to go where he could forget about his problems while Lila remained locked up inside the memory soaked house. An action-packed day in the ER certainly hadn't allowed him much time to think about Joey, or ponder about who had taken Molly and whether they were looking after her. He couldn't help but look forward to the following morning when he could return to the hospital and busy himself once more dealing with other people's problems. Problems that he actually knew how to fix.

Of course, he hadn't been able to completely forget about things. He'd probably checked his cell phone at least two hundred times during his twelve-hour shift, simultaneously hoping for and dreading any calls about Molly. Torturing himself each time he looked at his cell and was confronted by his background photo of a beaming Lila, Joey and Molly. A couple of times, convinced that the phone had somehow stopped working, he had called himself from the hospital's phone, only to be rewarded by the sharp icicle of pain that came from hearing the ring tone that Joey had chosen.

Climbing slowly out of the car, Eric walked to the door,

fumbling with the key, he eventually managed to get the door open. The second he entered he sensed something was wrong. There was not a single light on in the whole house, which was eerily quiet but for the sound of running water.

Up the stairs and down the hall to the master bedroom in seconds. "Lila?" he called as he headed straight towards the ensuite. "Lila?"

Upon entering the dark room he found his wife curled up in a ball on the floor of the shower. Arms wrapped loosely around her knees, head resting against the shower's wall, water pounding down upon her.

"Lila?" he called again. When she still didn't answer, he flicked on the lights and opened the shower door. Reaching a hand over to touch her shoulder, then snatching it quickly back, the water that ran over him was ice cold. Turning off the freezing water, which was pouring down on his wife, who apparently did not even notice the cold. "Lila!" he repeated more frantically this time, his fingers pressing quickly to her neck to check her pulse, he was about to say her name again when she finally stirred.

"Eric?" she asked, her voice faint and disoriented.

"It's me," he told her, grabbing a towel from the rack to wrap it around her shivering body. "Honey, what happened? You're freezing."

She looked up at him like she didn't know where she was or what was happening, and he noticed a new bruise forming in the middle of her forehead. Rubbing her briskly with the towel, trying to warm her, then lifting her up into his arms and carrying her to the bed. Laying her down he pulled up the covers and went to find her something to wear. Grabbing her pajamas from a chair, Lila lay limply on the bed like a rag doll, and he had to dress her as though she were Molly. Then he pulled the covers back up, tucking them in around her.

"Lila, what happened?" he asked again, lightly touching the lump on her ice-cold forehead. Obviously it had been a bad idea to leave her alone in their house so soon after the incident, and he cursed his own self-indulgence.

"I don't know," she whispered, her glassy eyes looking up at him, oblivious to the fact that she was shivering with cold.

"You're hurt. Did you fall?"

Shrugging helplessly.

"Have you eaten anything today?" he asked changing track. When she shook her head, "I'll make you something," he told her.

"I'm not hungry," she replied.

"You have to eat," he said firmly. "I'll be right back."

Her eyes fluttered closed and he pressed a kiss to her pale lips then left the room. Heading down to the kitchen he put on the kettle to make some tea, then set about warming up some soup that Savannah had sent home with him. As the meal was heating, he grabbed the phone and pressed speed dial one, absently stirring the soup as he listened to the phone ringing.

"Hello?"

"Charlie, it's Eric, I need you to come over."

"I'll be there in fifteen minutes," his brother told him, no questions asked.

Hanging up the phone just as the kettle started to boil. Unsure how he felt about turning to his brother for help with his wife, but Lila was slipping away and he didn't know how to bring her back on his own. Joey was gone and if they didn't get Molly back then he was afraid that his wife would never be able to come back from the dark, empty place she had retreated. Making a cup of tea and pouring some soup into a bowl, he balanced it all on a tray and carried it carefully up the stairs.

When he returned to their room, he saw Lila had fallen asleep, and was making soft snuffling sounds. Setting the tray down on the bedside table he began to gently stroke her hair, too drained to feel any anger towards her, now he just felt a guilty version of love, ashamed that he had ever, even inside his own head, blamed her for what had happened. Fingers brushing her skin, Lila was still cold, so he lay down on the bed beside her, pulled her against his own body, and finally fell asleep with his wife in his arms.

* * * * *

11:23 P.M.

Now she was really starting to get worried.

Parker hadn't come home. Neither had he called to say he was working late and going to spend the night at the station, as was his usual custom.

Tessa had tried calling him but his cell phone was off, and she just kept getting his voicemail time and time again. She'd also called the precinct, but had been told that Parker hadn't been there all day. Winter had called earlier to ask permission to spend the night at a friend's, Daniel and Matilda were still out on their date, so Tessa sat in her and Parker's bed, with the covers tucked up under her chin, alone in the dark, quiet house.

It wasn't that Tessa was afraid of the dark exactly. And she had lived alone in her old cottage for years, she was used to spending the night by herself, but her cottage had been decked out with a high tech security system she'd designed and installed herself. It had cameras, microphones, motion sensors, weight sensors, both the doors and all the windows were wired in, no one could get into that place without her knowledge. Now it was more the fact that she had grown accustomed to sleeping with Parker at her side, of his snoring, of his comforting presence, of the way he always calmed her down after a nightmare. Sniffing back tears, she wanted her husband to come home, she needed to talk to him.

Time to bite the bullet.

Picking up the phone, she dialed Skylar Wyatt's number and waited.

"Hello?" came Skylar's voice moments later, heavy with sleep.

"Skylar, it's Tessa," other than his mother she was the only person that he allowed to use his given name, everyone else called him Wyatt.

"What's wrong?" he asked, immediately awake, apparently a phone call from her at almost midnight could mean only one thing.

"You're at home." Somehow she'd been hoping that Parker had just become too caught up in work to call her, but if Skylar was at home in bed then Parker should be too.

"Yes. Tessa, what's up?"

"Parker never came home," she caught the hitch in her voice and steadied it. "I thought maybe you knew where he was."

"I haven't seem him since yesterday, he sent me an email saying he was following up on something else today. But that was this morning, I assumed he was at home by now," Skylar told her, and she could hear Parker's partner climbing out of bed and rummaging around for clothes. "I'm on my way over."

"You don't have to come," Tessa protested immediately, she was used to dealing with problems on her own.

"Don't argue with me, goldilocks," Skylar barked.

For once if felt good to relinquish control of the situation to someone else. "Thanks, Skylar."

"Anytime." Then his voice grew muffled, "it's Tessa. Parker never came home," he was explaining, apparently Casey was now awake. "I'm heading over there. No, no, you stay here, I'll call you." A bit more shuffling and then he was back, "is his car there?"

"No, it's gone."

"You tried calling him?"

"Keeps going straight to voicemail."

"And you tried the station?"

"Of course, he's not there." Then her voice dropped quiet, "Skylar, what if something bad happened to him? What if he crashed his car and he's lying hurt somewhere? What if . . ." gulping, "what if someone attacked him . . .?"

"Alright, alright," Skylar soothed. "Lets not jump ahead of ourselves."

She heard the thump of his car door slamming closed, followed by the revving of his engine, and was glad that he was coming over. If anything happened to Parker she didn't think that she could survive it, she had already lost so many people through the years, people that she'd loved and trusted. "Skylar, if something happened to him . . ." she let the sentence trail off because she knew he understood.

"I know, I know. Hang on, goldilocks, I'm on my way."

Long after he had hung up Tessa sat clutching the receiver, listening to the dial tone, and then, as she always did when faced with a crisis, she pulled on her mask of togetherness and went downstairs to wait for Skylar to arrive.

JUNE 17TH

2:47 A.M.

It had been a magical evening.

Things had started out a little awkward, neither he nor Matilda dated much, and both had a lot of baggage. They hadn't said a lot to one another on the car ride out to the estate where he, Tessa, and Emilie, had moved after Patrick walked out on them. Daniel and Tessa never called their parent's mom and dad, those titles implied certain actions and feelings, and Patrick and Emilie had never been interested in their children.

Out at the estate things had started to ease up. The enormous stone mansion had impressed Matilda, but Daniel had quickly bypassed the house with such bad memories, and taken them straight to the stables. Never having ridden a horse before, Matilda had been a little nervous at first, but he'd started her off on Caramel, the most easygoing, by the end he'd graduated her all the way up to Tessa's favorite horse, Jell-O. At dinner the ice had well and truly been broken, and they had chatted away like old friends, carefully avoiding any mention of either of their pasts.

They had been the last couple to leave the restaurant, and neither of them was ready for the night to be over yet, so Daniel had taken her back out to the estate. This time they headed to the stream that ran through the grounds, where he had tried to convince Matilda to go skinny-dipping with him. She declined at first, but soon followed him into the water fully clothed. Despite the warm night the water was icy cold, and Matilda had clung to him, giggling. Her wet clothes stuck suggestively to her body, her small round breasts pressed against his chest, her hips against his groin, and Daniel felt a tingling in his bones he hadn't felt in years. It had taken every ounce of self-control he possessed not to throw her down on the banks of the stream and take her right there, in the end, with the moonlight glittering on the water around them, he settled for kissing her.

His lips still tingled from that kiss as they walked, hand in hand, up the path to the front door of Tessa and Parker's house. It wasn't until he was sliding his key into the lock and swinging open the door, that he realized there was a light on inside the house. Tugging Matilda inside they found Tessa pacing nervously in the living room, dressed in one of Parker's old shirts, which swamped her tiny frame.

When they entered the room her head snapped towards them, eyes hopeful and then disappointed. "I thought you were Parker," she told them.

Frowning, "Parker's not home yet? Is he working?"

Tessa shook her head vigorously, sending her curls flying. "I don't know where he is," she whispered, her bottom lip trembled, and since Tessa never cried Daniel knew that his little sister was truly scared. Crossing to her he wrapped his arms around her. "Why are you wet?" she questioned, voice muffled against his chest.

Casting a guilty look Matilda's way, "never mind about that, tell us what happened." He led her to the couch, gently pushed her down, then sat beside her.

"Parker never came home," Tessa began shakily. "At first I thought he was just working, but he never called. I tried calling him, but I kept getting his voicemail, and when I tried the precinct they said he hadn't been in all day. In the end I called Skylar, he came over, he called hospitals to see if Parker was there, but he couldn't find anything. Something must have happened, Parker wouldn't just leave me without a word, he wouldn't."

"I'm sure everything's fine, Tessie," he soothed.

But his sister was not to be placated. "Parker's been acting so weird lately, maybe he's been working on something he didn't want to tell me about, and maybe someone did something to him."

"Tess," he started, Parker Bell was not his favorite person but he had never thought that the man would deliberately do anything to hurt Tessa. He'd thought that Parker understood that beneath her tough exterior Tessa was fragile and scared. He'd thought that Parker loved Tessa. But he did not think that the reason Parker had not come home was because something had happened to him. "I don't think that . . ."

Cutting him off, "maybe that's why he's been so on edge. He's back to bickering with you, he's hardly said two words to Matilda, and the other day with me . . ." she trailed off and tried to stand.

Grabbing her arm and turning her to face him, "did Parker do this to you?" he barked sharply, lifting the sleeve of the shirt to expose the bruises on her wrist he'd noticed the other night.

Wiggling free from his grip she went to stand in front of her wedding photo, staring at it so intently Daniel half expected the glass to shatter under such intense scrutiny. Glancing across to see how Matilda was processing the news, she was standing frozen in place, her mouth hanging slightly ajar with shock. Torn between whom to go to, when Matilda finally met his eye and gave a slight nod in Tessa's direction. Breathing deeply and fighting to keep his anger under control, the thought of Parker hurting his baby sister left him seething, but his anger wasn't what Tessa needed right now. Moving towards his sister he placed a hand lightly on her shoulder, she jumped and turned to face him.

Before he could offer any empty words of comfort Tessa planted her hands on her hips and fixed him with one of her determined smiles. "Parker's coming home, everything will go back to the way it was, everything will be okay."

Chewing on his lip as he watched Tessa turn on her heel and hurry from the room, moments later the sound of the vacuum cleaner hummed throughout the house. Tessa always cleaned when she was stressed, one of the ways she maintained control over her world. Daniel pondered how such a perfect day could end so horribly, and for a brief moment he wondered whether all of them were cursed. Whether it was their destiny to spend eternity alone.

* * * * *

8:34 A.M.

For some reason Tessa couldn't stop trembling.

Maybe it was because she hadn't slept in twenty-four hours. Maybe it was because she hadn't eaten anything in twenty-four hours. Or maybe it was because her husband had vanished and she was falling apart.

After Skylar had left, and Daniel and Matilda had returned from their date, which she felt bad for ruining with her depressing news, they had spent most of the night trying to reassure her that everything would be okay. Tessa didn't see how things could be okay, Parker was gone and she was positive that something bad had happened to him.

A knock sounded on the door and a moment later it swung open. "Tessa?"

Skylar was back, seconds later he and J.J. appeared in the doorway. "Hanging in there, goldilocks?" Skylar asked. "Hey, Daniel." Then he did a double take, "Matilda?"

Smiling warmly at him, "hey, Wyatt, long time no see."

Engulfing her in a giant hug. "This is Parker's twin sister," Skylar filled in for J.J.'s benefit.

"No kidding," J.J. was staring open-mouthed at Matilda.

"Parker didn't tell me you'd come back."

Tessa noticed Matilda's sad wince at that, but apparently Skylar didn't because he continued cheerfully.

"The last time I saw you, you were what, like seventeen. Wow

106

you have really grown up."

"You too." Eyes dipping to his left hand, "you're married?"

"Fifteen years," he grinned, "her name's Casey and she's a doctor. We have two kids, Sam's ten and Stacey is almost six. What's new with you?"

Matilda opened her mouth to answer but Tessa jumped in first cutting her off, she didn't have time to play catch up, "she's dating my brother." They all stared at her, Daniel and Matilda blushing. "Can we please get down to business. Have you found Parker? Do you know where he is?"

Sobering, "no we haven't found him. We've checked every hospital in the area and we have an APB out on his car, but so far nothing," Skylar told her.

Any hope she'd been clinging to melted away and she sank down onto the sofa. The cushions dipped as J.J. dropped down beside her, "we'll track him down, Tessa," he comforted, wrapping an arm around her shoulders and squeezing lightly.

"Something's happened to him. Did you check to see if he was working on anything that might be related?"

"There's nothing he was working on that would have led to him being hurt," Skylar reassured her.

"What about whatever it was he emailed you about?" she pressed.

"I don't know what it was he said he was working on," Skylar explained.

"What about his cell? Did you try to track it?"

"It's still turned off. Are you sure you haven't heard from him?"

Quickly becoming frustrated, "I would have told you if I did. Maybe his car crashed and it just hasn't been found yet."

"This is the city, Tessa, not the middle of the desert," J.J. reminded her.

Turning to glare at him, "well so far I don't see you offering any theories."

J.J. exchanged a glance with Skylar and she started to feel uneasy, Tessa didn't think she was going to like what they were about to say.

"I think you're overlooking something," J.J. begun carefully. When she raised a suspicious eyebrow at him he continued uncomfortably, "what if Parker left of his own free will?"

Staring at him incredulously, "you're saying he walked out on me?" J.J. grabbed for her arm but she dodged out of his grip and moved herself to the furthest corner of the room. "You're saying he walked out on his job? Does that sound like Parker to you?"

"Parker hasn't been himself lately," Skylar reminded as he followed her. "By his own admission he's tired, tired of everything."

"He wouldn't walk out on his job and he wouldn't walk out on me," she repeated stubbornly, shocked that Skylar of all people would suggest that he could.

"Wyatt's right," Daniel tried, "Parker hasn't been himself. The old Parker wouldn't leave you or his job. But the new Parker, the one who's barely acknowledged his sister after fourteen years, the one who almost crushed your wrists, who knows what he'd do."

Looking from Daniel to her and back again, "what do you mean Parker almost crushed her wrists?" Skylar asked.

Scowling at her brother, Tessa already regretted letting him drag out of her what Parker had done and said to her the last time she'd spoken with him. "It was nothing," she snapped.

Skylar wasn't placated and stomped to her, grabbing her arms and pulling up the sleeves of her sweater to stare intently at the ring of black and blue. "Parker did this?" he demanded.

"It's nothing," she muttered, yanking her arms free and gingerly sliding the sleeves of her sweater back down to cover her painful wrists.

"You should have told me, Tessa," Skylar told her reproachfully.

"It. Was. Nothing," she repeated tightly.

"And you should have gone to the hospital," Skylar looked as mad as she felt. "Those bruises look bad, you should have gotten x-rays, he could have broken something."

"Nothing's broken, and I don't see why you're angry with me," she bit out frostily.

Softening, "I'm not angry with you, Tess. I'm angry at Parker. And shocked. That he could put his hands on you . . ." he trailed off, his green eyes bubbling with fury.

"You'll let us monitor your bank accounts, just in case?" J.J. jumped in, veering the conversation in another direction.

Crossing her arms and pouting, "do whatever you want but I am telling you that Parker didn't leave on his own."

Skylar nodded placatingly, having tucked away his anger, but J.J. took a tentative step towards her. "Tess," he hesitated.

"What?" she demanded impatiently. She wanted them out there looking for her husband, not hanging around here asking ridiculously pointless questions.

"Is anything of Parker's missing?"

"No," she announced triumphantly, Skylar had forced her to check his wardrobe when he'd been here earlier. "Just his car."

"Is there any chance," J.J. cleared his throat nervously, "at all, that Parker might be seeing someone else?"

Recoiling as if he'd slapped her, sure she must have heard him incorrectly. "What?" she stammered.

"I don't want to upset you, but is there any chance that Parker could have run off with someone else?"

She lost it then. "You don't want to upset me?" Her two dogs, a Dalmatian named Ladybug, and a Golden Retriever named Buttercup, lifted their heads from where they were napping by the window. Sensing that she was upset, they crossed to her side, protectively placing themselves between her and the others and eyeing them warily. Tessa appreciated their support.

"Then why would you even suggest that?" she raved. "Am I the only one who actually knows Parker? We're talking about a man who risked his life numerous times to save me, a man who's responsible for taking countless criminals off the streets, a man who would do anything to help any one of the people in this room. And this is how you repay him? You agree with J.J., Skylar?" The look on his face confirmed that he did think it was a possibility. "What about you?" she turned on her brother. "You've always hated Parker, you think he's cheating on me four months after our wedding?"

"Tessie," Daniel tried to take a step towards her. "J.J.'s not saying that he is, just checking it out as a possibility. Maybe that would explain why . . ."

"I don't want to hear it anymore. Until you have something positive to say you can all get out." She begun marching to the front door and flung it open, the others trailing along behind her.

"Come on, Tess . . ." Skylar started.

Pressing her hands to her ears, "I don't want to hear it. Get out," she was shrieking now, quickly spinning out of control, and she could tell from the myriad of exchanged concerned glances that they were worried about leaving her alone like this. But alone was what she wanted, what she needed right now. "I mean it, just go, please," her voice dropping to a weary whisper.

Reluctantly they all filed out, Matilda paused in the doorway, "I don't think Parker would cheat on you, Tessa."

Glad that at least for the moment she had one person on her side but too worn out now to reply. When they were all gone Tessa closed and locked the door behind them, dragged herself up the stairs, the dogs at her heels, and down the hall to her bedroom where she practically collapsed on the bed. Pulling into her arms the soft, cuddly teddy bear, with fur the same caramel color as Parker's eyes, that he had given her for her birthday.

Before she could start to mope Tessa resolutely pushed to her feet, convinced herself that just as Parker had promised, nothing in the world would make him leave her, and headed for the bathroom where she proceeded to scrub the room from top to bottom.

* * * * *

11:19 A.M.

Wyatt felt bad about the way he'd left things with Tessa earlier. Already he'd tried calling her a dozen times, she hadn't answered once, was probably screening her calls so that she didn't have to talk to him. Despite all her pretence at projecting a strong, confident exterior, he knew that they had hurt her with their suggestions that Parker had deliberately walked out on her, and that he might be seeing someone else.

"Wyatt?"

Blinking, "yeah?"

"Thinking about Tess?" J.J. asked.

Nodding wearily. "She won't take my calls."

"Mine either. We'll sort things out with her," J.J. said confidently, but Wyatt noticed the doubt creasing the corners of his eyes.

The door swung open and Marty bustled in, short of breath, his lean frame weighed down with a heavy stack of papers. "Any news on Parker?" he asked immediately as he dropped the files on the table and plonked down into a chair.

"Not yet."

"How's Tessa taking it?"

"About as well as you'd expect," Wyatt sighed. "She's convinced that someone's done something to him."

"With her history can you blame her?" Marty asked, as he helped himself to a croissant and a glass of water.

Tessa's childhood friend had been murdered when they were eleven, as a teenager she had been abused by a teacher, and had been stalked by not one but two serial killers. When something bad happened in Tessa Bell's world, it was always because of a monster.

"No, I can't blame her," Wyatt answered, "but so far we have no evidence of foul play. He hasn't turned up at any hospitals, no bodies fitting his description have been found, his car is gone, for all intents and purposes it looks like he just up and left."

"That doesn't sound like Parker," Marty sounded doubtful.

"That's what Tessa said," J.J. chimed in. "She's convinced that his disappearance has something to do with a case he's been working."

Raising an eyebrow, "could it?" Marty asked.

"No," J.J. said firmly.

"What about the Abbott case?" Marty pushed, taking off his glasses to clean the lenses.

"The Abbott case that is so far going nowhere?" J.J. asked sarcastically. "We are nowhere near finding a viable lead to the pair that shot Joey Abbott and abducted baby Molly. We don't even know if we're after two females, or a male and female."

"One male, one female," Marty supplied as he slipped his glasses back on.

Eyes widening in surprise, "how do we know that?"

Smiling smugly, "we found hairs in the car, some belonged to the Abbott family, but we found a couple that didn't, we got lucky, some had roots attached, and we were able to get DNA. We're running it but since we didn't get any hits on the fingerprints, I'm not optimistic that it'll lead us anywhere. The bullet retrieved from young Joey's body has also turned out to be a dead end."

"Anything else useful on the car?" Wyatt asked.

"No," Marty confessed.

"Are we still thinking that the baby is alive?"

"No bodies found at the abandoned warehouse, checked the whole place, nothing. If they killed Molly Abbott they didn't bury her out there," Marty supplied.

"And we're getting nowhere with any suspect leads," Wyatt

added. "Unless Lila Abbott can give us a description of the couple that attacked her I don't think we're ever going to find that baby. It's been five days they could've taken her and gone anywhere in the world by now."

"Any leads from the press conference?" Marty questioned

"Not a viable one," Wyatt replied. At the press conference Eric Abbott had done the talking, Lila had stood there in a daze, beautiful but silent, staring out at the sea of cameras and microphones, but seeing nothing.

"The woman that Eric Abbott remembered from the hospital looks like she might be who we're looking for, if only we knew where to look to find her," Wyatt explained for Marty's benefit. "We checked it out, spoke with about twenty of the doctors and nurses who were working that day, still got a few to go. Some of them vaguely remembered her, but we got about twenty different descriptions. They checked their charts for that day and no one treated a pregnant woman, it looks like she came to check out the baby and the family, then disappeared. It took them a couple of days to get the security tapes together, but I got a call this morning saying they're in. I'll head over to the hospital and check them out, maybe we'll get lucky and find our missing pregnant woman who no one treated."

"Alright," J.J. stroked his thick brown beard. "We'll keep going with the little we have and hope for the best. I hate to say it, but if we don't get something in a day or so we might have to move on."

* * * * *

2:23 P.M.

Rows of people dressed in black filled the church.

It was fitting, Lila decided, black was the only color that perfectly represented what she was feeling.

They were sitting in the front pew of the small chapel, she and Eric.

Eric had his head in his hands.

She was unable to take her eyes off the small white coffin. How could it be white, she kept thinking. White was a bright color, a symbol of purity and faith and love and innocence, what did any of those things have to do with a dead child. The coffin should be black. Black was the color of anger and grief and guilt and death. White was for life and she no longer had one.

Registering a presence beside her, Lila turned to see her best friend, Savannah, giving her an uncertain smile.

"It'll be okay, Li," Savannah was saying. "The police will find Molly, they'll bring her back to you and things'll get better. I promise. You just need to give it time."

Lila didn't understand that. People kept telling her to give it time. Like if she reached some special number of days or weeks or months or years, then suddenly she would magically get better. Joey was dead and no amount of time was going to change that.

Maybe she started crying, she wasn't sure, suddenly she was just wrapped up in Savannah's comforting hug. "Oh, Lila, tell me how to help you," her friend was whispering against her hair.

Savannah was a good friend. Lila thought that it had been Savannah who had helped her get ready for the funeral. She had a fuzzy memory of standing in her bedroom, Savannah dressing her as though she were a child, while chatting away with forced cheerfulness.

They had been five, Joey's age, when they saw each other for the first time. It had been the middle of winter, and the day after she and her parents had moved into their new house. She'd spotted Savannah and the Abbott brothers snowball fighting in the Anderson's front yard. Lila had begged her mother, already fifty and very over protective after years of trying for a child, to go and join in the game, and from that day on the two had been firm friends and a perfect match. Both girls had been lonely, both were spoilt and bossy, and used to getting their own way. They fought like cats and dogs, but also got along like a house on fire. They were the sister neither had ever had.

Startled out of her reverie as she felt a hand clasp hers, Lila saw the minister come to the pulpit. Voices were jabbering but she didn't have the energy to figure out what they were saying and she was only vaguely aware of Eric sitting beside her. Lila felt herself once again unable to tear her eyes away from the small, white coffin. She felt like she had no control over her body, like she been turned to stone and forced to stare forever at her child's final resting place, as a punishment for her inability to save him.

A tug on her arm. Eric was gently pulling her to her feet and guiding her towards the coffin. Peering down at her little boy, he looked like he was sleeping, and she held her breath waiting for him to open his eyes, throw his arms around her neck and tell her he loved her. She wanted him back so badly. It wasn't fair, he was so small, so young, children weren't supposed to die. But whether she believed it or not, this was the last time she was ever going to see her little boy. Reaching over she brought her hand to his cheek, and then ran her fingers through his red curls.

Leaning down to lay Joey's teddy bear Snuggles down beside him she pulled back in shock as Joey's eyes opened. At first he smiled at her, but then it changed into a pout as he sat up, his eyes growing accusing he lifted his hand to point at her. "You killed me," he accused, then his eyes growing sad he whispered, "mommy why did you let them kill me?"

Backing away from the coffin, hands flying to her mouth. "No, no," she wailed. "I'm sorry, baby. I'm sorry, I'm sorry, I'm sorry."

Hands grabbed her shoulders, shaking her. "Lila, what is it? What's wrong?"

Pointing to the coffin where Joey still sat looking at her, "Joey . . . he's . . . he's mad at me," she stammered, oblivious to the horrified stares of her family and friends.

Eric shook his head sadly, "Joey's dead, honey."

"No," she protested wildly. "Don't you see him, he's sitting there. They made a mistake, they must have made a mistake," not daring to take her eyes off Joey in case he disappeared.

"I'm sorry, Lila," Eric murmured. He turned to the minister, "I think it's time."

"No," Lila tried to launch herself at the coffin to prevent the minister from closing the lid, but Eric still had a tight grip on her arms. "Let me go," she begged, raising her eyes to his and then realizing her mistake, when she looked back Joey was gone, and the coffin lid clunked shut with a finite thud.

"Come on, sweetheart," Eric tried to pull her back towards their seat.

Yanking free of her husband's grasp she collapsed against the coffin, beating it with her fists. "Joey," she shrieked. "Joey, please, come back. I'm sorry. Joey."

It was no use Joey was already gone.

Sinking to the ground, alone and lost, by the time Eric bent to pick her up she was already unconscious.

* * * * *

9:53 P.M.

"Do you remember what she looked like?" Wyatt hardly dared to ask the question. He was taking a break from reviewing hours of security footage to interview the last of the hospital workers who had been on duty the day that Eric and Lila Abbott had brought their baby daughter to the hospital to show her off to their friends.

Pondering, for what felt like the millionth time in the last few days, what kind of world this was, what kind of world was he raising his children in. A world where people stalked infants, where they shot preschoolers in cold blood, where proud parents weren't even safe taking their baby to the workplace.

Joey Abbott's funeral had been held earlier this afternoon. While he'd been squirreled away down here in the dark, watching hour after hour of sick people sitting in a hospital waiting room, J.J. himself had attended the funeral. They had hoped that whoever had abducted Molly might have turned up, but according to J.J., no such luck.

Apparently Lila Abbott had caused quite a scene though. J.J. said she had started screaming hysterically that Joey was alive and sitting up in his coffin talking to her.

Parker wasn't the only one who had taken the Abbott case hard. No one liked dealing with crimes against children, and Wyatt in particular could empathize with what the Abbott's were going through. This case was stirring up a lot of bad memories for him. At least he hadn't thrown in the towel like Parker had, just assumed he was the only one affected and walked off to leave everyone else to clean up the mess. Wyatt bit on his lip to stifle another wave of anger and resentment and fear. Not to mention the guilt. He was Parker's surrogate big brother, he was supposed to watch out for him, how could he not notice that Parker was teetering on the edge of a breakdown?

No, Wyatt told himself firmly, doing this to himself was not a good idea, neither was it productive. So far he had forbidden himself from thinking about Parker, which seemed to be working. There was no explanation for his disappearance that Wyatt could deal with. He couldn't accept that Parker would simply walk out on his life, but that meant wherever he was he wasn't there willingly, which was really no better. He figured the safest option, for the moment at least, was just to forget about it and wait to see what happened. Hopefully his partner had just taken a few days time out and would return on his own.

"Detective Wyatt?"

"Hmm?" he blinked, the stark grey room shimmering back into focus.

"Is everything okay?"

Focusing on the heavily lined face of Doctor Marcus Kane. In his early sixties, the man's face was a mass of wrinkles, but his pale blue eyes were kind, his manner easy and confident, his thick grey streaked brown hair perfectly combed into place. Dressed in bright orange suspenders, over an equally bright yellow shirt, his tie sporting kangaroo's throwing snowballs at one another, the only dull thing about him was his plain black pants. Wyatt guessed the guy was great with kids, and a hit with parents, the kind of doctor that made you feel safe and secure.

"Fine thanks," gulping down the last of his lukewarm coffee.

"You look a little pale," Dr. Kane remarked. "Have you been sleeping okay? Eating regular meals?"

What was it with doctors? Weren't they ever off? Casey was the exact same way with him and the kids. Everything must be related to a diagnosable and treatable condition. "I'm fine, thanks," he repeated more firmly. "Can you describe the woman you remember?"

"Like I was saying," the doctor frowned pointedly, clearly thinking he'd made his point. "I think she was tall, with dark hair. But like I said before, I wasn't really paying any attention. Things were busy, I stopped by for a minute or so to see the baby, and then I went back to treating patients. Maybe someone else might be able to provide a more detailed account of her appearance."

Thus far their mystery woman had been described as tall, short and medium height, Hispanic, Asian and white, with brown, red and blonde hair, with blue and brown eyes, and both with freckles and without.

"Actually you were my last, and it seems everyone else was as run off their feet as you were."

"This place is a circus," Dr. Kane agreed.

"Thanks anyway, Dr. Kane, hopefully I'll have better luck with the camera." The thought of watching more hours of tape distinctly depressing.

Taking the cue to leave Dr. Kane stood slowly, stretching his back so that it cracked. "Sorry I couldn't be of more assistance. And I was serious, you look terrible, if you want to stop by before you leave I can prescribe you something to help you sleep."

Wyatt watched the man's departing back and considered taking him up on his offer, then returned his weary eyes to the TV screen and pressed play.

Barely noticing when one of the security officers returned and plopped a new cup of steaming coffee onto the table. Wyatt grunted his thanks and let the boiling liquid work its magic and reinvigorate him.

These were the times when you needed a partner. Someone to make the tedious task somehow seem less dreary, someone to bounce ideas off, someone to rely on in case you missed anything on the blurry film.

And he was back to thinking about Parker. Apparently the tireder you got the harder it was to retain control of your thoughts. Centering his concentration back on the video, something caught his eye in the corner of the screen.

"Wait," he commanded.

"What? What is it?" the sleepy security officer asked.

"I think I found her."

JUNE 18TH

7:41 A.M.

"It's too quiet," Wyatt murmured, as they stood knocking on Tessa's front door.

It had been a long, sleepless night, close to midnight by the time he finally got back from the hospital. The tapes were already at the lab, awaiting someone who could work their magic on them, and turn them from grainy silhouettes into clear, identifiable people. Fingers crossed they would be able to get a picture of their babynapper out to the media, someone out there knew that woman.

"She probably just knows it's us," Casey countered. "I spent all day yesterday and half of last night calling her, and she just won't pick up."

"I'm worried about her, Casey," he said peering through the darkened windows, trying to see inside. "She hasn't spoken to Daniel or Matilda either."

Tessa was like the little sister he'd never had. Born the youngest of five boys, his mother had been desperate to have a daughter, an ally in the all male household. During her pregnancy she had been convinced that she was having a girl, decked the nursery out in pink, filled the cupboard with girl's clothes, and picked the name Skylar. When he'd been born, his mother had stuck with the name, and the pink nursery, and the clothes. Growing up he had hated his name, a girl's name as far as he had been concerned, and longed for a little sister.

"You know we do have a key," Casey reminded him when he banged on the door again.

"I know but she's already mad and if we go barging in there I don't think it'll help the situation." After several more doorbell rings, door knockings, and yelling, he was ready to give in and risk using the key.

"Tessa?" he called again once they were inside, "it's me and Casey. We just want to talk to you."

No answer.

"I'll look upstairs, you look down," he told Casey, already sprinting up the stairs. He hadn't gone more than a couple of steps down the hall when he found her, facedown on the carpet. "Casey," he screamed as he dropped down at Tessa's side, feeling her neck in search of a pulse, finding it fluttering weakly. There didn't seem to be any blood, and by the time Casey's footsteps sounded on the stairs Tessa was already coming to. "Careful," he cautioned as she tried to push herself up, helping her instead to roll over onto her back. "Take it easy."

"What happened?" Casey asked as she knelt down beside them.

"I was hoping you two would go away," Tessa groaned weakly.

"I found her unconscious," Wyatt explained, as he felt his heart rate slowly start to return to normal.

"Again? Tessa," Casey exclaimed as she took Tessa's pulse.

Too drained to protest, Tessa simply lay there while Casey checked her pulse, felt her forehead, and requested that she follow her finger. The sight of Tessa so listless scared him more than anything else. Ashen skin, overly bright eyes that seemed too big for her hollow face, shallow breathing, he didn't have to be a doctor to know that something was wrong with her.

"Is she okay?" he asked, as soon as Casey was finished.

Casey didn't answer, her attention focused solely on Tessa. "Tell me exactly what happened."

Rubbing wearily at her eyes, "I heard you two banging on the door," Tessa began. "I was waiting for you to leave, when I heard you breaking in here, I was going to go down and yell at you, then

I was opening my eyes and Wyatt was there."

Cringing at hearing Tessa call him Wyatt, apparently she was madder than he'd anticipated.

Making an attempt to stand, both of them put hands on her shoulders and pushed her back down. "I'd really like to get out of the hallway, if that's okay with you two," she huffed haughtily.

"Wyatt can carry you to the bedroom," Casey ordered sternly, in the 'don't argue' voice she used when refereeing their kids disagreements.

Tessa looked up at him with open betrayal in her tired face, it was like a knife through his heart, he loved both Parker and Tessa and would do anything to save either one of them.

"I'm worried about him too, Tess." Remembering the scared, sullen, little boy he'd first taken under his wing twenty-two years ago. The very idea that Parker could just walk out on the people who loved him left him feeling more betrayed than he could have imagined.

Relenting she held out her arms like a child and allowed him to scoop her up and carry her into the bedroom. Casey switched on the light as he settled Tessa on the bed, tucking her under the covers and catching sight of the bruises on her wrists. Forcing himself to take a deep breath and shove back down the anger that was welling up inside him. The Parker he knew would never lay a hand on another human being, let alone the woman he loved, and that he had done it was a testament to how much his partner had changed the last few weeks.

"I'm starting to get really worried about you, Tessa," he told her seriously, as she closed her eyes to avoid his gaze. "Passing out in shopping malls, and again today, throwing up, something is going on with you. Something other than the stomach flu," he added, anticipating her response.

"I think Wyatt and I should take you to the hospital," Casey chimed in anxiously, gently brushing Tessa's hair from her face.

Opening her eyes Tessa studied them both with her probing

blue stare, and then gave a resigned sigh, "I don't need to go to the hospital," she said at last. And before they could protest, "I don't need to go to the hospital because I already know what's wrong with me. I was waiting to tell Parker first but since he's not here . . ."

Feeling his stomach begin to churn as he sat down on the bed beside her and reached for her hand. His mind jumped from one farfetched conclusion to another, as he pictured every conceivable thing that could possibly be wrong.

"Whatever it is, Tess, me and Casey are there for you," giving her hand a tight squeeze.

"I'm pregnant."

* * * * *

12:57 P.M.

Aimlessly meandering through the house, Lila found herself, as she always did, in Joey's room. She had not changed anything since he had died, it was still exactly as it had been the day of the incident.

Eric was out somewhere but she couldn't remember where he'd said he was going. Work? Or maybe the grocery store? Barring the funeral, she hadn't left the house since coming home from the hospital. Eric had tried several times to coax her into going out, but she was scared that the further she went from the house the further she was moving away from Joey.

Eric had become even more worried about her since the funeral. He had hardly left her side all yesterday afternoon or this morning. So maybe she had asked him to leave? It was getting so hard to remember things. Maybe she was losing her mind.

Detective Bell hadn't turned up to the funeral like he'd promised. She'd been counting on him. She'd needed to see his eyes. Maybe something had come up. Maybe Detective Bell had found the baby. Maybe he'd called to explain and she'd forgotten. Her life seemed to have turned into a sea of maybes. The only thing left she knew for sure was that Joey was gone.

Curling up on the bed, she pulled several of Joey's stuffed animals into her arms and closed her eyes. Being in his room, surrounded by his things, was the closest Lila felt to Joey. She spent most of her time here on his bed, lost in wonderful memories. She remembered perfectly the first time he had called her 'mama', she remembered his first steps, his first smile, and his first day of preschool.

Opening her eyes, she let out a shrill scream as she saw Joey hovering above her. Face sulky, eyes accusing then he started to cry, and as he always did, asked her why she let those people kill him.

"I'm sorry, baby, I didn't mean to," she sobbed, squeezing her eyes closed. When she opened them again Joey's face morphed into Eric's and she let out another screech.

Staring at her angrily, "you killed him, it's your fault," her husband accused.

Pushing shakily to her feet, Lila staggered for the door. "I'm sorry, I'm sorry," she sobbed. Letting the door fall closed behind her, she turned only to meet Eric hovering above her.

"He's dead because of you! He's dead because of you," he started to sing.

"Please stop, please," she begged, pressing her fists against her temples, and stumbling down the stairs, thankful when Eric did not follow.

Making it through the back door on wobbly legs, she headed for the clubhouse she, Eric, Savannah and Charlie had assembled for Joey last Christmas Eve. Inside she flopped down, the bottle of sleeping pills tumbling from the pocket of her robe. Lila wanted to sleep. She was so tired. She wanted to see her sweet little boy again. Unscrewing the lid she tipped one into her hand, fingering it, the pills weren't working as well as they had been just a couple of days ago. Maybe she'd been taking too many? Maybe she wasn't taking enough?

She swallowed the pill.

Feeling no effect, she took another and then another, and then finally felt the comfortable lull of sleep wash over her. Letting the bottle slip from her hand, she allowed the blackness to pull her down and floated away.

* * * * *

1:19 P.M.

"Are you sure Lila won't mind us coming over for dinner?" Savannah asked him, as he drove her and Charlie home from the hospital.

"I'm sure she'll be fine," Eric answered, not even sure if Lila would notice the extra company, she was retreating further and further into a world he couldn't reach. "Besides you should tell her your news."

"I'm sorry we didn't tell you sooner," Charlie told him sheepishly.

"I understand," Eric answered automatically. And he meant it, kind of. While he did understand why his brother and Savannah hadn't told him about their engagement right away, it didn't mean that he wasn't a little hurt.

"It was just the timing felt wrong," Charlie added, sensing that Eric wasn't quite as understanding as he was making out.

"Really I get it," he snapped, a little more aggressively than he'd intended, and the car's occupants lapped into silence.

Charlie and Savannah had become engaged a few days before the incident and had been planning on throwing a party and announcing their news to the whole family. But then the world as they knew it had changed. Joey had been killed, Molly abducted, Lila had started falling apart, and they had decided to wait before telling anyone. If Eric hadn't accidentally walked in on them kissing in Charlie's office, Savannah wearing her engagement ring, he still wouldn't know about it.

It wasn't really his brother and soon to be sister-in-law that he was mad at. It was himself, Lila, the kidnappers, the world in general. In the six days after the incident Lila had continued to get progressively worse, her hysterical outburst and hallucinations at the funeral had really frightened him. Grief expressed itself in many different ways, he knew that, but that didn't mean he wasn't terrified. At the gravesite Lila had drifted into a near catatonic state. She hadn't spoken a word, had stared blankly through their friends and family, he'd had to lead her everywhere by the hand. When they'd finally arrived home, she'd taken a sleeping pill and gone straight to bed.

Pulling the car into the driveway, they all climbed out and trudged to the door, pausing while he fished his key out of his pocket.

"Lila? I'm home," he called once inside. One night he'd made the mistake of not announcing himself, when he'd walked up behind her in Joey's room she'd almost had a heart attack.

There was no answer. "She must be asleep," he muttered, heading to the stairs.

"We'll get started on dinner," Charlie told him.

Upstairs he went immediately to Joey's room. It was empty. Next, he tried their bedroom, it was empty too, ditto the ensuite. Starting to feel a little panicked, he tried the nursery, but again no sign of Lila, and he knew something was wrong.

Bolting down the stairs, "I can't find her, she's not up there," he called running into the kitchen.

"What?" Charlie asked.

"I checked every room, she's not up there," he repeated.

"Don't panic," Charlie tried to calm him. "She has to be around here somewhere, Savannah and I'll check down here, you check outside."

Nodding, Eric raced into the backyard, quickly skimming behind the fruit trees, the shed and the jungle gym. With no sign of his wife, he was about to head back inside when a thought occurred to him. Hunching over and wiggling through the tiny door of Joey's clubhouse he found Lila lying on the floor inside, an open bottle of sleeping pills at her side.

"Charlie," he screamed, dropping to his knees beside his wife, fingers checking for a pulse, cheek held above her mouth to check if she was breathing. Nothing and nothing.

"Charlie!" he screamed again, the world starting to spin. Forcing himself to calm down, he was not going to lose Lila too, but if he was going to save her then he needed to focus. Grabbing Lila around the waist, he dragged her from the clubhouse, lying her down on the grass outside just as Charlie and Savannah appeared from the house.

"I'll call an ambulance," Savannah yelled when she caught a glimpse of Lila's limp form.

Checking Lila's airway to make sure it was not obscured as Charlie knelt beside them asking. "What did she do?"

"Sleeping pills," he replied as he tilted back Lila's head, pinched her nose closed and covered his wife's mouth with his own. Breathing his own air inside her and willing her to take a breath and come back to him. "Check how many."

Charlie disappeared into the clubhouse, reappearing a moment later with the bottle and a handful of pills.

"I filled the prescription yesterday, it should only be missing one," he muttered as he put one hand on top of the other and positioned the heel of the bottom hand above her heart, pressing repeatedly to force her heart to continue to pump blood around her body.

"I've only got a couple left," Charlie said slowly.

Taking that in as he continued relentlessly with CPR, he was not going to let Lila die. Convincing himself this was all just a mistake. Even in her condition Lila would never do this, never try to kill herself. Surely life couldn't be this cruel. It couldn't take his son, his daughter, *and* his wife. It couldn't, it just couldn't.

"Ambulance is on its way," Savannah announced as she came running.

Glancing at his watch Eric saw that he had been doing CPR on Lila for several minutes, if she did not start to breath on her own soon she would be at high risk of sustaining serious brain damage or . . .

Just then Lila started to cough, as she struggled to suck in air, Eric held her face between his hands, "breathe in, breath in" he told her, weak with relief. Lila was breathing, she hadn't left him. Everything was going to be okay.

Charlie lifted Lila's wrist, "pulse is weak."

"Breaths are shallow," he added, as sirens sounded in the distance. "Come on, honey, hang in there," stroking Lila's hair back from her face. "Just hang in there. You can't die on me, Lila. You can't make me lose you too. I'll have nothing left."

* * * * *

6:34 P.M.

"Hello?"

The man on the other side of the door had a messy mop of sandy hair, a mass of freckles over both his face and his arms, and the brightest blue eyes Tessa had ever seen. He had on a friendly smile but she wasn't in the mood to entertain visitors.

"Is Parker Bell here?"

"No," she answered shortly.

"Do you know when he's coming back?"

"No."

Puzzled, "this is Parker Bell's house right?"

"Do I know you?"

Giving her what she assumed was what he thought to be his

most charming smile. "I think I'd remember someone as pretty as you."

Glowering, unfortunately for her mystery visitor flattery would get him nowhere. "Do you actually want something?"

Letting out an easy laugh, "maybe I should start from the beginning. Hi, my name's Caleb Brighton, I'm an old friend of Parker's."

"Really?" she asked suspiciously. "He's never mentioned you before."

Unfazed, "it was back when we were in foster care together, those weren't great times," electric blue eyes momentarily growing dark. "Parker was lucky, he got adopted, some of the rest of us weren't so fortunate. Anyway," brightening again, "I've been working on getting my life together and thought I'd track down my old friend and catch up."

"Everything okay, Tess?" Skylar Wyatt suddenly appeared on her front stoop, carefully eyeing the stranger with a calm green stare.

"Fine thanks, Skylar," relieved that she now had a reason for getting rid of her visitor, her stomach was starting to turn cartwheels, and she wondered how her own baby could cause her so much pain and discomfort. "I'll tell Parker you called," she announced dismissively to Caleb Brighton, and then as Skylar followed her inside, closed the door in his face.

"Who was that?" Skylar asked as he led the way to the kitchen.

"He *says* he's a friend of Parker's," Tessa replied. She had learnt a long time ago that it saved a lot of time and effort in the long run to be suspicious of everyone and everything. Some people might call her fatalistic because she was always waiting for the worst to happen, she called it being realistic since more often than not the worst did happen.

"You don't believe him?"

Shrugging as she resumed munching on the dry piece of cold toast she'd been eating for dinner before Caleb had turned up on her doorstep, and hoping that the baby let her keep it down. How did the baby expect to grow if it kept making her throw up everything she ate, at this rate they'd both waste away to nothing.

"You're being paranoid again," Skylar told her reproachfully.

"I like to call it being wary," she shot back.

"You can call it whatever you like but you can't keep living like this Tessa, at some point you're going to have to learn to trust people," Skylar admonished as he refilled her water glass.

"I trust people," she countered defensively.

Skylar raised a questioning eyebrow, "oh yeah, like who?"

Counting them off on her fingers, "you, Casey, J.J., Daniel . . . Parker," Tessa heard the vulnerability creep into her voice and hated it. She was tough, strong, independent, and more than used to going things alone. Skylar was like her big brother, but she did not need him to take care of her, she was quite capable of doing that herself. Taking a huge gulp of water to try and regain her composure, but it was already too late, she could feel tears begin to escape, slowly winding their way down her cheeks.

"Come here, goldilocks," Skylar murmured, as he pulled her against him. She rested her forehead against his chest for a second, before resolutely pulling away.

"Everything will be alright, Tess, I promise," he whispered, trying not to appear upset that she wouldn't let him comfort her.

"Parker wouldn't leave me," she told him defiantly. Tessa didn't think that Parker would leave her, but if history had taught her anything, it was that everyone she loved eventually went away one way or another.

"Shh, I know, I know," Skylar was watching her helplessly, wanting to help her but unsure what to do or say.

Meeting his eyes, "Skylar, do you really think Parker just left?"

Torn between his personal feelings on what he believed his lifelong friend would or wouldn't do, and his professional opinion as a police detective on the way things like this usually turned out. At last he let out a weary breath, and Tessa wondered whether he'd gotten any more sleep than she had the last couple of days. "I don't want to think he would just leave you."

"That's not really an answer," she gazed up at him.

"I know, it's just that I was thinking . . ."

"Thinking what?" she prompted when he didn't continue.

"Did Parker know you were pregnant?"

Immediately catching on to what he was implying, "no, he did not know. You and Casey were the first people I told."

"Is there any way he could have found out?" Skylar pressed.

"I don't see how," she answered haughtily. "I thought I might be pregnant about a week ago, I took a test, it said I wasn't. I wasn't convinced so I saw the doctor, had blood taken, and found out the day Parker disappeared that I was indeed with child. And since I'm only six weeks along, it's not like I'm showing yet. So sorry to ruin your well thought out accusation but . . ." Tessa trailed off as something occurred to her. Dropping into a chair and burying her face in her hands, it couldn't be, she was sure it wasn't, but maybe . . .

"Tessa, what is it?" Skylar asked gently, as he knelt in front of her.

"I threw the home pregnancy test in the garbage," she explained in a small voice. "I don't think he found it, but maybe he did. The instructions weren't there, he wouldn't have known how to read it," the world was beginning to rock dangerously.

Grabbing her shoulders, "hey, hey, it's okay, stay with me, Tess," Skylar commanded.

Taking several deep breaths. "You think that's why he's been acting so strange, because he was freaked out about becoming a father?"

"I don't know."

"But Parker'd be a great dad," she protested.

"I know that, and you know that, but Parker . . . have you told Daniel, Winter and Matilda?" he asked, abruptly changing the subject.

"Yeah," she gave a small nod. "They're all really excited. Well Winter and Matilda were, the way Daniel looked it was lucky that Parker wasn't in the room or I think Daniel would have decked him."

Skylar smiled, "he's your big brother, he's just looking out for you."

Picking at a loose thread on her amethyst blouse, eventually she looked up to meet Skylar's steady gaze, and knew that her own eyes betrayed the terror that was stewing inside of her. "I can't do this alone," she whispered.

"Hey," Skylar hooked a thumb under her chin so she couldn't look away, "you are not alone. You've got Casey, your brother, your niece, Matilda and me. I don't want you to ever think that you are alone."

"But I am alone," Tessa said simply, "I've always been alone." Pulling free from Skylar's grip she marched up the stairs, leaving Skylar kneeling on the floor and peering anxiously after her.

JUNE 19TH

9:19 A.M.

"You want to go out today?" Daniel asked Tessa, somewhat impatiently. He had already spent the morning trying to convince her to do something.

Matilda watched her sister-in-law shrug half-heartedly. Tessa had been in a funk since she'd told them she was pregnant, not that Matilda could blame her, mind you. Tessa had come home to tell her husband that she was pregnant with their first child, only to find that her husband had vanished off the face of the planet. If anyone deserved to be in a funk, it was definitely Tessa.

Still unsure of how she felt about her brother's disappearance. She wasn't convinced that something awful had happened to him as Tessa was, and she wasn't convinced that he'd left his entire life behind like Daniel was. Part of her believed that it was her own fault. She had run away, she had come back, Parker had run away.

It scared her to think of her brother as the 'bad' one, the one who ran away from his troubles, it was so unlike him. Growing up, running away had been her thing. Any time she felt stressed, or uncomfortable, or worse yet *comfortable*, she up and left for a few days.

The first time she had disappeared she'd been twelve, and had been living as Matilda Bell for two years. She had gotten a good grade on a saxophone exam and her family had gone out to celebrate, as was their custom when someone did something great. Later that night Luka delivered a speech telling them all how proud he was of her, he'd called her his daughter, and that had hurt her more than anything else. She wasn't a good daughter,

135

he deserved so much better than her, Laura too. They were too good to her, too kind, and she couldn't take it anymore, she had thrown some clothes in a bag and spent two days living in the park. When they had finally tracked her down, the Bell's hadn't yelled, hadn't punished her, they'd just hugged her and told her that they loved her and always would. Eight months later, this time after a perfect grade on a history paper, and another family celebration, she had disappeared again, four days this time.

But not Parker, he had never run from anyone or anything in his life. After she had killed Lachlan Mountain, the social worker, he had refused to leave her side, had held her hand and promised her that everything would be okay. When another social worker arrived and took them away he hadn't left her. When the social worker had explained that the Bell's wanted to adopt them so that they could be a family he had told her that it would just be the two of them, they wouldn't let another horrible couple hurt them. However, later on that first night, tucked up in their beds in their shared room, he had cracked a smile when Laura had appeared with two steaming cups of cocoa, and from that moment on life for him had been good.

"Come on, Tess," Winter was coaxing, "how about we go out to your place and go horse riding, you haven't given me a lessen in ages."

Feeling Daniel's eyes on her, Matilda felt a blush creep up from her neck to the top of her head and knew that she had turned bright red. Lips tickling as she remembered the soft, sweet feel of Daniel mouth against her own. Moonlight streaming down on them, his body pressed against her in the delightfully cold water, the raw desire in his blue eyes sending round after round of electrical currents coursing through her body.

"You're already a good rider, Winter." Tessa was not going to be convinced to lift her mood.

They all drifted into silence, Matilda's mind thinking back to her date with Daniel, the way he had intuitively known not to speak about her past, she'd sensed that his own past was a sensitive subject too. Unlike any other man she'd met, he hadn't pressured her to do anything she wasn't comfortable with. When he'd first suggested skinny-dipping she'd been initially horrified and declined immediately. Daniel had merely shrugged, pulled off his clothes and waded into the sparkling water.

Matilda had been shocked when she'd felt a stirring down low in her stomach as she watched the water drip from his hair, little beads glistening in the moonlight as they trickled down his perfectly toned chest and disappeared back into the stream. And at last, the lure had been too great to resist, and she had followed him into the icy water.

Daniel made her feel confident enough to experiment with pressing her body provocatively against his, her fingertips exploring his face and the hard curves of his chest. He had squirmed desperately against her, he had wanted her, but he hadn't pushed, hadn't put his own needs above hers, and she had enjoyed for once having power over a man.

"Maybe we could just stay in and watch a movie," she suggested, drawing her mind back to the present.

Once again Tessa lifted a disinterested shoulder, but Daniel and Winter jumped on the idea.

"That's a great idea, Matilda," Winter enthused. "We can watch Mary Poppins, that was my favorite movie when I was little." The girl's eyes dimmed a little as she mentioned her childhood. Daniel had explained to her that his niece's mother had died recently.

Before Tessa could protest, Winter had grabbed her arm and begun to drag her to the living room, chattering away in the upbeat manner only a teenager can achieve.

Daniel moved to follow them, but she grabbed his arm and leaned in close, feeling him move minutely away from her. "You want to go out later tonight?"

Hesitating before answering, "I don't really want to leave Tessa alone."

Pausing for a beat, then drawing in a deep breath, "Daniel, did I do something to offend you," she asked, almost afraid to hear the answer. He'd been a little distant since arriving home after their date, she had assumed that it just because of everything that was going on with Parker and Tessa but maybe it was something else.

His gaze softened, "you could never do anything to offend me," he pressed a tender kiss to her forehead, before almost running from the room.

More confused than ever Matilda followed the others.

* * * * *

1:48 P.M.

"Hi, honey," Eric tried to smile at his wife as she lay in her hospital bed.

The bruises on her face and body were slowly beginning to fade, the mottled colors contrasted with her pale skin and added to her haunted look. A pair of dead brown eyes stared back at him, and for the first time in their marriage, he was afraid of his wife. She wasn't the same woman she had been. It was like she had died right along with Joey.

Keeping his voice forcefully bright, "I thought that we could talk, does that sound okay?"

Lila nodded.

Wondering what was keeping Charlie. His brother had reluctantly agreed to talk to Lila in a professional capacity after yesterday's suicide attempt. Charlie felt that he couldn't be objective when attempting to help Lila, because as her brother-in-law he was emotionally involved. However, from Eric's point of view there was no one he trusted more to help his wife, than his brother. If anyone could reach Lila, it was Charlie.

"About what happened yesterday," he ventured.

"Yesterday?" she parroted back.

Gingerly sitting on the edge of her bed, "yeah, you remember yesterday?"

Her blank gaze conveyed that she did not, and he wished he could be so lucky. He vividly remembered crouching over her lifeless body as he performed CPR, the ambulance ride to the hospital, Jamie once again spiriting Lila away, this time to pump her stomach.

Gently he stroked her hair, which was spilled out on the pillow like a red halo. "You took some sleeping pills," he reminded her, watching closely for any spark of recognition about what she had done.

While he understood the desire to take his own life to escape the swamping grief, he did not understand how Lila could turn her back on him and Molly, especially now when the police were actually making headway. The only reason he had left Lila alone after her meltdown at Joey's funeral was because he'd received a call from Detective Wyatt. The detective had been vague, and Eric hadn't wanted to get Lila's hopes up only to have them dashed, so he'd gone alone. Detective Wyatt had managed to track down the old security footage from the hospital and found the pregnant woman. The picture he had of her however was very blurry, but Eric thought she looked familiar. If Lila could just hold on a little bit longer, then the police would find this woman, find Molly, and return her to them. Nothing could or would replace Joey, but at least they'd have their daughter back.

"Sleep?" Lila echoed, a little brighter this time, "I like sleep. Sometimes when I sleep, I have these wonderful dreams about Joey. Sometime we go to the beach and play in the waves, sometimes we're at the park running in the sunshine, one time . . ."

They both looked at the door as it swung open, when Lila saw it was only Charlie, she continued with her barely coherent rambling, "we were at the snow, building a snowman and throwing snowballs. But my favorite dreams are the ones where we play in his room, and I sit beside him on his bed and read him a story. Then he tells me he loves me and falls asleep in my arms, but sometimes . . ." she trailed off, her peaceful smile replaced by a worried frown.

"Sometimes what, Lila?" Charlie asked softly, as he took the room's one chair and pulled it close to the bed.

Lila looked small and frightened. "Sometimes my dreams are bad. Sometimes Joey's mad at me."

"How do you know he's mad?" Charlie continued calmly.

Sniffing, "he tells me."

"What does he say?"

Gulping, "he asks why I let them kill him, and then he says . . . he's says it's my fault, that *I* killed him."

"Do you think that's true?"

Her breathing growing shaky, Lila nodded slowly. "I'm his mother, it's my job to take care of him and keep him safe, and I failed."

Eric had never been more glad in his life that his brother was here, there was no way he would be able to deal with this on his own.

"But you tried to save him, didn't you?" Charlie reminded her gently.

Lila's face clouded over, and Eric thought she was about to start crying, but then she turned to look at him, her eyes meeting his for the first time since the incident. "Sometimes in my dreams you blame me too," she whispered.

Feeling his breath catch in his throat, a part of him did blame Lila, or at least it had, but he knew in his heart that it was not her fault. Caressing her cheek, "it was not your fault, Lila," he told her honestly.

"Make it stop," she begged, voice impossibly childlike. "Please make it stop, Eric. Make it go away. I don't want to hurt anymore."

"I wish I could, sweetheart," brushing his lips across her forehead. "I wish I could make it all go back to the way it was."

Lila was worn out, already drifting back to sleep, but Eric had to know, squeezing her hand he asked, "why did you do it, Lila? Why did you try to kill yourself?"

Confused, "kill myself? I just wanted to sleep. I like sleep," she mumbled, eyes fluttering closed, breathing evening out as she fell into a deep slumber.

The weight of the world lifting from his shoulders. Naïve or not he wanted, needed for his own sanity, to believe what his wife had just told him. Grinning at Charlie, "I knew she wouldn't try to kill herself."

But his brother's face was serious, "she needs help, Eric, real help, and I can't be the one to give it to her."

"She blames herself, that seems pretty natural to me. I blame myself and I wasn't even there," he countered, not wanting Charlie to ruin his brief happy mood.

"She doesn't blame herself, Eric, she blames Molly."

* * * * *

5:11 P.M.

"You again."

"I don't think I made a very good first impression last time," Caleb Brighton grinned back at her.

"Can't you take a hint?" Tessa growled. It had taken her most of the day to finally get rid of her well meaning brother, niece and sister-in-law, and she was looking forward to doing some well deserved moping on her own for a while.

"You're Tessa, right?" Caleb continued undaunted. When she didn't reply his eyes strayed to her left hand, "Parker's wife?" When she still didn't respond he finally seemed to take the hint, "okay, I can see it's not a good time." Giving her a hurt puppy dog look, just like one of Parker's, he turned and headed back down the garden path to the street.

Knowing she was going to regret this, "wait."

Stopping but not turning back around, Caleb waited.

"Parker's gone."

Confused, he spun around to face her, "what do you mean gone?"

"I mean gone," she repeated then headed back into the house, if Caleb was going to follow her, he could, if he wanted to leave he was free to do that too. Lately she was too weary to keep her paranoia at a safe level, she didn't even have the energy to go out and find Parker on her own. She had connections, some good, some not so good, it was a possibility that she could track him down. The only thing stopping her was a niggling doubt that Parker *had* left of his own accord. Everyone else had left her, what would make him so different that he should stay?

Just dropping into an armchair in the living room, when she heard the front door close. "Parker's really gone?" Caleb asked as he appeared in the doorway.

"Uh huh."

"Gone where? Like on a holiday, or ran off, or was abducted?"

"Like I don't know," she answered quietly.

Running his hands through his sandy hair, as he seemed to struggle to think of something to say. "The police know?" he asked at last.

"Parker *is* a police officer," she replied.

"That was his partner here the other day?" Caleb quizzed.

"Yeah, Skylar Wyatt."

"What do the police think happened?" Caleb finally entered the room and took the armchair next to hers.

"Well," she wavered, "they think that he just up and quit his life, ran off with another woman."

Scrutinizing her with an unreadable expression. "What do *you* think happened?"

"I don't think Parker would leave me," she replied emphatically, *at least I don't want to think that,* she amended to herself. Then abruptly asked, "so you knew Parker when you were kids? What was he like back then?"

"Tough and loyal," Caleb answered immediately, then seeming to realize what he said and what she had told him the police thought had happened, "at least he was loyal back then. After he and his sister were adopted I never saw him again."

"Matilda's here," Tessa told him. "Parker's twin sister, do you remember her?"

"She is? Yeah I remember her."

Tessa thought she saw something flash through his eyes, but then it was gone, and she assumed she'd just imagined it. "Yeah, she should be back soon, she and my brother and niece went to get dinner and pick up some movies, they're all intent on cheering me up. Anyway tell me more about Parker when he was a kid, did the two of you get up to mischief?" She was desperate for anything to bring her closer to her husband, who with each passing second felt like he was slipping further and further away.

Smiling thoughtfully, "Parker was eight when I met him for the first time, I was seven and had already been living there for a couple of months. We hit it off right away, became good friends, did everything together. Parker he was amazing, even at eight he would stand up for the smaller children, always putting himself between them and our foster father when he was on one of his rampages."

"Parker never told me that," Tessa murmured regretfully, she'd thought Parker had shared all of his history with her, apparently she'd been wrong. "He never told me his foster father hit him, only about the son."

"Malcolm," Caleb grimaced, "he was the worst. Parker always stood up to him though, even when he knew what was coming." Studying her with solemn blue eyes, "Tessa, don't give up," he reached for her hand, squeezed it gently. "If you think something

143

happened to Parker, then push the police to investigate it. If they won't then maybe there's another avenue you could explore."

"Tessie, we're home," Daniel announced, coming in through the back door.

Springing away from her like she'd suddenly caught fire, Caleb seemed genuinely startled by the sudden interruption.

"It's okay," she assured him, "it's only by brother and niece."

"Sorry," he apologized, giving her a lopsided grin. "I guess I'm a little jumpy today, I better be going."

"You can stay for dinner if you want," Tessa told him, but he was already hurrying for the front door.

"Maybe some other time." Glancing at his watch, "I didn't realize the time, I've gotta get to work. Give me your hand," he held out one of his own and with his other fumbled in his shirt pocket, pulling out a pen and scribbling down a number on the back of her hand. "Call me if you need anything, day or night, I mean it." Giving her a quick peck on the cheek, "bye, Tessa."

Flustered as she watched him disappear, starting when Daniel came up behind her. "Who was that?"

"An old friend of Parker's. He came by the other day when Skylar was here, and came back today," she explained as she closed the door.

Daniel wrapped an arm around her shoulders as they headed for the kitchen. "Come on, lets get some food in you, see if your baby's hungry enough to let you keep it down."

Nodding distractedly, Caleb's words still echoing in her head. He was right, if she thought that something had happened to Parker she should keep fighting, make Skylar and J.J. keep looking.

If there was one thing Tessa Allina Micah Bell never did, it was quit.

JUNE 20TH

10:17 A.M.

She and Joey were running in the park.

The sun was shining, the sky a brilliant electric blue.

The grass the brightest green she'd ever seen.

Butterflies flitted through the air, birds chirped.

She and Joey were laughing, and running, and rolling in the soft, sweet smelling grass.

Then everything faded to black.

"Joey? Joey?" she called. "Where are you, honey?"

The blackness swirled like a tornado.

When it stopped, she was in the grocery store parking lot.

Searching frantically for her son.

"Joey?"

He appeared before her, holding the baby in his arms.

Relieved, "there you are, sweetheart."

She tried to grab him but he moved away.

Following him, the faster she went the further away he got.

Something cold pressed against her head.

The gun.

"Give us the keys," a voice leered.

Then the kidnappers were standing beside Joey and Molly.

Their faces smooth, blank masks.

"Joey, come to mommy."

Shaking his head, his red curls bouncing. "No. You're not a good mommy."

Ever so slowly the kidnappers faces begun to change.

First, they took on Joey and Molly's appearance, but then

145

features begun to form, eyes, ears, nose, mouth, until she was looking at the man and woman who had killed her son.

Then the parking lot exploded with the sound of the gunshot.

Joey was on the ground.

He was red, so red, the color so bright it seemed to give off it's own light.

The kidnappers were walking away, the baby in their arms.

She was kneeling beside Joey, holding him, shaking him, begging him to wake up.

Screaming when his eyes popped open.

But this time the words he spoke were different. "Make them pay."

Lila woke with a start.

Sweating, shaking, breathless, hot and cold.

The faces of the couple that had taken her child from her seared into her mind's eye.

Cobwebs clearing from her mind she reached for the pad and pen in the drawer, quickly spilling down on paper a rough sketch of the killers.

When she was satisfied that her depiction of the faces was accurate she reached for the phone, realizing for the first time that she actually felt alive. Gone were the fear, the guilt, the emptiness, the blackness, the feeling of being lost in a desert, alone, mirages of hope popping up only to vanish when you got too close. In their place was anger. Pure, simple, anger, and Lila relished it.

About to dial the number, her hand froze when the door swung open.

"Hello, Mrs. Abbott, we need to talk."

* * * * *

12:43 P.M.

"It's me," Tessa announced unnecessarily into the phone,

careful to keep her voice down, she didn't want anyone to hear this particular conversation. She was supposed to be up in her room resting, the others were downstairs, but were likely to pop up at any second to come and check on her.

"At last count you owed me a favor," she reminded him. Tessa had decided to take Caleb Brighton's advice and look for Parker herself. If he had left her, so be it, but she was going to find out one way or another.

"Parker's gone."

Rolling her eyes in response to his answer.

"Why do people keep asking that? What do you think gone means?"

She was wound up so tightly these days it didn't take much to push her over the edge.

"I need you to use your people, see if anyone sees or hears anything."

Glancing around while she listened, careful to make sure Winter, Matilda or Daniel were nowhere within earshot.

"No, I don't want you to send out a search party, didn't anyone ever teach you about subtlety? Just tell your guys to keep an eye out. If something has happened to Parker, if someone attacked him," she kept her voice steady through years of practice, "I don't want them spooked and I don't want them catching on."

Lowering her voice further when she thought she heard someone coming.

"I am not being stubborn, I came to you for help didn't I? Don't call me unless you know something."

Tessa was just snapping closed the disposable cell phone, when Skylar's voice rumbled behind her, "you aren't doing something stupid are you?"

"I'm offended you would even suggest that," twirling her hair innocently.

Dubious, "who was that?"

"No one for you to concern yourself with," she told him

haughtily as she tried to barge past him.

"Let me see your phone," Skylar reached for it, but she swung her arm away.

"You have got no right to see that," she snapped at him.

Giving her a disapproving frown, "I care about you that gives me the right."

"Well who asked you to care about me?" She was close to tears again but she'd promised herself she wasn't going to cry until she was safely wrapped up in her husband's arms. Right now she didn't want anyone to love or care about her, she wanted to feel angry and alone, the only way she knew how to get herself and her baby through this in one piece.

Grabbing her arm, "are you trying to find Parker yourself?" Skylar demanded, apparently deciding to ignore her comment.

Yanking free, "well you certainly won't help me. You're the one who turned their back on Parker, you're supposed to be his best friend, how could you just abandon him when he needs you the most? How could you do that, Wyatt?"

"I thought we were past that."

Tessa could tell that she'd hurt him, but that was just too bad, he'd hurt her too. "I thought I was too, but it turns out I was wrong, I'm still mad at you. Something has happened to Parker and you're not doing anything about it," throwing her hands up in the air in frustration. Tessa hated it when she wasn't in control of everything that was going on around her.

"Last time we talked things were fine, what happened?" Skylar was standing beside her and looking at her with more kindness than she deserved.

She was probably being unfair to him. Skylar looked exhausted and had been working the Abbott case himself since Parker's disappearance, as well as taking care of his family and looking out for her. But that didn't mean she was about to let up on him, the one thing she wanted him to do, the one thing he could actually do to help her, he wouldn't. "I talked to Caleb," she answered wearily.

Puzzled for a minute before the name registered in his head. "The guy who was here the other day? The one who claimed he used to be a friend of Parker's? I don't trust that guy."

"I thought I was supposed to be the paranoid one," she returned dryly.

"I'm serious, Tessa," he bent over so that they were eye to eye, and she could see the black bags there, he must be more worn out than she'd thought. "You think something happened to Parker, well there's your answer. The guy turns up what? Two days after your husband disappears without a word."

Struggling for calm, "number one, you don't think anything did happen to my husband, you think he dumped me and the baby for another woman. Number two, why would Caleb Brighton do something to Parker and then come here to our house, that doesn't seem like the smartest thing to do. And number three," she huffed, "I already checked the guy out, and he's clean."

"You checked him out?" Skylar frowned.

"Of course I did," she scoffed. "Who do you think we're talking about here? You're the one who was chastising me the other day for never trusting anyone."

"Parker's been gone for over forty-eight hours now, you can officially file a missing person's report."

"Why bother? Parker is the police, his friends are the police, and you've already told me that you don't think it's worth the time and energy."

"Okay, okay," Skylar held up his hands in surrender. "Talk to me."

He took a seat on the huge mahogany box that sat at the end of her and Parker's canopy bed. She and Parker had picked out new bedroom furniture after the wedding, she'd fallen in love with this box the second she'd laid eyes on it. It was intricately carved with a wooded scene of trees, flowers, deer, owls, squirrels, Tessa had thought it was fitting since the woods had played such a big part in their shared past. Now Skylar sat on the box patiently waiting until she was ready to open up to him.

Unenthusiastically Tessa went to join him and taking a deep breath began, "Skylar, you know Parker. You know him because you're half the reason that he is who he is. Because of you and Laura and Luka, Parker learnt how to be loving, how to be responsible, how to be part of a family, there is no way he would give all of that up, his dream to have a family of his own." Restless she stood and began to pace, "Caleb said that if I think that something happened to Parker then I shouldn't give up. In my head I keep seeing all the horrific things that could have happened to him. Before I met Parker I was alone," her steely voice starting to hitch. "I love him, Skylar. I *love* him." Her hand moving subconsciously to cradle her stomach, "I need him and this baby needs him. How can you ask me to do nothing?"

Skylar came towards her but she pushed him away, she didn't want to be comforted, if she was going to find Parker then she needed to stay strong. "I'm tired, I think I'm gonna take a nap."

Waiting until she had climbed under the covers before coming to rest an uncertain hand on her arm. "Tessa, I'll look into it again. I'll get someone to go through your computers, see if that gives us any hints as to what might have happened, because believe it or not I really want to believe that Parker wouldn't leave us. But I need you to promise me that you're not going to do anything reckless. I can't be worrying about him and you as well as everything else." His emerald eyes were so imploring Tessa couldn't bear to lie to him.

Saved from having to promise something she couldn't deliver when Skylar's cell phone began to chirp out a tune that sounded like something Sam and Stacey had chosen. Glancing at the caller ID Skylar grimaced, "I have to take this, goldilocks, but we're not done."

Sighing with relief when he left the room, she waited until she could hear him talking in hushed tones, before pulling out her own phone, which she'd managed to tuck into her pocket without Skylar noticing. Thankfully he'd been too distracted to remember the phone, he would not be pleased to see her using an untraceable disposable cell. Not that the phone could lead back to the person who'd been on the other end or anything untoward, but it would certainly raise his suspicions that she was doing something she shouldn't.

Quickly closing her eyes and evening out her breathing when the door was eased back open. Skylar paused for a moment trying to decide whether she was really asleep or faking. Seemingly deciding that she was actually sleeping, he tiptoed over to close the blinds. Tessa felt his eyes on her, and then heard his half disappointed half worried groan before he finally left.

Once she was positive he wasn't coming back she dialed the next number on her list, she was going to find Parker no matter what it ended up costing her.

* * * * *

2:00 P.M.

"I got here as quickly as I could."

Lila Abbott looked up at him with surprisingly bright brown eyes. On the phone earlier, she'd sounded clear and concise, giving the bare bones version of her dream.

"Thank you for coming, Detective Wyatt," she gave him as close to a warm smile as he would expect her to muster under the circumstances. "I would have called you sooner, but I've had to spend the last couple of hours with the world's most boring psychiatrist."

Wyatt had been startled to receive a call from Lila Abbott, he'd heard about her apparent suicide attempt, but he had also been intrigued. Fascinated enough to postpone his discussion with Tessa, whom he was becoming increasingly concerned about. She was mad at him, fair enough, her husband was missing and he wasn't telling her what she wanted to hear. She was lashing out at him, once again, fair enough, her husband was missing and he wasn't telling her what she wanted to hear. But the problem with Tessa was that she was too smart for her own good, stubborn to a fault, and willing to do anything for someone she cared about. He couldn't be positive about whom she'd been reaching out to for help, but he knew it spelt trouble. She was deliberately putting herself and her unborn child in danger to find Parker, and he was terrified at just what she was bargaining with.

"Okay, Mrs. Abbott," he began, putting aside thoughts of Tessa, for the time being at least, he knew she was safe. On his way out he had instructed Daniel and Mattie that under no circumstances should they let Tessa leave that house alone. "Tell me what you remember."

A glimmer of excitement vibrating through the woman's wan frame, bearing witness to just what a beautiful, vibrant young wife and mother she had once been. If you took away the paling red gash on her temple, the yellowing bruises, hollow eyes, and gaunt face, Lila Abbott would have been a very attractive woman.

When Lila spoke, her voice was strong and focused, she sounded nothing like a woman who had tried to take her own life just two days ago. "I kept having this dream. At first Joey and I were playing, we were happy and laughing, but then everything would turn black," her own expression blackened. "When I could see again I was in the parking lot, but I was alone, Joey would be holding the baby. They were far away, I tried to go to him, but then the gun was against my head, just like it was that day. They told me to give them the keys and then they were standing next to Joey, I tried to get him to come to me but he said . . ." voice hitching for the first time, controlling it and continuing, "he said that I wasn't a good mother. At first the kidnappers had blank faces, no eyes or nose or mouth, just smooth skin, but this time they changed. First they were Joey and Molly, but then they changed again, and I saw their faces," Lila Abbott finished triumphantly.

"You remembered the faces of the people who attacked you and abducted your baby?" Wyatt confirmed, scarcely able to believe that they might get a happy ending after all.

Holding up the paper she clutched tightly in her trembling hands. "I not only remember them, I drew them for you."

Staring back at him were two somber middle-aged faces. The first was female, approximately late forties, with wide set eyes, a pointed chin and a high forehead. The second was male, also late forties, receding hairline, small eyes, large nose, and huge chin dimple. The pictures had been drawn with a black pencil, but around the edges of each sheet of paper Lila Abbott had added in descriptive detail. The female suspect had blue eyes and light brown hair, was approximately five foot five and one hundred and fifty pounds. The male suspect was roughly five foot seven, one hundred and eighty pounds, grey hair, brown eyes with a green and blue tattoo of a frog on his arm.

"That's very detailed." He couldn't quite contain his doubt, wondering if perhaps Lila Abbott's shock and grief-addled brain was simply creating it's own images to assuage its own guilt.

Offended, "I have a very good memory."

"Which only just returned to you over a week after what happened, and after you . . ." not quite sure how to say it, "ended up back in the hospital."

Thrusting the two sheets of paper at him, angry now, "these are the people who killed my son, do you really think I could forget their faces?"

"You did," he reminded her gently.

Cheeks heating, adding a touch of color and life to her features. "I had a concussion, retrograde amnesia, which means my memories from just before the accident *can* come back."

"I'm not saying it can't," he tried to soothe her, not quite sure just what her current medical condition was, but since she was still in the hospital he thought it best not to agitate her too much.

"When I turned to throw the keys I saw them," she spoke tightly, barely able to reign in her temper.

"And recalled them in such detail?"

"They killed my son," she screeched, hands balled into fists so tightly her nails pierced the skin.

Taking hold of her hands Wyatt gently eased them open, blotting at the blood with a tissue he retrieved from the table, Lila Abbott sagged wearily back against the mattress. "Are you positive that these are the people who killed Joey?" he asked. "Are you positive that you're not just seeing things the way you want them to be?"

This time she just stared at him tiredly, "they are the people who killed my son," she repeated more softly.

"Okay," Wyatt nodded his ascent. He'd compare Mrs. Abbott's sketch to the picture he'd got from the security footage at the hospital. If they could broadcast the drawings to the media they might get lucky, someone somewhere out there knew this couple. "You want me to find your husband, send him back in?"

Eyes growing distant, "he thinks I tried to kill myself."

"You took a lot of pills," he reminded her, pondering how he would feel if Casey ever attempted suicide. He loved Casey more than he could put into words, she was his wife, lover, friend, partner, and she'd given him the greatest gift he could imagine in their beautiful children. He didn't want to imagine his life without her.

"I wasn't thinking," Lila Abbott looked at him imploringly. "My memory was so fuzzy, I couldn't remember things, couldn't focus on things. I just wanted to sleep, to see my son, but the pills weren't working, I didn't know how many I'd taken. I just wanted to sleep and see my little boy," she finished mournfully.

Watching her battle tears and lose, Wyatt understood exactly what she was going through. Patting her hand comfortingly, "things *will* get better," he promised. "Never perfect, but better."

Standing to leave he was at the door when she finally spoke, "where's Detective Bell?"

Deciding that she deserved the truth. "Parker's gone missing."

Startled, "what?"

"We don't know where he is." If he found out Parker had simply walked out on Tessa he would wring his neck.

"That's why he didn't come to Joey's funeral like he promised," Mrs. Abbott murmured thoughtfully. "Did someone do something to him?"

"We don't know."

"Detective Bell is married, right? How's his wife?" Lila Abbott seemed much more in control now than she had a few days ago. Maybe the drug overdose, accidental or not, and remembering her son's killers had given her something to focus on.

"Tessa's hanging in there," Wyatt's concerns about her and what she was doing flaming back up.

"If she needs anything she can call me."

"That's sweet of you, Mrs. Abbott . . ."

"Lila," she interrupted.

"Lila, but right now you need to focus on getting stronger, ready for when we bring your daughter home to you."

A shadow crossed her face and Wyatt understood that she blamed the baby for what had happened. Another thing he understood all too well. In time she would learn, she would come to understand that loving Molly didn't mean loving Joey less.

After bidding her farewell and descending the hospital stairs, he needed a little exercise for the day, he drank in the warm sunshine. Jerking his wallet from his pants pocket, he found himself staring wistfully at her smiling little face in the old, creased photo. Resolutely he put it away and headed for the car, it may be too late to save some children, but it was not too late to save Molly Abbott.

JUNE 21ST

8:12 A.M.

Seemingly the baby was not pleased with their nighttime rendezvous.

Tessa felt awful this morning. This was the worst day yet.

In hindsight it probably hadn't been the best move to spend the night out looking for Parker, but she'd been backed into a corner. Skylar had promised that he'd keep looking, that he wouldn't give up on Parker just yet, but Tessa couldn't be sure that he'd follow through. She should give him credit, she supposed, he had sent someone by to collect Parker's computer like he'd promised. Of course Tessa had already been through the computer with a fine-tooth comb the second she realized Parker wasn't coming home, and had found nothing. She highly doubted that anyone at the crime lab was better with computers than she was, but she was grateful that at least they were starting to take things seriously.

After Skylar had left yesterday she actually had managed to grab a couple of hours sleep, she must have been more exhausted than she'd thought, because her sleep had been completely free of dreams. Then she'd been very sociable and had dinner with Daniel, Winter and Matilda, all of whom had been careful to avoid any talk of Parker.

Lingering in her room until she was positive that the house's other occupants were asleep before sneaking out. She'd driven around for a while, checking out any place she could think of that Parker might go, any place that was special to them, or to him, or even to her, but had come up empty. She'd then walked straight into the devil's lair to see if any of her connections had been able to come up with something. Unfortunately they too were at a loss, although he did promise her that he would keep his eyes open for as long as it took, and as long as she was willing to return the favor when the time came.

As her stomach heaved again, she was at least grateful that she now had the house to herself.

Daniel had to be at work early, and had dropped Winter off at a friend's house on his way, while Matilda had left on some mysterious errand about which she wouldn't elaborate. It had taken a fair amount of persuasion to get them to agree to leave her alone, apparently she had looked as bad as she'd felt, but in the end they had relented after she told them she needed peace and quiet in order to rest properly.

Debating whether or not it was a wise move to try eating something, then deciding no matter what mood the baby was in it was probably best to try to keep their strength up. Finding some crackers in the pantry she started nibbling on one as the doorbell rang. Tessa knew who it was going to be before she got there.

"Hello, Caleb," she said as she threw open the door.

Giving her one of his goofy grins, "I brought you a gift," holding up a stack of photos bound with a piece of string.

"What are those?" the combination of lack of sleep and lack of food in her stomach were making her mind sluggish.

Peering at her cautiously, but then forging ahead, "they're photos of me and Parker when we were kids. I thought you might like to see them."

Nodding her ascent, Tessa led him inside and down to the kitchen where she resumed munching unenthusiastically on some crackers.

"Are you feeling okay?" Caleb queried as he sat down at the table and untied the knot in the string.

"Upset stomach," she answered vaguely.

Not looking convinced but letting it drop. "When I got home the other day I couldn't stop thinking about you. I decided it might cheer you up to show you some pictures of Parker when he was a kid so I rifled through some boxes and came up with these. I was planning on bringing them by yesterday but I got held up with something."

Tessa felt a smile tugging at her lips as she flicked through the photos. There was little Parker and a sandy haired young boy with freckles who she assumed was Caleb. In one picture they were perched in a tree, leaning dangerously out of the branches they were sitting on, and looking like they might topple to the ground at any second. The next photo showed them wrestling in some mud, then swimming in a lake, and playing baseball in a field.

In each photo Tessa noted Parker's dark and hooded gaze. The way his smile never lit up his face, the way his arms and legs looked like sticks, the way his too big clothing hung off his gaunt frame, his messy mop of unkempt hair, his grimy face, and her heart broke. However awful and distant her own parents had been, they had always provided a nanny to make sure that she was clean and well fed, but before the Bell's Parker hadn't even had that. She'd thought that she made Parker happy, he'd told her he did, that having her made up for everything he'd missed out on the first ten years of his life, but if that were true then why had he gone?

"Hey," Caleb's anxious voice spoke up, "what's wrong?"

Mortified, she realized that she was crying, this darn baby in addition to hating food was also giving her awful mood swings. "I'm fine," she said quickly, brushing away the tears.

"I'm sorry, the photos upset you, that wasn't my intention," he mumbled awkwardly, obviously thrown by her tears and unsure how or what he was supposed to do to fix things.

"No," she reassured him, "they were great." In her effort to convince him that everything was okay, she made the mistake of standing too quickly, causing her baby to protest against the couple of dry crackers she'd snacked on.

"You don't look so good," Caleb stood too and grabbed her

arm as she teetered dangerously on her feet.

"I'm fine," she whimpered desperately as she tried to control her rolling stomach, her face felt like it was on fire, sweat pouring down her cheeks and mixing with the last of her tears. Taking several deep breaths, she thought it was working, but then had to wrench her arm free from Caleb's grip as she made a frantic dash for the downstairs bathroom.

Just managing to make it to the toilet before she threw up. The action didn't cause one iota of difference to her nausea, it was like however much she threw up the baby refused to be satisfied. Pressing her burning forehead against the cool tiles and hoping that Caleb had seen himself out. She was just regaining her composure when her stomach lurched again, and she was back to coughing and spluttering above the toilet bowl.

Then a hand was gently holding back her hair, its partner rubbing her back. "It's alright," Caleb murmured soothingly.

Stricken, embarrassed, mortified, humiliated, but ultimately too worn out to do anything about it. About to tell Caleb to leave her alone, but before she could utter a word another wave of nausea rocked her stomach, and before she knew it, she was throwing up all over again. Tessa wondered tiredly how her body kept managing to produce vomit when she was barely eating one meal a day.

"Done?" Caleb asked softly, and when she managed a nod, he helped ease her back so that she sat propped up against the wall, head resting floppily, limbs uselessly spent. Retrieving a washcloth from the side of the sink Caleb ran it under cold water and brought it back, blotting it over her sweat streaked face, pressing it to the pulse points in her neck and then draping it across her forehead and hunkering down beside her.

"Thanks."

"You know you look terrible," he told her mildly as he gave her one of his trademark grins.

"My baby hates me," she groaned softly.

"You're pregnant?" he asked, and seemed genuinely surprised.

Drained and shaky, she laid a hand against her stomach and begged the baby to give her a break, "six weeks,"

"The little guy just misses its daddy," Caleb told her reassuringly, as he rearranged the cloth against her head.

Mommy does too, she told her baby.

This was all so wrong. It shouldn't be a stranger here tending to her while she had her head in the toilet throwing up. It was supposed to be Parker. They were supposed to go through this together. The morning sickness, labor, middle of the night feeds, dirty diapers, teething, she wasn't supposed to have to do this on her own, and the simple truth was she couldn't.

* * * * *

9:12 A.M.

"Did the lab find anything on Parker's computer?" Wyatt asked as the door swung open, casting a shaft of bright light into the dim room where he'd been sitting for hours pouring through his and Parker's old case files. He was searching for something significant, something that jumped off the page and shouted 'I'm related to Parker's disappearance'. So far, of course, he had found nothing. But he had promised Tessa that he wouldn't give up and he was determined to keep that vow.

"Nothing," J.J. said, taking a seat next to him at the metal table and grabbing the file from the top of the pile, "but they're still going."

"They won't find anything," he swallowed the last of his coffee, and debated going to get a fresh batch. He hadn't been home last night. After his visit with Lila at the hospital, he'd come straight back to the precinct to update J.J. and compare the sketch with the picture of the pregnant woman from the hospital. The two pictures were remarkably similar, and convinced that Lila

Abbott had indeed managed to recall the faces of her attackers, they had plastered the pictures across the media.

"How do you know that?" J.J. asked crankily. His boss had also pulled an all-nighter, and his already famous temper was stretched to the limits.

"Because Tessa would never have given us the computer if she hadn't already been through it herself first." After eighteen months he thought he had a pretty good grip on the way Tessa's mind worked.

"Then why give us the computer at all?"

"She's throwing us a bone, rewarding us for playing along with her theory."

J.J. shook his head irritably, then softened, "how's she doing?"

"Stress isn't helping her morning sickness, or rather round the clock sickness, so not that great. She told you right?" he confirmed, with everything that had been going on he wasn't sure how many people Tessa had got around to telling about her pregnancy.

"Yeah," a ghost of a smile lighting his exhausted face, J.J. was a sucker for a baby. "She called and told me. It's not fair, Wyatt," the big man flexed his meaty hands them balled them into fists. "After everything she's been through, she finally lets herself be happy and it ends like this."

"At least she's not alone. Daniel's practically moved in there, and she has Winter and Matilda, not to mention she has her new best friend Caleb Brighton." Apparently Tessa's suspicions about the guy after their first meeting had quickly vanished, and he was now about the one person she was actually not angry with.

"Who's Caleb Brighton?"

"He's this guy who showed up at Tessa's house a few days after Parker left. At first Tess was her usual paranoid self, jumping to the conclusion that Caleb must have something to do with Parker's disappearance. But seemingly now she thinks he's the greatest thing ever."

"You run a background check on him?"

"Yes and so has Tessa," frustrated at his own helplessness. He was the kind of guy who liked, needed, to be in control of everything. He knew his suspicions about Caleb Brighton were completely unfounded but it didn't make him feel any better. "Besides," he said at last, "Tessa's strong and she's made it through worse than this before."

"That's what worries me. How much can one person be expected to handle, before they just break?" J.J. contemplated solemnly.

"Well what worries me, is what she's doing about it." Wyatt couldn't get Tessa's phone conversation that he'd walked in on out of his head. He'd missed the beginning, only walked in to hear her tell her mystery caller that she'd come to them for help, and that they weren't to call unless they knew something.

Arching a questioning brow, "what's she done now?"

"I walked in on her on the phone with someone."

"So?"

"A phone call she didn't want anyone to overhear," he emphasized.

Eyes widening as he caught on, "she's reaching out to him."

The 'him' they were referring to was an unknown, but assumedly male, person who may or may not be related to her abduction as a child, may or may not be related to an attempt on her life eighteen months ago, and who she may or may not have used for a favor in the past. That left them with a lot of unknowns, and no solid facts. "Parker's been looking for him."

"How? He had nothing to go on."

"It freaks him out that there's someone walking around out there who wants Tessa dead. He doesn't care how hopeless it seems, he needs to feel like he's doing something. If it was Linda wouldn't you do the same thing?"

"If it was Linda I'd hunt the guy down and kill him with my bare hands," J.J. growled. "But Tessa seems to trust this guy enough to go to him for help to find her husband. Are we sure that it's him who she was calling?"

"When I asked her about the call she got defensive, so I'm guessing it's something she knows we would disapprove of."

"We'll just have to sit her down and make her tell us who she's been calling, make her see reason," J.J. declared adamantly.

"Because Tessa is so big on sharing?" he asked, more sarcastically than he was usually prone to being, too many sleepless nights and worry filled days were taking their toll. "Come on, J.J., you know as well as I do that her MO says she's going to do something stupid. We've only known her eighteen months and she's already run off on her own after not one but two serial killers. If she finds out that someone has done something to Parker what are the chances she's going to come and tell us versus go after the guy herself?"

"Well we have to do something," J.J. flicked unseeingly through the next file in his pile. "Because what's really worrying me is what she's bargaining with."

The same thing had been worrying him too. If Tessa was dealing with criminals then there was no way they were working for free, and just what Tess had agreed to do in return scared him more than anything else.

"We already know the lengths she's willing to go to in order to save someone else," J.J. continued. "Plus she's desperate to get Parker back, she could agree to do almost anything."

"She has the baby now," Wyatt protested weakly. "It's one thing to risk her own life but she wouldn't risk the baby's." Even as he said the words, he wasn't sure they were true. Tessa would never intentionally hurt her baby, but she was more than likely to do whatever it took to get her husband back, even if that placed herself and her unborn child in harm's way.

Rolling his eyes, "when it comes to saving someone else's life Tessa is very conscientious, when it comes to protecting her own, she's severely lacking." Growing earnest, "she trusts you more than anyone else, Wyatt, you have to talk to her, convince her to let us do our jobs and bring her husband home."

"There are only three problems with that. First, Tessa's doesn't trust anyone. Second, at the moment she's pretty angry with me for betraying her so I don't think she'll listen to a word I have to say to her. And third, Tessa believes if you want something done right you do it yourself, so no way she's gonna sit back and do nothing and let us handle it." More than anything, Wyatt wished he had the magic words to say to Tessa to get her to see sense.

Heaving a gigantic sigh, "if Parker's just left, I'm going to wring his neck when we find him."

Wyatt nodded, "I think you'll have to get in line."

They both lapsed into silence and for the next couple of hours waded through umpteen case files. His eyes started to water from the poor light and skimming page after page, he needed the bathroom but couldn't seem to summon the energy to stand. Stomach grumbling from hunger, mouth parched and dry, Wyatt was just about to give in and ask J.J. if he wanted a soda when the door swung open to reveal an excited young officer.

Before he or J.J. could utter a word the young woman spoke, "we ID'd the abductors. We know who has Molly Abbott."

* * * * *

2:41 P.M.

It was hot.

Hot and sticky, and she was tired and irritable and miserable.

Yep, Tessa thought, that about summed up her life at the moment.

At least her stomach seemed to have calmed down a little, or maybe that was just because there was nothing left in it.

Before reluctantly leaving after she had assured him that she would be okay and that her brother would be home soon, Caleb had helped her to the couch and got her settled.

Once alone she had considered phoning to see if he had any information on Parker. Of course he would have called her the second he knew anything, and it wasn't a good idea to be contacting him too regularly. In fact, it had been eleven years since she had last turned to him for help. It wasn't something she liked doing or something she took lightly, but they had a delicate understanding based on mutual self-preservation. He could take her down just as easily as she could do the same to him. Their past was complicated but somehow they managed to make it work.

In the end, it became a moot point anyway. She couldn't call him because she didn't have the energy to make it up the stairs to her carefully hidden secret safe to retrieve one of her prepaid cells.

Instead, she'd drifted in an out of a fitful half-sleep. Dreams full of vivid images of death and destruction and blood. Tessa hated blood. It terrified her. Ellie had been in her dreams, crying pitifully like she had been that last night, the night before she was murdered. Dylan Riley had been there too. His taunting grin, his manic eyes, laughing and telling her she was only getting what she deserved, if she had of given her life to him he would have made her happy. Then the images had changed to Parker, drenched in blood, lying motionless on the floor in some indistinguishable room.

When she's woken to find a figure looming above her, for a second she'd thought her dreams had come to life, and she'd let out an ear-piercing scream, startling not only herself but also Daniel. After they'd both calmed down her brother had dragged out of her every detail of her dream, offered her the usual reassurances that he was positive Parker was fine, then insisted that they spend the rest of the day doing something together. Tessa wasn't exactly in the mood for that but she knew that Daniel was trying to make up for lost time. Her brother had been like that ever since he'd come back into her life six months ago.

As much as she'd tried to convince herself otherwise after Daniel had left, the two of them had been pretty close when they were kids, and she'd missed him more than she liked to admit.

So they'd played cards, had lunch, well Daniel had had lunch she hadn't wanted to risk eating anything, now they were watching a movie, and Tessa could feel her eyelids growing heavy. She was just starting to doze off when her phone started to ring. She cast a hopeful glance at Daniel, her cell was all the way over on the other side of the room.

Daniel rolled his eyes and punched her lightly in the arm, but obediently went to retrieve the phone. She had a couple of missed calls from when she was sleeping, and a new email was the source of the current ringing. When she saw who the email was from her heart froze.

"What's wrong?" Daniel quizzed, instantly concerned.

Ignoring him, her fingers were shaking so badly she could hardly open the email. When she did finally manage to read it, she was so repulsed she tossed the phone away from her like it had suddenly erupted and started spewing lava.

More concerned, "Tessie, what's wrong?"

She couldn't answer. The room was quickly draining of all oxygen.

Grabbing her shoulders and turning her to face him. "Tessie, you're scaring me, who was that?"

Her worst fears were coming true.

Giving up on her, Daniel went for the phone instead, his eyes growing wide as he read the email. Then he was back at her side, engulfing her in a hug. "I'm sorry, Tessie," he told her, squeezing her tighter.

Wildly pushing him away, lurching to her feet and pacing frantically. It couldn't be true, there was no way.

"Tessie, I'm so sorry," Daniel lingered near her, unsure whether she wanted him to comfort her or not. "I didn't want it to be true, I really didn't."

"It's not true," she declared.

Confused, "what do you mean?"

"Exactly what I said," she insisted, "it's not true."

"That was an email from Parker," Daniel remained baffled, although now a little wary, as though she might be starting to lose it. "The email said that he wasn't coming back."

Staring at her brother as though he were an imbecile. "That email was *not* from Parker."

"Tessie, it was Parker's email address," Daniel said gently, reaching for her hand.

Snatching it away before he could touch it. "Parker would never leave me," she maintained adamantly.

"Honey, I know this is hard for you to hear," he began carefully, "but Parker left you. Maybe he found out about the baby, maybe he had another woman, maybe he just up and left. I don't know why he left and I don't really care, but this is an email from his address and it says in his own words that he is not planning on coming back."

Tessa could see that her brother was trying really hard to remain calm for her benefit, but the gesture did little to ease her jangled nerves, the email made her more confident than ever that something bad had happened to Parker. "Read the email again," she ordered Daniel.

"I don't need to, I know what it says. Tessie, I'm sorry, but he's gone . . ."

"Yes he is gone," she interrupted. "And we have to find him." Snatching the phone from Daniel's hand, and jiggling it in front of his face, "he called me Tessie. He never calls me Tessie, in fact you are the only person who has ever called me that," she elaborated when her brother didn't seem to catch the significance.

Daniel studied her with thinly veiled concern. "Honey, I think you're only seeing what you want to see," he ventured.

Fired up, feeling more energized than she had in weeks. She was ready for a fight, Caleb was right, if she was going to get her husband back then she was going to have to fight for it. "Have you ever heard him call me Tessie?" she demanded.

Hesitating, "no," Daniel answered reluctantly.

"Then why would he suddenly start calling me that when he sends an email saying goodbye?" she asked triumphantly.

Remaining unconvinced, "maybe he was trying to distance himself from you, make it easier to walk away."

"Or maybe," she shot back, stubbornness ran in her family's genes, "someone forced him to write that, someone that doesn't know us as well as they think they do."

"Daniel? Tessa?" Matilda's voice called through the house.

"In here," Daniel answered.

Sensing the tension the moment she entered the room. "What's going on?" Matilda asked.

"Tess got an email," Daniel explained, "from Parker."

Hand flying to her mouth, "what did he say?"

With an anxious glance her way, "he said he wasn't coming back," Daniel responded. "I'm sorry, Mattie."

Matilda staggered backwards, "he left on purpose?" she asked in a small voice.

"It seems so."

"Tessa, I'm so sorry, I can't believe he would do that," Matilda looked positively devastated.

"He didn't do that," she countered.

"Tessa thinks," Daniel explained patiently, "that the email proves someone did something to Parker because in it he called her Tessie, and since he never calls her that, she is assuming that it confirms her theory."

Scowling at both her brother and Matilda. "I don't care if either of you believe me or not, but Parker did not write that. Something's wrong, and I'm going to prove it, to you two, to Wyatt and J.J. and everyone else." Her carefully crafted shell was beginning to crack and she could feel tears building up, but she was not going to let them make her cry.

Storming for the door, ignoring Daniel and Matilda's calls for her to wait, she didn't stop until she was safely inside her car. Roaring out the driveway it wasn't until she'd been driving for several miles that she realized where she was heading. Or at least where she would be going if only she knew where it was. Caleb was the one person who had supported not only her, but Parker as well. Since she had no idea where Caleb lived, Tessa drove out of the city and when she had reached the quiet country roads, she pulled in behind some trees so that she was hidden from sight, turned off the engine, and wept.

* * * * *

11:32 P.M.

Addressing the small gathering, Wyatt summarized what they knew so far. It had been a busy day, but a fruitful one.

"Thanks to a tip we received earlier this afternoon we have identified the kidnappers as Jim and Polly Matijevic. We've spent the day compiling all the background we can on them. Jim Matijevic is forty-eight years old, five foot eight, one hundred and eighty-five pounds, with grey hair, brown eyes, and has a green and blue tattoo of a frog on his left forearm. Polly Matijevic, born Polly Upton, is forty-six, five foot four, one hundred and fifty-five pounds, blue eyes, light brown hair. The descriptions of Jim and Polly Matijevic match with the descriptions that Lila Abbott supplied of the couple that attacked her.

"They have been married for twenty-six years, and to all intents and purposes appear to be an average couple. Jim, second son of Kristina and Alfred Matijevic, both now deceased, older brother is married and lives in Italy with his wife and two kids. We contacted the brother, he hasn't spoken to or seen Jim in a couple of years, and couldn't really offer any information other than to say he couldn't imagine his brother shooting a child and abducting a baby. Currently Jim works as a fourth grade teacher, coaches the local kids soccer team, attends church every Sunday, no criminal record, not even any parking tickets.

"Polly, only child, father deceased, mother is in a nursing home, she suffers from dementia and wasn't able to provide anything helpful, just kept telling us that Polly used to love knitting when she was little. Polly was a housewife for the majority of her married life, volunteers with a charity that helps families with terminally ill children, someone comes and sits with the kid, reads to them, gives the parents a break. Seems like a model mom, attended all her daughter's school events, plays, dance recitals, baked home made chocolate chip cookies for her church's bake sales, again no criminal record. They seemed like exemplary citizens, so we started thinking what could make a perfect couple capable of killing a five-year-old child and abducting an infant.

"The Matijevic's had one daughter, Alaina, who is now deceased, committed suicide approximately six months ago, and that is where things start to get interesting. Once we had names and identities for the abductors we went back to the Abbott's, Dr Abbott believes that Polly Matijevic is the pregnant woman that approached his family at the hospital shortly after Molly's birth, and paid an inordinate amount of attention to the baby. Beth said that the majority of people who abduct an infant are either trying to replace a baby they've recently lost or they cannot have their own kids. Since we know that the Matijevic's have, or had a daughter, we're thinking that possibly they were trying to replace Alaina.

"Beth also told us that many infant abductors plan their crimes in advance, and that sometimes they target a specific baby. If so then the Matijevic's came into contact with the Abbott's some time before the visit to the hospital after Molly was born. Since the hospital seems to be the common link, we went back a couple of months and checked out all of Eric Abbott's patient files, it turns out that he was the doctor who treated Alaina Matijevic after she slit her wrists. She lost too much blood, there was nothing the doctors could do for her. It was her mother that found her in the bathtub, called 911, rode with her in the ambulance, it would have been very traumatic for her. Once we showed him the file Eric Abbott remembered the family. Apparently Polly Matijevic was so hysterical in the end they had to sedate her, but not before she caught a glimpse of a pregnant Lila Abbott.

"Dr Abbott remembered that Lila, who would have been five months along, had come to see him at the hospital that day because he'd missed an appointment with their ob-gyn. He'd been held up trying to save Alaina Matijevic, when Lila arrived she and Eric argued about him balancing his responsibilities more equitably, so as not to miss important family occasions. So we're assuming that Polly Matijevic linked her daughter's death with the unborn Abbott baby, she then comes back after the baby's born, under the guise of being a nervous but excited first time mother. She then learns Lila's routines, follows her, and convinces her husband that they can replace Alaina with Molly, have a second go at raising a child. We're unsure whether shooting Joey Abbott was planned or whether something spooked them.

"When we do locate Jim and Polly Matijevic we need to be careful about how we approach them. I don't think that they'll hurt the baby, but they will most likely believe that they are now Molly's parents, and that they can provide a happy, loving, nurturing home and family for her. Our main problem at the moment is locating where they might be hiding out, so far there's no sign of them at their home. We've talked with neighbors, co-workers, friends, no one has been able to provide any ideas as to where they might have gone. We're hoping that they haven't gone too far away."

Drawing to a close, throat dry, the adrenalin buzz that came with progress on a case the only thing keeping him awake after over forty-eight hours without sleep.

"We want everyone to be properly prepared for what we're going to encounter when we track down the Matijevic's, our main aim is to get that baby out alive, return her to her parents."

As everyone filed out J.J. came over, "go home, Wyatt, get some sleep."

He couldn't go now, not when they were so close. "I'll crash here."

J.J. looked like he was going to disagree, but seemed to think better of it and merely nodded and headed off, to sleep in his own office Wyatt surmised.

Possessing the ability to sleep anywhere and anytime, Wyatt balled up his jacket and stretched out on the floor in the small conference room. There were two things he needed to do before he could attempt to rest. First, he called Casey, gave her a quick update on the case, and received a quick update on her and the kid's day, then promised that no matter what he would be home for dinner tomorrow night. Then he tackled the next, slightly harder, task. Dialing and waiting.

"Hello?"

"Daniel, it's Wyatt, I just called to check on Tessa."

A whoosh of air came down the line.

Instantly on edge, "what's wrong?"

"Tess doesn't want me to say anything."

Tired and not in the mood for word games. "It's about Parker?"

"Yeah."

"Well?"

"Tessa got an email from him."

Wyatt felt a tightening in his chest, "and?"

"And it said he wasn't coming back."

The words he'd been both dreading and hoping for. If Parker had gone off on his own it meant at least he wasn't in danger, it also meant he didn't know his oldest friend as well as he thought he did.

"Only Tessa thinks," Daniel continued, "that the email wasn't really from Parker, because in it he calls her Tessie."

That sounded like Tessa, she was an expert at denial. "Let me talk to her."

Clearing his throat, "that's going to be a problem."

Getting a sinking feeling in his gut, "why?"

"Because Tessa's gone. I don't know where she it."

"What?"

"She freaked out when Matilda and I wouldn't go along with her theory and ran off. I haven't heard from her since and she's not returning my calls."

"How long has she been gone?"

"About eight, nine hours."

Stressing about what Tessa was up to was the last thing he needed at the moment. "Call me the second you hear from her. I mean it, Daniel, the *second* you hear from her."

"Will do," Daniel sounded as worn out as he felt. "If she calls you first same goes, call me."

"Yeah," he agreed, not that there was much chance of Tessa calling him. "Night, Daniel."

"Night," Daniel echoed then was gone, to spend the night waiting for his sister to come home Wyatt assumed.

Laying his cell phone down on the rough carpet, closing his eyes, shutting down his mind, letting sleep trickle in, until it filled up his head and he drifted off.

JUNE 22ND

3:09 A.M.

The house looked so innocuous.

A simple white farmhouse. Wide veranda, flowers boxes at the windows, tall trees providing shade, tidy paddocks surrounding the house. It could quite easily be the setting of a wholesome family movie, instead inside lurked a hidden evil.

Following more hours of tedious paperwork they'd managed to track down the house where Jim and Polly Matijevic were hiding out. Wyatt had just managed to fade away into a deep, restful slumber when a chirpy young officer who looked like he'd come straight from a spa, awakened him to announce that the abductors had been located.

After thirty-six hours locked up indoors, Wyatt had to admit it felt nice to be out in the open again. On the drive over J.J. had explained how they'd managed to find the house. They had checked it out initially, since it used to belong to Polly Matijevic's grandmother. The reason they hadn't checked it out in more detail was because the house had changed hands so many hands. First it had gone to Polly's uncle, who had died young and left it to his son, who had also died young, and childless, and the house had come to Polly. She and Jim had lived in it for a couple of years but they'd sold it to move closer to the city after Alaina was born. The house had remained out of the family for two decades, before being recently repurchased by Alaina. It was the house where Polly had found her daughter, unconscious and bleeding in the bathtub.

They'd spoken with the neighbors who reported that a couple had moved in a week ago with their newborn baby. At first nothing had seemed suspicious, the couple was quiet, kept to themselves, but were polite, had declined dinner invitations, but had agreed to attend a small gathering the following weekend with a couple of families in the neighborhood.

Gun held low, hoping that he wouldn't need to use it, Wyatt knocked on the front door. "Police."

There was scuffling in the house, the drawn curtains in the window closest to the door rustled, moments later the door swung open to reveal a timid Polly Matijevic.

"May . . . may I help you?"

"Mrs. Matijevic?"

"Yes?" she answered uncertainly as though it might be a trick question. Her eyes darted past him to the officers that swarmed her yard.

"Is your husband home?"

"He's . . . he's sleeping . . . upstairs."

"My name's Detective Wyatt," holding up his badge. "We need to talk to you about Molly Abbott."

Panic flittered through her eyes, and deep in their blue depths a detachment from reality. A part of her knew that she had committed an unforgivable act, the other part believed her baby daughter was asleep in the house. "I . . . I don't know who that is."

"May I come inside?"

"I . . . I don't think so," her gaze locked on the other officers.

"I have a warrant for you and your husband's arrest," keeping his voice calm despite his pounding heart. "I'm here to take Molly Abbott back to her parents."

Springing to life as if a switch had been flipped, "no, you can't take her, she's mine." Polly tore back into the house taking the stairs in bounding leaps, Wyatt hot on her heels, the other officers right behind him.

At the top of the stairs she veered right, down a corridor and threw open a door, trying to slam it behind her, but his longer legs had caught up to her, and he pressed his weight against the door sending her skittering back into the room.

Taking a second to survey the room, a pink girly nursery. Fairy princesses and castles had been stenciled lovingly onto the walls, teddies and stuffed animals were piled about, the bookshelf full of picture books, the furniture all co-ordinated.

Polly stared back at him breathlessly, and a little wildly, the room's only other occupant a figure in a rocker, partially hidden in the shadows by the window, Wyatt assumed it was Jim. There was no sign of the baby, who was probably clutched in Jim's arms, but neither were there any signs of weapons.

"We're just here to get Molly, we don't want anyone to get hurt," Wyatt spoke soothingly.

"No, she doesn't belong to you," Polly protested.

"She doesn't belong to you either," Wyatt reminded her. "I know that you love her, I know that you think that you can give her a wonderful home, but her family miss her and want her back. Molly's mom and dad, they love her too, and they want to bring her home. They want to see her grow up, they want to see her fulfill all the hopes and dreams that they have for her. You know what it's like Polly, to lose a child, to have them ripped away from you, it's like losing a piece of your heart, you don't ever get over it. It's not natural, a parent isn't supposed to bury their child. You know what that pain is like, you lost Alaina. I'm asking you not to let Eric and Lila Abbott lose Molly, they love her, just like you loved your daughter."

Polly was looking from him to the rocker and back again, debating her options. "It's not fair," she whispered softly. "I loved Alaina. I loved her so much and it still wasn't enough."

"I know, I *know*. But you can give the Abbott's their daughter back. If someone could have saved Alaina, spared you all that pain, you would have wanted them to do it." He was getting through to her he could see it in her eyes.

Still wavering, Polly took a tentative step towards the rocker but paused.

"You know it's wrong Polly," he pushed a little harder. "To keep a baby from its mother."

"I'm her mother now," she protested lamely.

"You know that's not true," Wyatt contradicted. "Molly has a mother, her name is Lila Abbott, and she misses her daughter." Deciding to take a leap of faith, "Lila misses her baby so much that she took too many sleeping pills, if her husband wasn't a doctor she would have died."

Glittering eyes, "she tried to kill herself because her baby was gone?"

Wyatt nodded, watching the wheels turning in Polly's head, her mind thinking of her daughter who had taken her own life.

Arms outstretched, another step towards the rocker, reaching for the baby . . .

"No!"

Gun drawn, Wyatt spun around as a manic looking man charged at him, grey hair a wild halo around his head, fists barreling.

"Freeze," he yelled.

The man ground to a halt, his brown eyes darting around the room, lingering on no one point for more than a millisecond. The man was clearly Jim Matijevic, and he had clearly long ago lost touch with reality.

"You can't have her," Jim screeched, his whole body trembling violently.

"Sir, please get down on the ground, hands out in front of you," Wyatt ordered calmly.

"You can't have her," Jim repeated. "I won't let you take her."

The situation was quickly spinning out of control, he began to repeat his request, "sir, please get down . . ."

"Jim please," Polly interrupted, "maybe we should give her back, she needs her mother . . ."

"She has her mother right here," Jim gestured frantically at the rocker.

"Mr. Matijevic . . ." Wyatt tried again but was cut off once more by Polly.

"It's time, Jim, it didn't work, I'm sorry," Polly was crying now, tears streaming down her face.

Frenzied, his breathing harsh, Jim looked at his wife, then at Wyatt and the other officers, their drawn guns pointed directly at him.

"Mr. Matijevic, please get down on the ground," Wyatt directed.

For one moment the room seemed to freeze, there was not a single sound, not a single movement, both Jim and Polly seemed to recognize that there was no way out of this for them. Then with a ferocious scream Jim broke the spell, and with amazing agility he leapt across the room, diving for the rocker. "If I can't have her no one will."

The room erupted into noise, Jim's screams, his wife's desperate pleas for him to stop, the police's orders to stop, Jim disregarded them all, his focus solely on the baby. Just as he was about to reach the rocking chair Wyatt realized he had no choice but to shoot the man before he could hurt the baby. About to pull the trigger, when Polly pushed the chair sending it flying across the room, stuck out her foot and sent her husband careening through the window. Glass shattered everywhere, a thud as the body landed on the ground below them, the baby started to scream, Polly moved towards the rocking chair.

"Mrs. Matijevic, don't touch her," he commanded, gun pointed in her direction.

The woman nodded and remained still while an officer put her in handcuffs, and began to lead her from the room. "I took good care of her," Polly sniffed as she was taken away.

"If Jim Matijevic is down there," Wyatt glanced out the window at the still body lying on the grass, "and Polly Matijevic is in the hall," he mused to no one in particular, "then who's in the chair?"

Moving towards the rocker Wyatt couldn't quite contain the involuntary gasp, as he quickly snatched up the crying baby.

"What?" asked one of the other officers, as those remaining in the room came to see what had captured his attention.

"Oh my . . ." one trailed off, turning a little green.

Another coughed and spluttered, and then hurried from the room.

"That is sick," the last said with a disgusted grunt.

As he carried Molly Abbott through the house, past the woman who abducted her, past the dead body of the man who in the end would rather have her dead than let her go, Wyatt decided it was a good thing she was just a baby. Molly would never remember the abduction that left her big brother dead, she would never remember the events of the last ten days, nor she would ever remember that she had been cradled in the arms of a mummified body.

* * * * *

6:34 A.M.

"What's taking them so long?" Eric was pacing restlessly up and down the hall, popping out the door to check the street every couple of seconds like some sort of demented cuckoo clock. "They should be here by now."

Awakened from a dreamless sleep a couple of hours ago, when Detective Wyatt had called to say that Molly had been found. Not only had she been found, but she seemed perfectly healthy, and as happy as an infant was capable of being. At the time he hadn't known whether to laugh or cry, and thought he might have done both. Detective Wyatt had said that he would bring the baby right over, but that had been an hour ago and there was still no sign of them.

"They'll be here soon," Charlie replied, with surprising patience considering it was probably the hundredth time in the last hour that he had said those words. After the call from Detective Wyatt, Eric had phoned his brother, who had promptly turned up with Savannah. So promptly in fact, that Eric surmised that Savannah had been spending the night at Charlie's, which in turn reminded him that Lila still did not know about her brother-in-law and best friend's engagement.

Speaking of his wife she was sitting on the sofa, demeanor composed, a little too composed considering the circumstances.

After what he still wasn't sure was a suicide attempt or an accidental overdose, Lila had changed once again. No longer did she seem lost in a world he couldn't reach, a world haunted by terrifying hallucinations of a Joey who blamed her for his death, now she was calm.

Too calm.

She had calmly explained to him her dream where she had seen the faces of the couple that attacked her. She had calmly explained to the psychiatrist who had assessed her exactly what had been going through her mind when she had swallowed the pills. She had spent the previous day calmly scouring the house from top to bottom. She had nodded calmly when Detective Wyatt had shown them photos of the couple they believed had abducted Molly. She had sat there calmly while Detective Wyatt told them that the couple had targeted Molly after he had tried and failed to save their daughter. And she sat calmly now waiting for their daughter to be brought home to them.

Eric found it unnerving, and almost wished for the old, hysterical Lila to return, he was beginning to hate calm.

"Maybe something happened on the way here," he knew he sounded irrational, but he had already lost one child and every second that Molly was out of his sight was a second where some potential danger could befall her. "Maybe something happened to Molly and they had to take her to the hospital."

"I thought Detective Wyatt told you that Molly was okay?" Savannah was sitting beside Lila on the sofa and peering at her anxiously like at any moment she might break down in tears, or scream, or do *something* besides just simply sitting there.

"Maybe something changed." Wrenching open the door with more force than was necessary and stalking down the drive to the street, scanning right and then left, and upon seeing nothing stormed back into the house. "I'm going to call and see what's holding him up," he announced, pouncing on the phone.

"I don't think that's necessary," Charlie insisted.

Starting to dial then pausing, "was that a car?" Dropping the phone and hurrying back to the front door, certain that he had heard a car clumping over the broken concrete block in the driveway. But once again, it was nothing.

"Maybe we should do something while we wait," Charlie suggested when he re-entered the living room.

"I could bake cookies," Lila proposed, as though she didn't have a care in the world. Not a hair in her red ponytail was out of place, her brown eyes were clear and focused, the jeans and shirt she'd thrown on in a hurry after the phone call were completely free of wrinkles.

Needing desperately to crack her infuriatingly calm exterior. "Charlie and Savannah are engaged," Eric announced, and couldn't quite hide a satisfied smirk when Lila's face sprung to life.

"You're engaged?" Lila echoed, crestfallen.

"We wanted to tell you, but we . . . it didn't seem . . . we didn't want to . . ." Savannah stammered helplessly, looking to Charlie for support.

"We didn't think it was the best time," Charlie supplied, throwing a glower Eric's way.

"How could you not tell me? I'm supposed to be your best friend."

"With everything that was happening, we weren't sure how you would react," Savannah implored softly. "I should have told you. I'm sorry, Li."

Savannah reached out a hand towards Lila but she sidestepped neatly out of reach and pulled her mask of composure back into place. "That's okay," she said stiffly. "I'll go start on the cookies."

Guilt knifed sharply in his heart as he watched his wife disappear down the hall. His own selfish desire to force Lila down to his ramshackle frame of mind had only ended up heaping more pain on everyone involved. His wife might be sporting a calm and cool exterior, but she still bore the physical and emotional scars of what she had been through. The bruises on her hollow face, now more yellow than black, were still visible, her clothes hung off her emaciated frame, her hands constantly trembled.

He was starting after her, when a knock sounded at the door, and everything else flew from his mind.

His baby was home.

Flinging open the door, he was greeted by a grinning Detective Wyatt, cradling a soundly sleeping Molly in his arms.

Neither of them spoke, the detective held out the baby, and with shaking hands, Eric reached for his daughter. As he took her, Molly's big brown eyes opened and she gurgled, Eric hadn't realized how much he missed that sound until he heard it. Marveling once again at her tiny fingers, her little arms and legs that kicked out in the weird way only a baby's could. Running his hand over her soft head, breathing in the clean baby smell, Molly gurgled again and then gave him her first real smile. She'd smiled before, little baby smiles, but this was a real smile, a genuine smile, a heart-warming smile.

And reality began to sink in.

Eric had his daughter back, safe and sound, but things were still far from being right. They'd missed out on ten days of Molly's life, which for an infant who was growing and changing with each new morning, was more like a year. Joey was dead, and Molly or no Molly nothing would change that. Lila was still far from being okay, she was merely substituting one method of denial with another. As for himself, his family was more important to him than anything else in the world, and it was shattered beyond repair. He was eternally grateful to have his baby daughter back, but it only served to remind him just how broken things really were, and he felt himself plummeting quickly towards despair.

Molly chose that moment to grab his finger. Wrapping her tiny hand tightly around it, her big brown eyes looked straight into his, and he knew that they could make it. It might take years to fix their family, but he wouldn't let things be completely hopeless.

"Thank you," he told the detective, the words didn't seem like enough.

"You're welcome," Detective Wyatt gave him a weary smile, looking like he was half dead on his feet.

"Did they take good care of her?" he had to know that his daughter had been looked after for the ten days she had been away from them.

A shadow flickered through the detective's face, but Eric couldn't read it, and it was quickly replaced by a firm smile. "They looked after her. Fed her, cleaned her, cared about her in their own way."

The knowledge that the abductors had loved his child as if she were their own both comforted and repulsed him. "Come in," he invited, closing the door and leading the detective to the living room, where both Charlie and Savannah ambushed him in their enthusiasm to see the baby. "Charlie, Savannah, this is Detective Wyatt. My brother and his fiancée, Lila's best friend," he made the introductions.

"Call me Wyatt, everybody else does."

Eric nodded, catching sight of Lila hovering silently by the door. "She's home," unable to wipe the grin off his face. His wife didn't move, "don't you want to hold her?"

Dawdling over to him, Lila's gaze flitted to anything but the baby, her calm façade had vanished, she was now back to twitchy and nervous. Stopping beside him, close but not too close, she held out her arms but as he was about to place the baby in them, she suddenly pulled away.

"No," she screeched, "I don't want to hold her, Eric."

Frowning, "she's our daughter," he said firmly.

"Eric, don't," Charlie warned.

Disregarding his brother. "She's just a baby, Lila, it's not her fault what happened to Joey."

"Yes it is," Lila insisted wildly. "I was trying to get her out of the car, that's why they shot him. If I'd just let them have her then Joey would still be alive," the tears that had been welling up began to tumble out.

"You can't know that, Lila," he tried to reason with her. "They wanted Molly, they might have shot Joey anyway."

"All you care about is Molly, what about Joey? He's dead, he's not ever coming back," Lila sobbed.

"But Molly did come back and she's all we have left now."

"Well I don't want her," the words shooting out of her mouth like flaming arrows. "I don't want her, I want Joey. I want my little boy," and with that she flew from the room.

"Lila," he started after her, but a hand grabbed his elbow.

"Let her go."

Spinning around expecting to meet Charlie's eyes, but it was Detective Wyatt who was gazing at him intently.

"Let her go," Wyatt repeated.

About to protest but the look in Wyatt's green eyes stopped him. It was a look of understanding. Not the general understanding of what it must be like for a parent to lose a child, but the deeper understanding that came from personal experience.

Instead of following his wife, Eric squeezed his daughter tighter in his arms, and wondered whether perhaps she might have been better off with the couple that had taken her, than growing up in this house that would be forever haunted by the ghost of the older brother she would never know.

* * * * *

8:19 P.M.

"Where have you been?"

Swarming at her the second she was through the door.

Half-heartedly raising a shoulder, "out."

"Out?" Casey exploded. "That's not an answer, Tessa. No one's spoken to you in over twenty-four hours. Do you know how worried we all were? I've called you about a hundred times. You can't just storm out and not tell anyone where you're going."

"Gee, sorry, *mom*, I didn't realize I needed permission to go out, I thought I was a grown-up," Tessa threw back sarcastically, she was not in the mood to be treated like a three-year-old.

"That's not funny, Tessa. You have to accept that you're not on your own anymore. There's people that care about you, you can't just disappear," Casey snapped, grabbing her arm when she tried to push past. "I mean it, Tessa, you can't keep doing that, running off when things don't go your way." Casey glared at her, Tessa simply glared straight back.

"Maybe we should all just sit down and take a break," Maisy piped up. Maisy was a year older than Tessa, a cheerful, bouncy redhead, who worked CSU with Marty Jenkins, she and Maisy had become good friends over the last eighteen months.

Tessa felt the fight drain out of her. Once again, it hadn't been a restful night. After receiving the email claiming Parker was never coming back, she'd driven out to her estate, bypassing the mansion to head for the stables, grabbing her horse, Jell-O, and riding out to her favorite place in the woods.

A place where she had spent many hours, alone, thinking, when she was a kid.

It was one of the few places where Tessa actually felt at peace. Unfortunately, the place hadn't been peaceful enough, she hadn't managed to get more than an hour or so worth of sleep spread over eight or nine. Originally she'd planned on spending tonight there also, but in the end had decided she wasn't going to relax no matter where she was and thought the baby at least deserved a sleepless night in a bed rather than on the floor in the tiny wooden shack.

"I'm sorry," she sighed at last. "I should have told someone I was okay."

Softening, "you should have told someone where you were." Casey scrutinized her carefully, "you don't look so good, you know."

"So I've been told." Tessa pulled her arm free and dropped down onto the sofa, thinking of Caleb, she'd been hoping that maybe her one ally had been by to try to see her. "Where's Daniel and Winter?"

Plopping down beside her, Casey clasped her hands tightly in her lap to prevent them from performing their doctor tasks. "Daniel's taking Winter to a friend's house, she doesn't know about your little disappearing act. You look tired did you sleep last night?"

"Not really." As if on cue a giant yawn tore across her face.

"Have you eaten?"

"I'm too afraid to," even the thought of food made her nauseous.

"Have you been drinking enough water?"

Tessa shrugged, to be honest she couldn't remember the last time she'd had a drink, her mind had been too full of other, more pressing, things.

"You need to keep drinking or you're going to become dehydrated. Do you have a headache? Dry mouth? Dizziness?"

"All three."

"Then you're already dehydrated," Casey threw her hands in the air in exasperation.

"I know." Tessa was already well aware of the symptoms of

dehydration, but at the moment knowing and caring were two different things.

Pushing to her feet, "you know for a genius, you can be really stupid sometimes," Casey huffed as she headed for the kitchen.

"Casey's pretty mad at me huh?" Tessa rested her head against the back of the sofa and closed her eyes.

"Wyatt told us that you've been calling *him*," Maisy accused as she sat down beside her.

Choosing to ignore that, she was not going to get sucked into a discussion on that particular topic. "Where is Skylar?" she asked instead.

"Upstairs, asleep." Unlike Casey who was going with angry, Maisy sounded hurt as though Tessa was deliberately shutting her out.

"He found the Abbott baby?"

"Yeah, in perfect health. He took her home to her parents and then came straight here to see if anyone had heard from you. He's exhausted, hasn't slept in a couple of days, he crashed upstairs," Maisy paused and Tessa could feel her studying gaze. "You shouldn't be calling him, Tess, it's dangerous."

"I think Tessa wants to get herself killed," Casey announced from the doorway.

Opening her eyes, "you know that's not true, Casey." Tessa pressed her hand to her stomach, "I would never put this baby at risk."

Striding into the room, glass and jug of water in hand, "and just how long do you think your luck's going to last? You keep putting yourself in dangerous situations and sooner or later you're going to end up dead. Here," Casey poured a glass of water, "drink this. All of it."

Complying Tessa drank the whole glass, and realized just how thirsty she actually was. "And just what do you suggest I do, Casey?"

"Let the police handle it."

"You mean Wyatt and J.J.? Two of Parker's best friends who think he left me for another woman because he found out I'm pregnant with his child. Yeah they're going to be real helpful." Tessa hated to admit it but Skylar's betrayal cut more deeply than she would have thought. From the first time they'd met she'd felt comfortable with him, even after she started dating Parker and things had been a little awkward, with Skylar she'd always felt at ease.

"That's not fair, Tess," Casey refilled the water glass, apparently an argument did not diminish her mothering instinct.

"You're right, Casey, it's not fair. It's not fair that my husband goes missing and everyone he knows, including his *sister*, think he just took off," Tessa snapped.

"I thought Matilda was on board with your theory that someone did something to Parker?" Maisy queried.

"She was until I got that email, now she agrees with the rest of you that Parker's left on his own." If it wasn't for Caleb, then she wouldn't have anyone on her and Parker's side.

"Tessa," Casey started, gently now, sitting beside her and wrapping an arm around her shoulders. "I know you don't want to believe it but Parker is not coming back, it's just you and the baby now."

Feeling herself start to slip, the tenuous hold she had on the gate that was keeping her emotions in check was faltering. Tessa wasn't usually one to cry, and already she'd spent most of the last two days in tears, it seemed like she shouldn't have any left by now.

"I don't want to sound harsh, Tess, but I love you and I can't stand to see you torturing yourself like this. You need to start getting used to Parker not being around, you have to start accepting that he's not coming back," Casey was staring at her with pity.

That was it.

The thread snapped.

It was like Tessa moved outside her own body and was watching what happened. She watched herself throw the glass, still full of water, against the wall. Watched it shatter into a thousand tiny glass raindrops, catching the light and glowing like mini rainbows. She watched herself start to scream and objectively noted the hysteria in her own voice.

"I don't want to hear that anymore," Tessa screeched, hands pressed over her ears. "I'm sick of everyone telling me that Parker left me." Maisy and Casey were staring at her with open panic, as though she was about to break. Objective Tessa guessed they weren't far wrong. "Parker didn't walk out on me, someone took him. I don't understand why no one wants me to do anything about it. How can you ask me to just sit back and see whether he turns up on his own . . .?"

"Tessa?"

Twirling around to see Skylar watching her closely, looking refreshed from his nap.

"Sweetheart, what's going on?" He took a step towards her, while casting a glance at his wife for some cues as to what had set her off.

"Tessa's upset . . ." Casey began.

"Don't talk about me like I'm not here," Tessa interjected frantically, scanning the room, looking for something that wasn't there. "Please just go, I don't want to see anyone right now. I just want to be alone, like Casey so thoughtfully pointed out that I am now . . ."

"Tess," Skylar grabbed her flailing arms, pulling her towards him, "you need to calm down . . ."

"Calm down? Calm down? How am I supposed to calm down?" beating her fists against his chest.

"Honey, look at me. It's not good for you or the baby for you to be this worked up," Skylar soothed.

As quickly as her outburst had come, it was gone, leaving her drained and shaky. Taking her silence as a sign, Skylar tried to pull her into an embrace but now she was embarrassed, Tessa usually made it a point not to let anyone see her with her guard down.

Overwhelmed with the need to be alone she wiggled free from Skylar's grasp and flew from the room, ignoring the concerned protestations of Skylar, Casey and Maisy. In her room, she flung the door closed behind her and threw herself down on the bed, reaching for her teddy bear.

When she had first learned she was pregnant, she had dreamed about this bear, the bear Parker had given her, a bear that she wanted to pass on to her baby. She had imagined herself and Parker standing over the baby's crib, the bear in the corner, simply watching their child sleep. That dream seemed to be slipping further and further away.

Taking several slow, deep breaths, she refocused herself. She could deal with alone, it wasn't like she'd had no practice at it, and it wasn't like she was going to be alone forever.

Patting Ladybug's and Buttercup's heads as they nuzzled against her lap, picking up on her distress. Reaching for her phone, she dialed the number of the one person she still had left who believed in her and Parker; Caleb Brighton.

JUNE 23RD

5:42 A.M.

"She still asleep?"

Surprised, he hadn't expected anyone else to be up this early, "she's still in bed, whether she's asleep or not I have no idea." Daniel sat down opposite Matilda at the kitchen table, where she offered him a steaming cup of hot chocolate.

"Bad dreams, that's my excuse, what's yours?" Matilda asked as she blew on her cocoa to cool it.

"My sister," Daniel sighed. At least Tessa was home again, but by the time he'd dropped Winter off at her friend's and returned, she'd already shut herself up in her room. Wyatt and Casey had still been here and had told him about Tessa's breakdown, which bumped his stress level up a couple of notches. He'd tried to talk to her, but of course she had ignored him, and he'd spent the night listening out for any signs that she was sneaking out of the house. "I'm afraid to let her out of my sight, she's lucky I haven't chained her to the bed."

"Tessa has a knack for getting herself into trouble I take it," Matilda smiled wryly.

"You could say that," Daniel smiled back. Then they both lapsed into silence, sipping their drinks and thinking their own thoughts.

"Did I do something to upset you?" Matilda asked abruptly, attempting nonchalance but failing dismally.

Only half surprised. "No of course not," he assured her. "Why do you ask?"

Arching a brow at him to let him know she knew he was lying. "You've been vague with me, ever since Parker vanished. You remember that night, the night of our first date, our *only* date. Admit it, Daniel, you've been avoiding me, and I think I deserve to know why. If you don't like me, if I'm not pretty enough, or I won't have sex with you . . ."

"Hey, hey," grabbing her hands, which she was waving wildly as she spoke. "I think you're the most beautiful woman I have ever seen. And after everything my sister has been through, I would never pressure a woman to sleep with me, especially one I cared about. I'm sorry I've been a little vague with you . . ."

"Then you admit it?" Matilda confirmed with uncertain triumph.

"Yes I admit it. I mean I have been preoccupied with Tessa and that brother of yours, but that's no excuse. I'm sorry."

"Why?" she begged, vulnerability creeping into her face.

Not quite sure how to explain, "it felt like we were all cursed."

Staring at him incomprehensively, "cursed?"

"Tessa has been through so much, she finally gets a chance at happiness, a husband who loves her, a baby on the way, and what happens, everything falls apart." Shrugging helplessly, "it just seemed like maybe none of us were meant to be happy, that maybe we were all cursed."

"So you basically started ignoring me because you were scared that you'd develop feelings for me only to have everything fall apart?" Matilda blushed.

"I've already developed feelings for you," Daniel told her. Picturing her pressing her body against his in the water out at the estate. Her clothes clinging to her slender body, the cold making her cheeks pale and accentuating her full lips.

Sobering, "I'm pretty much a failure at being part of a family," Matilda warned him mournfully. "I have no idea who my father is, my mother is a drug addict who got arrested and sent to jail when Parker and I were three months old, she robbed a gas station with us in the car. We were bounced from foster home to foster home until we were ten, all were poor, some of the homes were okay, the last was horrific, I never had anyone to nurture me. And even though my adoptive parents were wonderful, and loving, and generous, I still never learned how to love them."

"You think growing up in foster care is the only way to be screwed up?" Daniel scoffed. "My family had money and we were still horrendously dysfunctional. Patrick and Emilie, my parents, they fought all the time, and I mean all the time, huge screaming matches. Emilie was an alcoholic and a drug addict. She suffered from depression and never spent any time with Tessa and me. Patrick left when I sixteen, Tessie was ten, we never heard from him again. After that Emilie got worse, hardly even left her room anymore. When I turned eighteen I decided to leave and take Tess with me, Emilie freaked out, declared if she couldn't have Tessie then no one would. So she drugged Tessa and tried to drown her in our bathtub, now she's in a psychiatric hospital. After that I left, it was the only way I could think of to keep Tessa safe. Because of that decision Tessa ended up being abused, so believe me I know all about growing up hard."

Considering this, "when I was fourteen," Matilda added, "my mom got out of prison, came back to see me and Parker. Claimed she'd changed, said she wanted to be a part of our lives, she didn't want us back permanently, she just wanted to get to know us. Parker of course wanted no part of her, said she'd never change, warned me about getting involved with her. I didn't listen to him, started hanging out with her, believed every word she fed me. She ended up getting arrested again, sold drugs to some of the kids at my school."

Not to be outdone Daniel expanded his own tangled family tree, "Tessie and I have, or rather had, a sister. Her name was Cordelia. She was a monster, when our parents found out they were pregnant with Tess she insisted they abort the baby or she would leave forever. They wouldn't, she did. She came back six months ago. When I told you the other day that I had killed someone in self-defense it was my own sister. She tried to kill

Tessie. I ended up shooting her."

Scowling, Matilda opened her mouth to say something, but seemed unable to think of any words to speak and snapped it shut again.

Realizing just what they were bickering about Daniel started to laugh, "are we really bragging about who has the worst family, and who's childhood was more screwed up?"

Joining in his laughter, "I think so," Matilda agreed.

"I'm serious, Matilda, I really like you, it was stupid of me to try and hide from that. I really want to keep seeing you, see where things go." Catching the insecurities that flew across her face he added, "we can take things as slow as you like."

Waiting on tender hooks, Daniel was sure Matilda was going to say she couldn't handle a relationship right now, when her face finally softened, "that sounds like a plan," she smiled at him.

Tugging on her hands, which he still held, he brought her around the table and sat her down on his lap. Tucking her hair behind her ears, "you really are beautiful," he told her, "I wish you'd believe that."

"I like hearing you say that," she stated shyly.

Taking her face in his hands he slowly brought his lips to hers, making sure to keep the kiss gentle and unassuming. After a few seconds Matilda deepened the kiss, bringing her hands to his head and tangling her fingers in his hair. It turned out he'd been wrong too, he hadn't just started to develop feelings for her, Daniel was pretty sure he was already in love with her.

Everything else fled his mind. There was nothing in the world but him and Matilda . . .

* * * * *

4:12 P.M.

"Mrs. Matijevic?"

Dull blue eyes looked up to meet his, and Wyatt was struck for the first time about how weird it felt to be conducting an interrogation without Parker by his side. Once again, his thoughts strayed back to Tessa, and the fragile grip she had on her emotions right now.

"Where . . . where is she?" Polly asked desperately. "Where's my baby?"

Drawn back to the moment, Wyatt took a seat opposite her. "She isn't your baby," he reminded her.

"She's my . . . my granddaughter," the woman declared, wringing her hands.

"I'm sorry Polly, but she wasn't. She is the daughter of Eric and Lila Abbott, her name is Molly . . ."

"No," Polly interjected frantically, "her name is Breanna, and she's my daughter Alaina's daughter."

Reaching over and placing his hands over Polly's, gently easing them apart before the woman could dislocate her own fingers. "Alaina's baby died, Polly," he said softly. "Alaina went into premature labor, her baby never had a chance, it died. Breanna died, and Alaina became depressed. Your daughter committed suicide . . ."

"No," Polly interrupted again, pleading this time. "Jim said she wasn't really dead, just in a state of suspension," tears began to flow down her cheeks. "He said if only we could get Breanna back then Alaina would come back too, and we did. We got Alaina's baby back for her and she came back. You were at the house, you saw her, my daughter came back to me because we got her baby back for her."

Staring deep into her eyes, Wyatt could see that somewhere along the line of tragic events that had led her to this point, Polly Matijevic's mind had disconnected from reality. "That's not true, Polly," he pressed on carefully, "Alaina never really came back. You just stole her body from the graveyard and mummified her." Wyatt shivered as he remembered the grotesque body's lifeless hands clutching the screaming infant. He didn't think he'd ever be able to erase that picture from his head.

"We had to," Polly protested. "Jim said she wasn't really dead, if we left her there she would have run out of air, been dead for real. We did what we had to in order to get our daughter back."

"You killed a little boy, Polly," Wyatt reminded her.

"No, that was Jim, I was . . . I was getting Breanna, he didn't want to do it, it was an accident."

"You came to that parking lot with a gun and the intention of abducting a baby . . ."

"He didn't want to shoot that little boy, he had to," Polly repeated. "He had to. She wasn't going to let us take Breanna, so Jim had to do something. If we didn't take Breanna, then we wouldn't be able to get Alaina back. They didn't want her, they didn't deserve her, she was better off with us," Polly challenged.

Frowning, "what do you mean?"

"At the hospital, the day that Alaina almost died, he was her doctor, he did everything he could to try and save her, but then he gave up and he told us that she was dead. His wife was there, they were arguing, she was angry that he hadn't been there for her doctor's appointment, that he cared more about his job than their baby. She called the baby Molly, it was a sign, her name being so much like my name," her eye begging him to understand. "I remembered them, I kept coming back to the hospital, waiting for them to show up with the baby, and then when they did," her face shining as she spoke of the child, "she was so beautiful. I knew as soon as I saw her that she was meant to be with us, with Alaina. I knew that such a perfect child would bring my own daughter back to me."

"You started stalking them?"

"Not stalking," Polly admonished. "I had to find the right time to take her. They didn't deserve her you know. Dr Abbott was always working, Mrs. Abbott was always too busy with the boy, they didn't love her like she deserved. They didn't love her like we did, like Alaina did. They didn't need her, we did, she was better off with us. I want to go home now," Polly announced.

"Mrs. Matijevic, you can't go home," Wyatt reminded her. "You've been charged with murder and kidnapping."

Suddenly looking as lost as a small child, "where's Jim?"

"I'm sorry, Jim's dead."

Looking crestfallen, "where's Alaina?"

"She's dead too." Worried about the woman's state of mind, Wyatt was about to call for help when she sprung up from the table.

"There's too much blood," Polly shrieked, staring at something on the floor that only she could see. "Quick call an ambulance, there's too much blood. She cut her wrists, why did you do that Alaina? I would have helped you, why didn't you come to me?" Throwing herself against the wall, banging her head against the hard concrete and sobbing wildly, manically.

Wyatt wrapped his arms around her chest and hauled her into the middle of the room. Hysteria giving her additional strength, Polly swung and kicked her legs, sending the table and chairs clattering as the door swung open and reinforcements ran in.

As Polly Matijevic was dragged away, Wyatt found himself thinking once more of Tessa. Of how many things one person could be asked to bear before they just collapsed under the pressure. Replaying last night's scenes of Tessa's breakdown in his mind. Awakening to the sound of her hysterical shrieks, he'd hurried downstairs to find her ranting uncontrollably, Casey and Maisy looking on in shocked horror. He had attempted to calm her down, but once again, she had rejected his efforts at comfort and bolted for her room. Unwilling to leave her alone in that condition, he and Casey had cleaned up the shattered glass shards, and waited until Daniel returned.

Tessa was as close to losing it as he'd ever seen, and given some of the things he'd seen her deal with, that was saying a lot. Wyatt prayed that Tessa would have the strength to make it through this, for her sake as well as her unborn child's.

JUNE 24TH

9:31 A.M.

"Tessa? Hello?"

Not in the mood for visitors, she had ignored the insistent banging on the front door, but now whoever it was had let themselves in. If people continued to insist on breaking into her house, then she was going to have to start bolting herself in, something along the lines of the security system she used to have at her cottage.

"Tessa? It's Caleb."

Lifting a weary head from the arm of the couch. Caleb had joined the list of people she was unhappy with. She'd called him two days ago and left him a message asking him to come over. Reaching out to people was something she almost never did, and when he hadn't replied it had only reinforced in her mind the importance of replying only upon herself.

"Hey, the door was unlocked so I . . ." Caleb trailed off as he reached the living room door and caught sight of her stretched out on the couch, his face creasing with concern, "are you feeling okay?"

Looking back at him Tessa realized how much he reminded her of Parker. The way his brow furrowed, the way he worried about everything, and she remembered how sweet he'd been the other day when she'd been sick.

Mustering a smile for him, "I'm alright, just tired."

Crossing to her, "the baby okay?"

"It let me eat without throwing up yesterday," not that she'd had much of an appetite anyway. Caleb grew uneasy and tentatively sat in the armchair opposite her, Tessa pushed herself

201

up so that she was sitting, ignoring the swimming in her head. "What's up?"

"I need to apologize to you."

Confused, "for what?"

"I upset you the other day," Caleb elaborated, "with the photos of me and Parker when we were kids. That's why I didn't call you back right away, I had to work up the courage to come and see you again. I didn't mean to upset you, I just wasn't thinking straight. You were already stressed about your husband going missing, and your baby, your morning sickness, I shouldn't have sprung those photos on you, I didn't mean to upset you with them."

"You didn't upset me, I loved them, really," she reassured him, relieved when his stressed face slid into one of easy grins. "You want something to eat?"

"Sure."

"I've got homemade doughnuts in the kitchen."

"Doughnuts are my favorite, especially homemade ones, my mom used to make them all the time before she died."

"I'm sorry," Tessa remembered the thousands of time she had wished her own mother dead when she was growing up. "How old were you?"

A faraway look in his blue eyes, "I was seven."

"Your dad wasn't around?"

"No."

Tessa noted the way Caleb's eyes clouded over at the mention of his father, and wondered about the relationship between them. "I'll go get the doughnuts," standing too quickly Tessa felt herself sway and had to fight not to pass out. These dizzy spells were getting worse and more frequent.

Grabbing her arm and holding her up. "Are you okay?" Caleb quizzed.

Brushing away his concern, "fine, just a little dizzy. What would you like to drink?"

Keeping a hand out in case she toppled. "Whatever you're having will be fine."

Caleb followed her to the kitchen and took a seat at the table, while she got the doughnuts out and poured them each a glass of milk. He'd gobbled down two doughnuts, and half his drink, before she'd even taken a bite. "These are amazing," he marveled reaching for a third.

"Thanks," she smiled, taking a tentative bite and begging the baby to be good today.

"Where's everyone else?" Caleb asked, wiping away his milk moustache.

Rolling her eyes, "out, thank goodness. Daniel has been pretty much glued to my side, I know he loves me, but right now I just need space."

"You're close with your brother?"

"Kind of," she and Daniel had a very complicated relationship. "We are I guess, well we used to be, and I think we're getting back what we had, but Daniel's been gone so long it's hard to get used to leaning on him."

Caleb nodded understandingly. "How's Parker's sister Matilda?"

"She's okay, we don't know each other too well. She's pretty devastated with the idea that Parker just up and left."

"The others still all think he left on his own?"

Feeling the usual rush of betrayal as she thought of Daniel and Matilda and Wyatt and J.J. and their refusal to believe that something had happened to Parker. "Yeah, especially since . . ." Tessa hesitated, nervous about the possibility of alienating her one ally by telling him about the email.

"What is it?" Caleb reached out a hand and lightly rested it on her arm.

Sighing, "after you left the other day I got an email, supposedly from Parker, telling me that he isn't coming back."

"Supposedly?" Caleb raised a questioning eyebrow.

"In the email Parker called me Tessie, he has never once called me that. In fact the only person who calls me that, who has ever called me that, is my brother," Tessa watched Caleb closely to gauge his reaction.

Chewing on his lip as he reacted to this, "you're sure that the email wasn't from Parker?"

Tessa nodded.

"Then I believe you, I still don't think Parker would walk out on you," he smiled confidently at her, and squeezed her arm with the hand that still rested there.

Relieved Tessa smiled back, and was about to say something when they heard a car pull up in the driveway, startled Caleb snatched his hand away and looked at his watch.

"I'm sorry, Tessa, I have to be somewhere in like fifteen minutes, I didn't mean to stay so long."

This time she followed Caleb down the hall to the door. "I'll see you later?" she asked, hating that it came out sounding a little desperate, but she really needed to be around people who believed in Parker right now.

"Of course," Caleb assured her leaning in, and for a second Tessa thought he was going to try and kiss her, but then he simply pecked her cheek and with a wave of his hand was hurrying to his car.

Making her way back down to the kitchen, she found Daniel munching on a doughnut. "You had company?" he asked indicating the two glasses of milk.

"Yeah," she nodded, a little perplexed by Caleb's sudden departure. "That old friend of Parker's."

"Everything okay?" Daniel checked.

"Yeah, fine." As she took a seat beside her brother and partially listened to him babble away about his day, Tessa wondered whether Caleb simply kept coming back because of Parker, or if he was starting to fall for her.

* * * * *

12:27 P.M.

Ramming his shoulder fruitlessly against the metal bars. Since he'd already done this about a thousand times, the movement sent bright stabs of pain through the bruised joint. When the poles refused to give, he let out a frustrated growl.

Parker felt like he was losing his mind.

It had been eight days since he'd been grabbed and knocked unconscious, waking up here locked inside a metal cage in someone's basement. After checking himself for injuries, of which apart from the one on his head that had knocked him out he didn't seem to have any, he had spent hours screaming for help and trying to break free. The cage was sturdy, their location obviously remote, and he was provided with plenty of food and water, it seemed like whoever had abducted him planned to keep him here for some time.

The masked man came twice a day with a tray full of food, and despite Parker's efforts to engage the man in conversation, he never spoke a word.

At first he'd wracked his brain trying to think of anyone who would do this to him, any criminal with a grudge, anyone related to a case he was working on, but he kept coming up empty.

Now however all he could think about was Tessa. She must be going crazy worrying about what had happened to him. Parker hoped that she didn't think he had simply walked out on her.

He had been close, had even packed a bag and taken it with him on the way to the Abbott house the night he had been abducted. He hadn't really wanted to leave forever, just take a couple of days to sort things out in his head.

It had been Lila Abbott who had changed his mind.

The way she'd looked into his eyes and told him that they were just like her son's. The comment had broken him, when he'd heard it he'd known, known instantly, that all he wanted was to fix things with his wife.

Parker felt his cheeks heat with shame as he thought of the way he'd spoken to Tessa, the way he'd treated her those last few days. He couldn't blame Tessa if she was happy to be rid of him after the things he'd said to her. After all the time it had taken him to get her to trust him, Parker was afraid it would break her if she thought he had abandoned her. At least Tessa had Wyatt and Casey, and Daniel and Winter to look after her. Matilda too.

Another thing for Parker to feel guilty for. He'd treated his sister just as badly as he'd treated his wife. Mattie had come back to see him, to try and make things right between them, and he had brushed her off and barely said two words to her. His sister's reappearance on top of everything else he'd been dealing with had just pushed him over the edge and he'd lashed out at everyone he loved.

Parker believed, had to believe, that he would make it out of here alive. To make things right with the people he loved. To hold Tessa in his arms again, to breathe in the fruity scent of her shampoo as her hair tickled his nose, to feel her small body pressed up against his, to tell her that he loved her.

When he heard the sound of the lock wiggling in the basement door Parker knew he had to get out of here. He could try to build a rapport with his captor and work on talking his way out, but if it came down to it, Parker was willing and prepared to do whatever it took to get home to his wife.

* * * * *

7:43 P.M.

"Hey, Tessa."

Elisabeth Bennett beamed at her from the front doorstep, and Tessa wished she had followed her instincts and ignored the doorbell. "What do you want?" she asked flatly. They both knew Elisabeth was not one of her favorite people, it was nothing personal, Tessa just didn't like psychiatrists.

"Just checking up on you," Elisabeth kept her bright smile pasted on her face.

"Well I'm fine, thanks," Tessa began to close the door, but Elisabeth stuck out a hand and stopped her.

"Tessa, wait, everyone's really worried about you, I just want to talk," Elisabeth pleaded.

Not in the mood for a fight, Tessa released her grip on the door and retreated into the house. "They sent you huh? I wondered why Daniel, Matilda and Winter all suddenly had to go out tonight, since usually it's a battle to get them to leave me alone." Tessa plonked herself back down onto the sofa and tucked her feet up underneath her.

Closing the door behind them and following her into the living room, Elisabeth took the seat beside her. "Everyone's really worried about you," she repeated.

Wearily closing her eyes, "I didn't ask them to worry," Tessa sighed.

"They care about you." Elisabeth reached a hand over to rest it on her knee, but when Tessa opened her eyes to glare at it she pulled it back. "I care about you too, Tessa."

Rolling her eyes, Tessa wasn't in the mood to indulge Elisabeth's apparently offended feelings.

"I thought things were getting better between us," Elisabeth had on a hurt puppy dog look that reminded Tessa of Parker. When Tessa didn't respond she continued, "I wish you'd talk to me, Tessa, it might help."

"And what is it exactly that you want me to say?"

"Just talk about how you're feeling."

"How I'm feeling? How do you think I'm feeling? I find out that I'm pregnant and then my husband disappears. I think I probably feel about that the same way that any normal person would. Look it's fine that you talked to Parker, that you helped him, that's great, he believes in you and I was okay with asking you to help him, but we both know that it was for Parker's benefit not mine. Parker thinks that talking to a shrink helps, based on personal experience I disagree."

"Do you want to tell me why?"

Tessa raised an eyebrow, but decided this time to indulge Elisabeth, "because they don't do anything. No offence, but psychiatrists, they're all talk, they never actually do anything and they don't change anything. You tell them your problems but that doesn't mean that they go away." Tessa felt a sudden need to tell Elisabeth of her first experience with a shrink, and too weary to fight it started the story. "After Ellie died my grandparents sent me to see a trauma counselor. His name was Wayne Hickory," she had to stop to take a steadying breath.

"What did he do?" Elisabeth pushed softly.

"After Ellie died I wouldn't talk to anyone, every time my grandparents took me to see Dr Hickory I just sat there quietly. At first it annoyed him, but then he saw it as an opportunity," Tessa shuddered involuntarily. "He was creepy, he was always watching me with these beady eyes. One day he told me he had a new idea of something to try, he told me to go and lie down on the couch and he started explaining to me this fantasy he had about taking a schoolgirl's virginity. When he tried to climb on top of me, I kicked him in the groin and banged on the wall until the receptionist came in. Even at eleven I was paranoid, carried a tape recorder on me, I left it on the desk and walked out. I never told anyone what happened, the receptionist and the doctor must have made some sort of deal, because the guy just disappeared."

"Oh, Tessa, that's terrible," Elisabeth exclaimed.

Shrugging, "then there was Dylan Riley."

"I know that you've had some terrible experiences," Elisabeth said gently, "but that doesn't mean that all psychiatrists are perverted criminals."

"I know that," Tessa snuggled down deeper into the soft cushions. "Did you see someone after you were attacked?" she asked, indicating the scar on Elisabeth's cheek, and wondering whether Elisabeth would answer, psychiatrists loved asking questions but rarely answered them.

"I talked to a close friend." Leaning over, "you know, Tessa, sometimes it can help to just talk to a friend, it doesn't have to be a therapist, just someone you trust."

"Talking doesn't help, Elisabeth, and you're naïve to think that it does. You keep acting like seeing a shrink is the equivalent of a small child who thinks the world can be made safe by the comforting words of a mother."

Sobering, Elisabeth pressed her hands to her stomach and Tessa remembered that she too was pregnant, a couple of weeks further along than herself. "Speaking of mothers, I must admit that I'm terrified of becoming a mother. My mom she wasn't the most nurturing of people. She hated my father, used to spend most of her time screaming at him, about everything, she never had any time for anything else, her hatred for him certainly outweighed her love for me and my sisters. It scares me to death that I might turn out like her."

"My parents used to fight all the time too, at least they did when Emilie was lucid enough, half the time she was too drunk, or too high, to focus on anything, and she certainly didn't spend any time thinking of me and Daniel. When I was really small I used to sit at my window every night and wait for the first star to come out, and then I'd wish that for just one day Emilie would be a real mother," Tessa blinked in surprise that she had just shared something so personal.

"You're going to be a great mom," Elisabeth assured her. "Really, Tess, you're the most generous, caring person I know."

Appreciating that, but doubting the validity of it nonetheless. "So are you, Elisabeth, and you're lucky, you don't have to do it alone."

"I'm really sorry that Parker's gone, Tessa," Elisabeth sympathized.

"He didn't just leave, Elisabeth, something happened to him," she insisted.

"Wyatt and Daniel told me about the email that you got," Elisabeth ventured carefully.

Frowning, "that email was not from Parker."

"Wyatt and Daniel said . . ."

"I don't care what they said," Tessa interrupted, feeling hysteria brimming. "He did not send it. Have you ever heard Parker call me Tessie?" she demanded.

Shaking her head, "not that I recall. Casey is very concerned . . ."

"I don't care what Casey is concerned about," she interrupted again. "Casey and Wyatt and Daniel and Winter and Matilda and you, can think whatever you want. You're the ones betraying Parker not me. I don't care if I'm the only one who believes it, but something has happened to my husband and I am not going to rest until I find him."

JUNE 25TH

3:27 A.M.

"Skylar!"

Wyatt turned to see Tessa rushing towards him and snapped an arm around her waist as she tried to pass.

About half an hour ago he had been woken from a deep sleep for the second time in two weeks by a frantic call from Tessa. Apparently she had received a call from someone claiming that they'd located Parker's car. Although Tessa hadn't said who the mystery caller was, Wyatt was pretty sure he knew, and that no good would come from it.

On the phone he'd told her to wait at home and he'd let her know what happened, he hadn't really expected her to comply but she had turned up just as they were about to pop the trunk. "Tess, just wait for a second," he said, trying desperately to keep a hold on her squirming form, Tessa may be tiny but she ran miles everyday and was surprisingly strong.

"Did you find anything?" she asked frantically.

"We only just got here," he explained, indicating himself, Marty, and the two other officers. As soon as he'd gotten off the phone with Tessa, he'd called Marty, and then J.J., before heading straight here. After they'd checked inside the car Marty had taken a number of photos, before announcing they were ready to check the trunk.

"Where are Daniel and Matilda?" He'd been hoping they might have come with Tessa, depending on how things turned out, she may need the emotional support.

"They were still out on their date when I left," she replied distractedly.

"Wyatt," Marty called, "ready when you are."

"Ready for what?" Tessa demanded, still trying desperately to wriggle free from his grasp.

"Hang on a moment," he called to Marty, and motioned for one of the officers to come and keep a hold of Tessa, if Parker's body was inside that trunk that was not an image Tessa needed in her head. Passing Tessa to the cop, she barely noticed, her gaze riveted on the car.

Treading slowly across the across the grass to where Parker's car had been left, hidden from the road behind a bank of trees, a short way outside the city, where the houses became few and far between. Despite the early hour the air was hot and muggy, his shirt was already soaked with sweat, though whether from the heat or stress, Wyatt wasn't quite sure.

Attempting to stop the tremor in his hands, Wyatt didn't know how he would live with himself if his best friend's body was inside this trunk. Tessa had kept insisting that Parker would never leave on his own, he'd dismissed her as paranoid because there was no evidence of foul play. But if she was right and someone had hurt Parker, and he'd done nothing about it, he didn't think he could ever forgive himself.

Reaching the back of the car he nodded to Marty, who was perched next to the driver's door, ready to pull the switch. Upon Wyatt's signal Marty did so and the trunk popped open, not enough to reveal anything though, and Wyatt waited until Marty and the other officer had joined him before opening it up the rest of the way.

Letting out an involuntary gasp when he looked inside.

Tessa managed to break free of the cop's grip and rush up beside him. Looking inside she swayed, and when he wrapped his arms around her, she rested her forehead against his chest for a moment before determinedly pulling away.

"I told you," she practically shouted, bordering on hysteria. "This proves that something happened to him."

Gripping her arms and bending down, trying to force her bloodshot eyes to meet his. "Look at me, Tessa, come on, goldilocks, this doesn't prove anything. The car is empty, there's no blood, no sign of a struggle, no sign that he was run off the road, it looks like it was dumped here."

Eyeing him defiantly, "yes," she agreed, "dumped here by whoever took my husband."

Scrutinizing her carefully, the bluey green eyes that looked back at him were dull and empty with black bags underneath. The few curls that had escaped her ponytail hung around a face that was even whiter than usual. Her pixie like face was thinner than usual and she looked worse than she had the morning they'd found her unconscious in her house, the morning she'd told them she was pregnant. And the reality of how they'd found Parker's car tonight really sunk in. "Who called you?"

Feigning innocence, "what do you mean?"

Tightening his grip on her arms, "it was *him* wasn't it? You called him for help and he managed to find Parker's car?"

"I don't know what you're talking about," Tessa huffed and tried to get free from his grasp.

"Yes you do, Tessa," keeping hold of her. "And he wouldn't do this for free. What did you offer him in return?"

"Don't, Skylar," she whispered, "you're hurting me."

Refusing to let go of her, "come on, Tess, you've made a deal with the devil. You've got a baby to think about and you're out there making a bargain with a criminal, and not just *a* criminal but one who tried to burn you alive. What are you thinking?"

"Wyatt," Marty cautioned coming up beside them. "Ease up on her."

Tessa's eyes were welling up with tears, but he was tired, and worried, and far too wound up to behave sensibly at the moment. It wasn't that he'd wanted to find Parker's lifeless corpse locked in a trunk, but right now it seemed better than the idea that he deliberately left Tessa and the baby. That Parker had left him.

After everything he and Parker had been through together, Wyatt found it almost incomprehensible that his best friend of more than twenty years, could leave without a word.

"You live in this world of your own where reality doesn't exist," he ranted, focusing his mixed emotions on anger, and aiming them at Tessa, since she was the most convenient target at the moment. "You keep pretending that nothing ever happened, Eleanor, Dylan, Cordelia, this. You keep refusing to deal with it. You keep refusing to come to us for help, to *me* for help, yet you'll go to *him*? Are you insane?"

As he watched Wyatt could see the strain and exhaustion of the last couple of weeks come crashing down upon her, and with a strangled sob Tessa fell against his chest. Wrapping his arms around her to keep her upright, Wyatt realized he was clinging to her as tightly as she was clinging to him. Holding her shuddering body until her flood of tears eased to a trickle, his anger dissipating, "shh, I'm sorry, I'm sorry. It's going to be okay, we'll take the car back to the lab, we'll find something, anything, that points us in the right direction, I promise," he whispered reassuringly in her ear. "I just need you to trust me okay? No more going to him for help, you need something you come to me, okay? Okay?" he prodded when she didn't respond.

She whispered a muffled acquiescence against his chest, but refused to lift her head.

"Come on, I'm gonna take you home." He had just swung her up into his arms when someone called his name. Looking up to see Daniel and Matilda sprinting towards them, both concerned, both looking from Tessa to the car and back again.

"We got Tessa's message, came as quick as we could, what did you find?" Daniel asked, placing a comforting hand on his sister's shoulder.

"Nothing," Wyatt assured them. "The car was empty."

Matilda sagged with relief, and Daniel gave her a quick hug before reverting his attention back to Tessa, who kept her face buried in the crook of his neck, and raised a questioning brow to silently ask about his sister's wellbeing.

Wyatt shook his head, "I know Beth went to see her last night but I'm not sure how that went. It might be a good idea to ring her, see if there's anything she can give Tess to help her sleep, something that's safe for the baby. She's completely wiped out, Daniel," he added as he placed Tessa in her brother's outstretched arms, she simply rested her head on Daniel's shoulder and lay there.

"Alright, thanks, Wyatt. You'll keep me posted?" he nodded a head in the direction of Parker's abandoned car.

"Of course. Look after her." Wyatt watched as Daniel carried Tessa back to his car, settled her in the back and climbed in after her. Matilda climbed into the front, and moments later the car pulled off into the night. As he watched it go, he wondered how they were going to get Tessa through this if Parker never turned up.

* * * * *

4:42 A.M.

This couldn't be happening.

Parker couldn't really be gone.

Tessa's mind was reeling, unable to properly comprehend what was happening. Her head had been spinning ever since Skylar had opened the trunk of Parker's car. Thankfully her husband's body hadn't been in there, but Tessa was positive that something awful had happened to him. Someone had taken him from her and she didn't know how to get him back.

"Tessa?" a gentle voice spoke above her.

She jumped as a hand touched her.

"It's okay, Tessie," Daniel soothed. "It's only Beth."

Oh right, she thought, she vaguely remembered Daniel

215

speaking to Elisabeth on the phone in hushed voices on the ride back home from where Parker's car had been dumped. She'd been distracted, forgotten this, preoccupied with trying to control the panic inside her that continued to swell larger with every passing second.

"I'm just going to check you out, Tess, make sure you're okay," Elisabeth explained.

Too drained to protest, Tessa barely registered Elisabeth pulling her arm from under the blankets and pressing her fingertips against her wrist to take her pulse, or strapping on the blood pressure cuff to check her BP. She couldn't seem to stop shaking. Daniel had covered her with blankets but it hadn't made one ounce of difference. She wished her trembling could shake all the bad thoughts right out of her head.

"I'm going to listen to your chest now," Elisabeth's calm voice continued. "Daniel, can you help her sit up?"

Her brother's arm slipped around her shoulders, lifting her to a sitting position and keeping her upright when she would have fallen back against the mattress. Tessa flinched slightly as Elisabeth pressed the cold stethoscope against her back to listen to her heart and lungs. Voices murmured as Daniel rested her back against the bed, and she assumed that Elisabeth was relating details of her condition to Daniel and Matilda. Tessa didn't care how she was doing, if Parker never came back then she doubted she'd ever care about it again.

"Tess?" she felt Elisabeth's hand on her shoulder. "Can you open your eyes for me?"

Shaking her head. Tessa didn't want to open her eyes. She wanted to keep them firmly closed and pretend none of this was happening.

"That's okay," Elisabeth assured her. "I'm going to give you something to help you sleep now, okay?"

Shaking her head again. Tessa didn't want to sleep. Had been fighting it with every drop of energy she had left. Tired as she was she knew that with sleep would come dreams. Most likely bad dreams. And she didn't think she could handle nightmares right now.

"You need sleep, honey," Daniel told her gently.

"Your body needs time to recharge, regain some strength," Elisabeth added, softly stroking her hair.

Tessa knew they were right but that didn't make her any less scared. She heard a strange whimpering sound, and it took her a moment to realize it was coming from herself.

"Shh," Elisabeth comforted, "it's going to be okay, Tessa."

"I won't leave you, Tessie," Daniel reassured her. "I promised you I wouldn't and I won't, I'll be right here by your side."

Her brother had promised her that earlier, when she'd become hysterical because he was going to leave her side for all of five minutes to go to the bathroom. Tessa had known she was being irrational, but Parker was gone and she couldn't bear to lose anyone else, she wanted all her family and friends to glue themselves to her.

If she'd had more strength she would have begged Daniel to call Skylar and Casey and Maisy, and make them come over. Skylar had scared her earlier with his angry outburst, and she couldn't deny she was still mad that he hadn't taken Parker's disappearance seriously from the beginning, but that didn't change the fact that he was her surrogate big brother and she loved him just as much as Daniel and wanted him here with her so she could keep an eye on him and make sure he didn't leave her too. Her best friends had also hurt her, but that didn't change the fact that they were her best friends and she didn't know what she would do if anything ever happened to Casey and Maisy.

"Tess?" Daniel pressed.

Hesitantly she nodded her consent. They were right, she did need sleep. If she was going to find the person who had taken her husband from her then she needed to be able to focus, and without some proper rest she couldn't.

"Good girl," Daniel kissed her forehead.

Elisabeth took her arm again, "I'm just going to swab your shoulder," she informed as she wiped Tessa's shoulder with a cold alcohol wipe. "Okay, sweetie, now a sharp prick," Elisabeth continued as the needle pierced her skin. "You're going to start feeling sleepy now, don't try to fight it, Tess, let yourself rest."

Reaching for Daniel's hand as sleep began to crash down on her, her brother tucked the covers up around her chin and lay down beside her.

There had to be a way to find who had taken Parker. There had to be a way to get him back. There had to be. She couldn't survive otherwise. She'd be stuck in this deep abyss, crushed by a blackness so black it seemed alive, forever.

He had to come back to her. He just had to. He would come back to her. She wouldn't believe anything else. She'd get some sleep and then she'd formulate a plan to get her husband back.

* * * * *

10:38 A.M.

Still left reeling from this morning's events, not to mention those of last night.

Matilda wasn't sure whether to be happy or sad that her brother's body wasn't found inside his car. She was still having a hard time coming to terms with the fact that Parker was really gone, although not as hard a time as Tessa was having.

Her sister-in-law hadn't spoken a word on the ride home last night, just burrowed into Daniel's arms and stayed there. When they'd reached the house Daniel had carried her upstairs while they waited for Beth, whom they'd called from the car, to arrive. The only time Tessa had made a sound was when Daniel had attempted to leave to go to the bathroom. She'd completely freaked out, clinging to him and bursting into a fresh batch of tears. It had taken close to fifteen minutes and a number of reassurances from Daniel that he wouldn't leave her side to console her.

Beth, Parker's shrink friend, had given Tessa a sedative and she had finally drifted off to sleep, still clutching her brother's hand. Daniel had spent the last few hours stretched out on Parker and Tessa's bed, holding his sister while she slept. Right now, he was off collecting Winter from her friend's house, and she was sitting with Tessa. As she sat, gently stroking Tessa's blonde curls, Matilda thought about her date with Daniel last night, and of what might have happened if they hadn't received Tessa's message.

For their second date, Daniel had taken her on a picnic at what used to be his and Tessa's favorite place when they were kids. He had somehow managed to find out her favorite foods and prepared them all. After eating, they taken a walk in the surrounding woods, and climbed a small hill where they had watched the sunset.

As they had lain there together, on their backs in the grass, watching the stars slowly blink on one by one, Daniel's hands had gently begun to explore her body. At first she had shrunk instinctively away from his touch, but he had moved slowly, taking his time, letting her adjust, and before she realized it she was enjoying the ticklish feeling of his hands against her bare skin. When he had leaned over and kissed her she hadn't protested, neither did she object when he began to tug at her clothing. If they hadn't received Tessa's frantic message about the discovery of Parker's car, Matilda didn't think she would have stopped Daniel no matter how far things went. That thought terrified her.

Voices sounded downstairs, so Matilda carefully disengaged her hand from Tessa's grip and quietly slipped from the room, closing the door behind her.

"Winter, there is absolutely no reason to cancel your party," Daniel was saying as Matilda came down the stairs.

"No reason? What about Tessa losing it?" Winter raved back.

"She wouldn't want you to cancel it." Daniel countered.

"She doesn't know what she wants right now," Winter returned.

"Hey guys, keep it down," Matilda cautioned joining them in the kitchen.

"Is she still asleep?" Daniel asked, immediately lowering his voice.

Matilda nodded as Winter asked, "she really let you drug her?"

Daniel had explained to her that ever since their mother had drugged and tried to drown Tessa, she had avoided all medications.

"She's barely slept in weeks, she needed to rest, and for the last time we are not going to cancel your party," he gave his niece a stern look before softening, "Tessa will be okay, Winter, she has all of us to get her through this."

Winter nodded but didn't look convinced. "I'm going to call Vanessa," she announced and hurried up the stairs.

"Didn't she just come from Vanessa's?" Matilda asked as she set about making coffee.

"Yeah she did," Daniel plonked wearily down in a chair, propped his elbows up on the table, and rested his head in his hands.

"You told her about the car?"

"Uh huh, she took it pretty well, she's just worried about Tess." When she didn't respond Daniel looked up, "I'm sorry, Mattie, I haven't even asked you how you're doing."

"You've been preoccupied with your sister," she told him, but kept her back turned so Daniel couldn't see the tears sparkling in her eyes.

"Yeah I have but that's no excuse," Daniel came and stood behind her, hands on her shoulders, gently kneading. "Are you okay?"

"I'm okay," she assured him, "I just don't know what's worse, thinking he's dead or missing, or thinking he's just gone off somewhere to start a new life without any of us."

"Something else is bothering you."

Tiredly she leant back against Daniel, who immediately slipped one arm around her waist, the other brushing her hair away so he could rest his chin on her shoulder. "If we hadn't of gotten that call from Tessa last night then we probably would have ended up having sex."

"Maybe," Daniel replied noncommittally.

Turning around to face him, "what do you mean maybe?"

"I mean," he paused to drop a kiss on her forehead, "that we would have done whatever you were comfortable with."

"Sex still scares me, terrifies me really," she told him.

"I don't care, Mattie, I'm not with you to sleep with you, I'm with you because I care about you, because I think I'm falling in love with you."

Stunned, "you're . . . you're what?" she stammered.

"Falling in love with you," Daniel dipped his head and softly pressed his lips against hers.

Too shocked to respond, Matilda had never ever had a man say those words to her, and she wasn't sure how she felt about it. She knew that Daniel warmed something inside her she'd thought was frozen, but she'd never really thought that falling in love was something that would ever happen for her. With a shudder, she gave in and tentatively kissed him back, deciding that she had nothing to lose by letting herself fall in love with Daniel Micah.

* * * * *

4:11 P.M.

Parker had managed to piece together most of what had happened the night he'd been abducted. After leaving the Abbott house ten days ago he'd driven out to the country to think, and after realizing that the only thing he wanted was his wife and child in his arms he'd headed straight for home.

When he'd found the pregnancy test in the garbage, it had completely freaked him out. He and Tessa had only been married for four months and hadn't yet talked about trying for a baby.

Parker didn't know who his own father was, and despite the wonderful influence of his adopted father, he had massive doubts about his own abilities to parent a child. When Tessa had suffered such violent morning sickness, a part of him, for one brief second, had actually thought it might be better for everyone if she miscarried.

Realizing he had wished his own baby dead, especially after witnessing the pain of the Abbott's as they grieved their son, had made him push away everyone that he loved. Some people may believe that a fetus was not really a baby, he did not, whether he felt ready for it or not he believed that the child growing inside his wife was already a living person, and one that deserved two parents who loved it unconditionally.

Heading for home to apologize to Tessa and tell her that he loved her and knew about the baby, he had stopped when his headlights had illuminated what appeared to be a body lying at the side of the road. Pulling over to check it out, he'd found the body of a man lying face down in the ditch, as he'd reached to pull out his cell phone something had whacked him on the back of the head, knocking him out.

When he regained consciousness, he'd found himself bound with ropes and bouncing around in the trunk of a car. He hadn't been gagged and when he'd started to call for help, he was pretty sure he had heard laughter coming from the car. Queasy, dizzy, and stiflingly claustrophobic, he must have passed out again because when he'd next woken up he'd been here in this cage, in this basement, wherever that may be.

"I have a surprise for you."

Surprised, Parker looked up to see his masked captor standing by the far wall. He must have been too caught up in thinking about Tessa and not heard the man's entry.

"Talking to me today?" Parker asked calmly, very conscious of the fact that everything he said and did could push his abductor either of two ways, it could convince the man to let him go or to kill him.

The man said nothing simply reached up and pulled on a string, parting a pair of thick black curtains to reveal a row of television screens.

Parker frowned, confused, "are you going to tell me what's going on?"

Taking his time to cross the cold basement floor to hover just out of reach of the cage. "You must be missing your wife."

Nodding uncertainly, unsure where this was heading. "Of course."

"Then you should enjoy this."

"Enjoy what?" The black ski mask worn by his captor made him feel like he was talking to a shadow, the dull light in the room added to the effect.

Lifting a gloved hand in which he clutched a remote, the man clicked a button and the screens on the wall began to flick on one by one. Each one displayed a different view of his own house. Parker saw his living room, the hall, the den, the kitchen, both the front and back yard and finally his and Tessa's bedroom, where his wife was curled up in a small ball on the bed.

A sharp stab of love and longing and guilt shot through him at the sight of Tessa, and he leaned forward against the bars of the cage as though that could bring him closer to her. Remembering the last time he had seen her. She'd been in their bed then too, in a fitful slumber, the sheets tangled around her. She'd been burning up, her skin flushed red and hot beneath his touch, he'd retrieved a cold washcloth from the bathroom and attempted to cool her down. Then straightened the covers, tucked her in, kissed her forehead, and gone to get ready for Wyatt to pick him up. That could well be their last interaction and Parker was pretty sure

Tessa didn't even remember it.

"If you lay a hand on her . . ." he growled fiercely at the masked man, desperate to wrap his hands around his captor's neck.

Snickering, "I don't think you're in any position to threaten me."

It took every ounce of energy Parker possessed to keep from battering on the bars until they buckled and launching himself at the man. The only thing stopping him was that he knew it would be pointless, brute force wasn't going to get him home to his wife, staying calm was.

Biting his tongue and sucking in a calming breath. "I'm a police officer," he reminded the man, he'd lost count of the number of times he had already said this, trying to start a conversation. "You're not going to get away with this, my family and friends are going to be looking for me, doing everything they can to find me."

Even though Parker couldn't see his face, he could hear the smirk in the masked man's voice, "I don't think so."

Wary, "what are you talking about?"

"It turns out all your so called 'friends' and 'family'," the man did air quotes as he spoke, "really aren't all that loyal to you. They don't think they need to be looking for you, because they don't think anything happened to you. They all believe that you simply walked away from your life."

Assuming that his abductor was saying this to rattle him. "They would never in a million years believe that I would walk out on them."

"My time certainly does fly when you're having fun," the man mocked.

"I don't believe you."

Shrugging, "I don't care what you believe, it's what they believe that's important."

"That would never happen," Parker insisted.

"Well happen it did, that's what they believed even before the email."

Getting a sinking feeling in the pit of his stomach, "what email?" he asked. The first thing he'd done after awakening in the basement was check his pockets for his cell phone, of course it had been missing.

"I thought it would be nice if you sent your loved ones an email saying goodbye and telling everyone that you weren't ever coming back. Didn't want to leave them hanging."

Parker was starting to believe the lunatic, and the betrayal of the people he loved was like a weight pressing down on his chest. "Tessa knows that nothing would make me leave her," he stuttered desperately.

"Right now your wife is the only one who believes that."

The momentary relief he felt hearing that Tessa hadn't given up on him was quickly pushed away when the man continued.

"In fact she's so adamant that you wouldn't leave her, that she's pushing everyone else away because they don't agree with her. She's determined to deal with this on her own."

Sighing, that was exactly what Tessa was like, and for a brief moment, Parker found his thoughts straying to his wife's connections. He knew the lengths he would go to in order to save Tessa were almost boundless, and he was pretty sure that she would do anything to find him, including seeking help from a man who had tried to kill her.

"Not such a chatterbox now, huh, Detective? Feeling hurt, disillusioned, betrayed, offended, insulted, wounded?" the man chuckled delightedly.

Studying the man, it was hard to get an accurate read on him due to his ridiculous black clothes and mask. Parker wasn't sure that he was going to get an answer to his question but he had to ask, "who are you? Why are you doing this?"

Ignoring the first question, "I'm doing this for exactly the reason you think I am. Revenge."

"Revenge? For what? How is it revenge when I don't even know who you are or what I'm supposed to have down to you?" Parker asked, desperately trying to make sense of the irrational actions of what was clearly a lunatic.

Instead of answering his captor crossed slowly to the glowing screens and stopped in front of the one that showed his bedroom, where Tessa was still asleep on their bed. Raising his gloved hand the man gently traced a finger over Tessa's form. Then with a click of a switch, a close up of his wife appeared on the largest of the monitors. Tessa had her hands pressed palms together and tucked under her cheek, her face was paler than normal and seemed thinner, making her already enormous blue eyes seem too large for her face.

Seeing his wife so vulnerable, asleep in her own bed, in her own home, completely unaware that some monster had a camera hidden in the room made him snap. Before he knew what he was doing, he was screaming, "I swear to you, if you hurt her, if you hurt one single hair on her head I will kill you. Do you hear me? I will kill you, I will tear you to shreds."

The masked man simply laughed. "My plan for revenge seems to be working perfectly."

* * * * *

9:23 P.M.

Rolling over in bed, she got a fright when she didn't bump into her husband's body.

With a weary sigh, Tessa pushed back the blankets and stood, making her way to the window to stare out at the clear night. The air coming through the crack was muggy, but despite the heat, Tessa couldn't stop shivering.

The house was unusually still and she decided to get herself a glass of ice water and enjoy the peace and quiet. Wrapping her arms around her chest as she headed for the door, preoccupied with everything that was going on, when she pulled back the door she let out a startled scream.

The face on the other side of the door was one that she would never forget. One that was burned into her head for all eternity, but it was also one that couldn't be here.

"You . . . you can't be here," she stammered.

He said nothing, simply grinned at her, his hazel eyes glowing unnaturally in a face that was as white as paper.

He reached his hands towards her, clamping them around her arms, and she struggled to breathe as he started dragging her back to the bed. Throwing her down on top of the covers and climbing on top of her, keeping her pinned down, and leaning in close to brush his lips across hers. "I've missed you, Tessa."

Wondering why she wasn't fighting back, kicking, biting, scratching, yelling, something, anything.

"Don't you want to say hello to an old friend?" he asked with mock disappointment.

"We're not friends, Dylan." Tessa thought she said the words aloud, but maybe it was only in her head. "You're dead."

He smiled at her, "yes I remember that night," he said sociably. "You shot me."

"It was your gun," she reminded him. "It was an accident."

"Who cares?" Dylan shrugged indifferently, then his face changed into the horrible sneer she knew so well. "I've been waiting a long time for this, eleven years in fact. And this time there's not going to be any knight in shining armor to come running to your rescue."

As his hands begun to roam her body, Tessa squeezed her eyes closed, popping them back open a moment later when the pressure on top of her disappeared. Sitting up quickly Tessa saw she was no longer in her and Parker's house, now she was in her old bedroom in the mansion. As she threw back the covers and sprung out of bed she saw that she wasn't alone, her sister

Cordelia was sitting in the corner.

"Hi, little sister," Cordelia stood and moved towards her.

Sinking wearily back onto the mattress. "I'm too tired to deal with you now."

"I hear congratulations are in order."

Tessa eyed her warily, "what do you want?"

Cordelia's face twisted into a snarl, "I enjoy seeing you suffer. You were always so smug and self-righteous, everyone always loved you, and now your own husband can't even stand you."

Squeezing her eyes closed again when she opened them this time she was in another old mansion. It was dark, there were no lights on and outside a thick layer of clouds obscured the moon. By memory, she made her way to the door and through the long winding hallways, heading for the front door.

"Tessa."

Spinning around at the sound of the voice. Unable to believe her eyes, before her stood her childhood friend, dark blonde hair in braids, dark blue eyes bright, looking just as she'd looked the last time Tessa had seen her alive. "Ellie?"

"It's me," her friend beamed.

"What are you doing here?"

"I missed you." Then Ellie's face fell and her bottom lip trembled, just like it used to when they were kids and she didn't want to go along with one of Tessa's plans. "Why didn't you save me?"

Tears pricked her own eyes, "I tried, Ellie. You know I did."

"Tessa."

This time it was Parker calling her. Tessa looked around but couldn't see him, she turned back to Ellie, "do you know where my husband is?"

"I never got to have a wedding," Ellie responded dismally.

She loved Ellie but her best friend was dead, there was nothing she could do to help her, but Parker, he could still be out there somewhere, waiting for her. Leaving Ellie behind she ran through endless corridor's, calling as she went, "Parker? Where are you? Answer me."

Eventually she found herself in front of the basement door. The door was splattered with blood. With a shaking hand she turned the knob and her worst fears were confirmed. In the middle of the floor was a body, it lay on its stomach, face turned in the opposite direction, but Tessa knew who it was. In this house of death nothing but bad things ever happened. With baby steps she moved closer until she had crossed the room, then plopped down beside the body. With clawing hands she grabbed his shirt and rolled him onto his back. For a moment she was too stunned to make a sound as she took in the hole in his chest and the bloody pulp that used to be her husband's face.

And then she was screaming.

And screaming and screaming and screaming.

"Tessa, Tessa, hey, it's okay. You're just dreaming."

Gasping and disoriented, Tessa sucked in one nauseous breath after another, as a pair of hands untangled her from the sheets then gripped her shoulders, kneading gently. When she had recovered sufficiently she opened her eyes to see Caleb Brighton's anxious face inspecting her carefully.

"Are you okay?"

Jerkily nodding her head, when she had enough control over her breathing she asked, "what are you doing here?"

Giving her a shy smile, "I came to see you. Your brother let me in after giving me the third degree. He had to pop out for a minute, I was just coming up here when I heard you screaming, you sure you're alright? Here."

Taking the bottle of water from Caleb's outstretched hand and swallowing a couple of mouthfuls. "I'm fine," she assured him, "just a bad dream." When Caleb raised a questioning brow she elaborated, "we found Parker's car this morning."

"No . . .?" Caleb hesitated not wanting to say the word.

"No, no body," she confirmed.

Taking this in, "so he's still out there somewhere."

Tessa shivered as she thought of her nightmare and Parker's bloody body missing its face.

Caleb noticed and smiled sympathetically, "that what your dream was about?"

Not wanting to get into a discussion about her past, "just some old demons."

"You're exhausted, you need to sleep," Caleb told her softly, smoothing one of her curls.

"I'm afraid," she almost whimpered, fighting sleep because she was terrified by the prospect of more nightmares.

"You never have to be scared when I'm here," he reassured her, tentatively placing an arm round her shoulders. When she didn't protest he settled her in his arms and began to stroke her hair. "I won't ever let anyone hurt you."

* * * * *

10:07 P.M.

As Parker watched the screen, which he had been staring at with every fiber of his being since it turned on, he saw another person enter Tessa's bedroom.

A man.

He couldn't see the man's face because he kept his back to the camera. But he watched as Tessa thrashed in her sleep then woke screaming from a nightmare, watched as the man comforted her, watched as she settled into the man's embrace, and fell back into a fitful sleep. And he prayed that somehow he could make his way home to his wife before it was too late.

JUNE 26TH

8:52 A.M.

He hadn't moved a muscle all night.

His gaze had remained riveted to the screen.

Parker watched Daniel return to Tessa's room and the mystery man leave. His brother-in-law remained at Tessa's side throughout the night, consoling her, when she awakened screaming and breathless, no less than four times. He'd left a short while ago, and on the other monitors Parker had seen him drive off. Almost immediately another car had pulled into the driveway and a man knocked on the front door.

* * * * *

8:54 A.M.

Dragging herself down the stairs when the doorbell chimed.

Tessa had been awake when Daniel left her room a few minutes ago, she just hadn't been in the mood for conversation. She wasn't sure where he was going, or where Matilda or Winter were, but she didn't really care. She welcomed the solitude. She still felt a little groggy from the drugs that Elisabeth had given her, and most of the events of the last twenty-four hours were a little blurry.

Opening the door, she couldn't help but smile when she saw Caleb, two cups of coffee and a bag of doughnuts in his hands.

"I come bearing gifts," he grinned and held up his treats. "Feeling better?"

"I'm fine," she assured him, closing the door behind him as he

231

entered and trailing along after him to the kitchen. She sunk into a chair as she watched him putter about, getting plates and napkins, and wondered tiredly when he had become so familiar with her kitchen.

* * * * *

9:01 A.M.

Watching as Tessa picked idly at an iced doughnut. Wanting nothing more than to reach through the screen and run his fingers through her silky soft hair, trace his fingertips across her face, press his lips to hers.

Parker twisted desperately, trying to get a glimpse of the man in the kitchen with his wife by rotating his head, as though that might somehow manage to change the camera angle.

Wringing his hands anxiously around the metal bars as he watched the man take the two cups and move to the counter. A frown forming when he realized what the man was doing. Watching with excruciating helplessness, as the man tipped a small amount of white powder into one of the cups, stirring it carefully until it was dissolved.

Then he looked right up at the camera and grinned.

Suddenly violently ill as he realized just who this man was. The sandy hair, the bright blue eyes, the millions of freckles, the easy smile. There was no one else it could be.

Everything fell into place, and Parker knew exactly what was going on, and exactly what his abductor planned to achieve. Fighting not to throw up. No longer worried about whether or not he would make it out of this basement alive, now he was worried about whether Tessa would make it out of this alive.

* * * * *

9:13 A.M.

Squinting, her vision blurry, Tessa was struggling to concentrate on what Caleb was saying. Taking another sip of coffee, the strong liquid as bland as water in her mouth. Her morning sickness appeared to be back, her stomach feeling like a spinning top.

"Tessa, you okay? You're not looking too good."

Trying to focus on Caleb, she could hardly keep her eyes open. "I'm fine." Deciding she was just shrugging off the after effects of yesterday's medications, she rose to her feet, thinking maybe some fresh air could freshen her up. Teetering dangerously when she took a step, Caleb was at her side in an instant, his arms wrapped around her waist.

"Hey, easy, you alright?"

Clinging to him with one hand, the other pressed to her head where a headache was pounding. "Just a little dizzy." The world stopped rocking slightly when Caleb eased her back down into her chair, and she clenched her eyes closed.

"Maybe I should call an ambulance," Caleb knelt in front of her, his hands on her knees.

"No," Tessa forced her eyes back open. "I'll be okay. I think I just need to sleep."

She tried to stand but Caleb stopped her, "here I got you," he said, slipping an arm beneath her knees and the other behind her back, lifting her easily and carrying her towards the stairs.

"I'm sorry," she murmured, her head resting listlessly against his shoulder, she didn't have the energy to lift it. "This is the second time I've almost passed out on you."

"You have nothing to apologize for," he assured her as he bumped her bedroom door open with his foot and set her down gently on the bed. "I am always here for you when you need it."

Before unconsciousness came once again she heard herself whispering something completely out of character, "I trust you."

* * * * *

9:26 A.M.

He'd almost lost it when he'd seen Tessa collapse, but the sight of him cradling her was worse. Parker's stomach twisted itself into knots as he watched the man lay Tessa down on the bed, then lean over her unconscious body and kiss her. As once again the man turned to face the camera, to smile and wave, then stretched out beside Tessa, pulling her into his arms, Parker found himself screaming.

* * * * *

12:34 P.M.

Knocking on the door Wyatt wasn't sure it was a good idea to be here. Wasn't sure it would do any good either, but he had to do something. He couldn't stand by and watch the Abbott family be destroyed like his own had almost been following a similar loss. If there was any possible chance that he could help the Abbott family to heal just a little then he would take it.

"Detective Wyatt," Eric Abbott said, surprised, as he pulled open the front door, then with a hint of panic in his eyes, "what's wrong?"

"No, nothing's wrong," Wyatt assured him as he gave the man a discreet once over. Eric appeared to have aged years in the last four days, since Wyatt had returned baby Molly to them. "I just came to talk to Lila."

Eric nodded and held the door open wider to let him in, leading him to the living room. "Can I get you a drink?"

"No thanks," taking a seat. "How's Molly?"

"Doing fine."

"And Lila?"

Saying nothing, just gazing down into the bassinette and placing a hand inside, "not so well. She won't feed her or change her, she won't even touch her." Eric looked over at him with hopeless eyes, "I don't know what to do."

Giving him an encouraging smile, "believe me, I know what you're going through, it just takes time," Wyatt promised. "I know it sounds trite but it's true."

"You lost a child."

They both turned to face Lila Abbott as she stood in the doorway. Clad in jeans and a t-shirt, the clothing a couple of sizes too big, the bruising on her face had now almost vanished, she looked stronger, more in control.

"Her name was Serena. She was three. This year she would have celebrated her fourteenth birthday." Eleven years later and it was no easier to talk about now than it had been back then. Wyatt still missed his little girl. Her winning smile, her enormous brown eyes, her corkscrew curls. The way she lit up every time he walked into a room. The way she entwined her twig-like arms around his neck so tightly that even when he let go she continued to hang there.

The baby began to fuss, Lila took no notice her gaze fixed firmly on him. Eric discretely picked up the child and slipped from the room as Lila sat opposite him.

"How did she die?"

Drawing in a deep breath before answering. "It had to do with a case I was working on. A man who had killed his wife and two little stepsons, because she was planning on filing for divorce and suing for custody of his daughter. He decided to make things personal. He hated me. Threatened me, stalked me, eventually found out about my family. One day he followed my wife and daughter to a gas station, when Casey went to pay she left Serena in the car, he jumped in and drove off. The police managed to find him, chased him for a while, in the end he drove into a concrete wall killing himself and Serena instantly."

Lila looked stricken, "I'm sorry."

Nodding sadly, "me too. Every day of my life. I think about her all the time. What would she be like now? Would she be good at school, at sports, maybe be creative? Would she be stubborn or easygoing, would she be a laugher or a sulker? She was the sweetest little girl, I know whatever she would have done it would have been with her whole heart." Looking the woman directly in the eye, "more nights than I can count, I've laid awake feeling guilty about Serena's death. I should have protected her, if I wasn't a police officer then it wouldn't have happened, if I'd filled up the car with gas like I was supposed to then Casey and Serena wouldn't have been there that day. You can't play that game, Lila, my daughter is gone and your son is gone, nothing that we do is ever going to change that."

"What happened? After?"

"I almost quit my job. I couldn't drive a car. Every time I climbed inside I just froze. My wife became depressed, wouldn't even get out of bed. Just before Serena was killed we found out we were pregnant with our second child." Feeling his cheeks heat with shame as he remembered. "I hated that baby. I didn't want a new child I wanted my daughter back. I was determined that I would never love that baby because if anything happened to it, I didn't think I could survive. It wasn't until seven months later when Casey went into labor, and I was forced to drive her to the hospital, that I actually faced my fears. When the doctor placed my son in my arms, it was like a crack in the wall I'd built around myself. It didn't mean that all the pain and guilt went away, but it was a start, and now Sam and his little sister are the light of my life. I still think about Serena every morning when I get up, and every night when I go to bed, and many times in between. I still hurt, I still feel guilty, I would still do anything to get her back, but I can live too."

Lila was biting her lip, teardrops ready to spill at any moment,

"I blame her. I blame Molly. If I hadn't been trying to get her out of the car then they wouldn't have shot Joey."

Shaking his head, "doing that will destroy you, and Molly. I blamed Sam for a while, convinced myself that if Casey hadn't been pregnant, hadn't been tired and feeling sick, then she would have taken Serena with her to pay. Doing that, blaming anything and everything, is only a way to put off dealing with what actually happened. A way to put off moving on."

"I'm scared," she whispered pitifully.

"I know you are. Moving on is terrifying because it feels like letting go. But whether you want to acknowledge it or not, you still have a husband and a daughter who depend on you. You've already lost Joey, don't lose Eric and Molly too."

"We don't want to lose you, Lila," Eric announced quietly from the doorway.

Looking from him, to her husband and child, and back again.

"There's no easy answer, Lila, but the only way to have a future is to let go of the past," Wyatt told her as she stood and took a hesitant step towards her family.

Leaving the young family to begin the healing process, a process that from personal experience he knew would never end, Wyatt crept quietly to the door, and found he had to force himself to climb back into the car. Whenever he talked about Serena his old phobia of driving had a sudden spike.

Pressing on, Lila wasn't the only person he needed to see today. Earlier this morning he had received a call from Tessa. He'd almost dropped his phone when he'd seen her name pop up on his caller ID. Tessa was still angry with him, and had barely said two words to him since Parker had disappeared. When he'd gone over to check up on her yesterday, after Parker's abandoned car had been towed, she'd still been passed out from the drugs Beth had given her, but Daniel had kept him updated on how she was doing.

Wyatt was becoming more and more concerned about Tessa's

increasingly erratic behavior and fragile emotional state. He knew what she'd dealt with as a kid, and he'd seen her deal with things most people couldn't even dream of. But this time was different, this time she seemed to have lost her focus, and if Parker didn't come back then Wyatt didn't know how to help her find it again.

It wasn't just the fact that Tessa was losing it that was worrying him, it was also that she kept alienating herself from everyone who loved and cared about her. He understood why she was doing it, putting her trust in Parker had been an enormous step, and for him to then disappear just like everyone else she'd ever trusted, it had shaken her. Again, he understood why she was doing it, but it wasn't going to get her through this.

Apparently, there was still one person left who Tessa was speaking to, Caleb Brighton. Who seemed to be forever hanging around, apparently he'd already been over twice since they'd discovered the car. There was still something about that guy that Wyatt didn't trust. Parker hadn't talked a lot about his time in foster care, but Wyatt was sure that he would have mentioned Caleb if they had been as good friends as he claimed.

Turning into Tessa's driveway, he noted that all the other cars were gone, and wondered what exactly it was that she wanted to talk to him about. Deciding it was better to wait for Tess to let him in rather than risk her wrath and use his key he knocked and waited patiently.

When finally she did throw open the door, he only just managed to control a gasp from escaping his lips. She looked abysmal. Her normal sparkly bluey-green eyes were dull and lifeless, her white blonde curls hung limply around a face that was almost translucent and so bony it seemed as though there wasn't an ounce of flesh on it.

"Tessa, you look . . ."

"I know," she interrupted, "terrible."

"Are you feeling okay?"

"Not really," she admitted tiredly, brushing at her bleary eyes.

As he followed her indoors, he made sure to stay right by her side, to catch her in case she fell. He wasn't sure she could make it to the sofa, but somehow she managed, and Wyatt let out a sigh of relief when she dropped down into the deep cushions.

"I'll get you some water," he told her and left her there while he went to the kitchen and retrieved some iced water from the fridge. Upon his return Wyatt saw that Tessa had closed her eyes and appeared to have dozed off, settling into a chair to let her sleep when her eyes struggled open.

"Wyatt?"

"I'm still here," he assured her, still a little hurt to see she was still calling him Wyatt. As much as he couldn't stand his given name, he kind of enjoyed Tessa calling him that, she was the little sister he'd always wanted. "What did you want to talk about?"

"Did you find anything in Parker's car?"

"No," he answered reluctantly, not sure how much more bad news Tessa could handle. "But we'll find him, I promise. I already looked through mine and Parker's old case files, but I'll go through them again, maybe something will stand out this time around."

She nodded half-heartedly and shrunk back further into the sofa.

"What's up, Tess?" he pushed gently.

Inspecting him with a glum expression. "I want you and Casey to take the baby."

Sure he hadn't heard her right. "What?"

"I want you and Casey to take the baby," she repeated.

"Tessa," Wyatt shook his head, "you're only saying that out of fear."

"No I'm not, Skylar," she eyed him determinedly. "I've thought it through, I cannot raise a baby."

"You're going to be a great mom," he soothed.

"You have got to be kidding," she scoffed. "Even Parker knows I'd make a terrible mother."

"What?" he frowned, confused, perhaps Tessa was finally admitting to herself that nothing sinister had happened to her husband, that he had simply left of his own accord.

"He didn't tell me," she explained mournfully, "that he knew I was pregnant. I think you were right, Parker found the pregnancy test, he thought it said I was pregnant. That's why he was freaking out, because he was worried about bringing a baby into our family, because he knew what a horrible mother I'd be."

More than a little worried. "You don't really think that, do you?"

Her arched brow confirmed that she did indeed believe it.

"Honey, you have to know that's not true."

She looked at him doubtfully.

"Tessa, it is *not* true," he said emphatically. "You are going to make a great mom."

"If you don't want the baby that's okay. I can put it up for adoption. It's just that with so many bad families out there, I want to know that it goes to a good home. To someone who'll love it like it deserves. Just because it has a mixed up mom and dad doesn't mean that it should have to suffer . . ." she was rambling.

"Hey, hey," kneeling in front of her to try to catch her eye. "You're only two months pregnant, you have plenty of time to make a decision."

"I've already made my decision," she declared.

Thinking about the mysterious Caleb Brighton. "Did you talk to Caleb about this?"

Furrowing her brow in concentration, "I don't remember."

"What do you mean you don't remember?"

Rubbing at her head, "I can't seem to keep things straight in my head right now."

Concerned about that. Tessa was a genius with a photographic memory, that she couldn't keep simple conversations straight in her head was extremely worrying.

"But," she added defiantly, "I know that I cannot raise a

baby."

Despite her protestations, Wyatt knew she was making this resolution because she was tired and scared and overwhelmed, and that she had not considered all her options. Taking hold of her hands, "Tess, if when the baby is born you feel like you still can't deal with it, then Casey and I will help you in whatever way we can, okay?"

"Okay," she echoed in a small voice.

Wyatt could see he was losing her, her gaze had become unfocused, she'd sunk further back into the cushions, her hands were resting limply in his hold. "Come on, you're exhausted," scooping her up into his arms, expecting her to protest, more concerned when she didn't.

"Where's Daniel?" Tessa asked as her head drooped against his shoulder.

"I don't know, sweetheart. Out somewhere. You want me to stay with you till he gets back?" he asked as he gently placed her on the bed and tucked her in.

"Uh huh," her head almost split in two by a gigantic yawn.

Settling onto the bed beside her, she immediately nestled into him, grabbing his hand and pulling his arms tighter around her then clinging to him. Absently stroking her tangled curls, Wyatt thought she was asleep when she peered up at him.

"Skylar?"

"Yeah?"

"Do you think Parker really loves me?"

Squeezing her lightly, "he loved you from the second he first saw you."

Bobbing her head tiredly before resting it on his shoulder. It was gut wrenching to see Tessa, who was usually so strong and tough, reduced to a quivering huddle in his arms. Within minutes she was fast asleep, and Wyatt again found himself thinking about what he would do to Parker if his best friend had deliberately walked off and done this to Tessa.

* * * * *

8:42 P.M.

"Did you guess it was me? Did you guess it was me? Did you guess it was me?" He was literally clapping his hands and bouncing up and down he was so excited.

Parker still couldn't believe this was happening. Never in a million years would he have guessed that this could ever happen. "I don't understand why you're doing this, Lachlan."

Lachlan Mountain's freckled face continued to beam at him. "Actually I go by Caleb now. A fresh name for a fresh start."

"I don't care what you're calling yourself, Lachlan, this doesn't make any sense." Parker had never met Lachlan Mountain but he was so eerily similar that he had known who it was immediately.

"It makes perfect sense," Lachlan countered with a pout. "Because of you I lost everything that was important to me, and so I am going to do the same to you."

"How am I responsible for what happened?"

In an instant Lachlan's face clouded over, as though hit by a sudden hurricane of rage. "You know *exactly* what you did."

"I was not responsible for your father's death," Parker told him calmly. "What happened was an accident."

"She shot him," Lachlan reminded him coldly.

"She thought he was going to hurt her, she was only trying to protect herself."

"My father would never hurt anyone," spitting the words out as though the idea were preposterous. "He was only there to help her."

"She knows that now, but at the time she didn't. You know what happened to her there," Parker held Lachlan in a steady gaze, "Matilda would never hurt anyone on purpose."

Stalking over to the cage, taking care to stay just out of reach.

"You talk like your sister just gave him a black eye, she killed him. Shot him straight in the heart. Watched him die in the driveway."

"Lachlan, it was an accident, a horrible accident," Parker said but Lachlan had gotten a faraway look in his shockingly bright blue eyes.

"Everything was ruined after that. My mother was never the same. She never recovered from her husband's murder. I ended up being placed in foster care, becoming one of the children my father made it his life's work to save." His gaze grew even darker, "and it was all because of your sister."

Still a little hazy on exactly what Lachlan hoped to achieve. "So how exactly does kidnapping me get you revenge?"

A horrible smile spreading across his face, Parker couldn't decide if it was a sane smile or a manic one, or which was the better option. "It helps me get revenge because Matilda loses the only person she ever loved, and you lose that beautiful wife of yours."

"If you hurt Tessa," Parker threatened once again.

"You're one to talk, I've seen the bruises on her arms," Lachlan glared, a hint of possessive fury in his eyes.

A sharp stab of guilt caught him in the heart. That he had inflicted physical pain on his wife was something he would never forgive himself for. That he had inflicted emotional pain on her was even worse. "That was a mistake, but if you hurt her . . ."

"Relax, relax," Lachlan snickered, "I haven't laid a hand on her."

"You've been drugging her," he incredulously reminded Lachlan.

"I just need to keep her a little out of it, don't want her getting suspicious or starting to patch things up with her friends. Anyway," Lachlan continued, "I don't plan on killing her. I plan on making her forget all about you and fall in love with me. I'm already her new best friend."

"How did you even manage to get her to let you in the door?"

Tessa was the most paranoid person Parker had ever met, and it wasn't like her to let her guard down around anyone.

"I told her that we were old friends, that we lived together in the same foster home, even showed her some photos I made up on my computer of the two of us as kids. Right now she's really looking for a friend, someone who's on her side, who's supporting her."

Parker cursed his own stupidity. It was his fault. He'd been so wrapped up in himself he hadn't really thought about how his actions were affecting Tessa. He knew better and yet he'd done it anyway. And in doing so, he'd left her vulnerable, alone and completely susceptible to Lachlan's lies.

Still he maintained that Tess would catch on to his game. "Are you insane?" Parker roared. "Tessa will never believe that I left her on purpose. She will certainly never ever love you. And are you forgetting the fact that she's pregnant with my baby?"

Smiling smugly, "oh that's right I forgot to leave the sound on for you."

"What are you talking about?"

"You didn't hear the conversation Tessa had earlier today with your friend Skylar Wyatt," Lachlan paused.

Parker remembered watching Wyatt visit with Tessa, remembered the glassy look in her eyes, the lifeless way she'd laid in his partner's arms when he'd carried her upstairs. It had been reassuring, albeit only slightly, to know that Wyatt was looking out for Tessa. Parker knew that no matter how hard Tessa worked at pushing people away, his partner wouldn't budge. He had assumed that Wyatt had just been there to check up on Tess, to make sure she was hanging in there, but seemingly he had been mistaken.

"Apparently," Lachlan drew the word out, "Tessa doesn't want to keep the baby, she wants to give it to your partner and his wife."

Perplexed, "why would Tessa want to give away our child?"

"Well, you see your wife thinks that you knew she was pregnant and the reason you were acting so weirdly before you disappeared was because you knew that she would be a terrible mother."

"What?" he gulped in a small voice. Parker knew he'd treated Tessa badly those last few days, and it had been about the baby, but it was because of his own crushing insecurities about being a good father, he had not a single doubt that Tess would make a wonderful mother. Lachlan was still grinning delightedly, and the pleasure he seemed to be taking in all of this fuelled Parker's anger. "You are insane, Lachlan, this is never going to work, you are never going to get Tessa to fall in love with you."

"Oh it's going to work, and I'll tell you why," Lachlan grew sinister. "How many times have you thought of me in the last twenty-one years?"

"Mattie and I thought of you a lot," he answered honestly. "My sister never recovered from what happened. She blames herself, it doesn't matter that it was an accident, that she was just a child. She took a life, killed a man. We used to talk about you all the time, wonder how you were doing, what had happened to you after your father died. But you have to understand that our foster father was sexually abusing Matilda. He brought his friends over, she didn't know your father was a social worker, she thought he was another one of our foster father's friends come to hurt her."

"I've thought about *you* every single day," Lachlan spat out as though Parker hadn't spoken. "Every day for twenty-one years, and that is why my plan will work. Because I have invested everything I am in doing this and I have nothing to lose." His smile returning, "and it's already beginning to work. Right now Tessa doesn't have you, all her friends and family keep insisting that you walked out on her, probably to be with another woman, and I am the only person on her side, the only person that she trusts."

"Tessa doesn't trust anyone," Parker contradicted.

"Well she trusts me, she told me she did, and I am going to make her fall in love with me. Then you're going to lose your family to me."

JUNE 27TH

Tessa felt a little more clear-headed this morning. Maybe it was the fact that she'd actually had a good night's sleep. Maybe it was because she had made a decision about her baby's future. Or maybe it was because Caleb had once again shown up bright and early with breakfast.

"You're looking better today," Caleb told her with a smile, as he set a plate of steaming waffles in front of her.

"I feel better," Tessa confirmed. "I'm getting closer to the end of my first trimester, so hopefully things will start to settle down," to emphasis her point she took a big mouthful of waffles and prayed that the baby would accept them.

"Your brother was a little reluctant to leave us alone," Lachlan sat beside her and began wolfing into his breakfast.

That was putting it mildly.

When Caleb had shown up again this morning, minutes after Matilda had taken Winter out to buy the last minute things for her party tomorrow, Daniel had gone bananas. He'd ranted at Caleb, asking why the man kept showing up and hanging around Tessa. Then he'd taken her aside and told her that he'd been talking to Wyatt about Caleb, and that Wyatt didn't like or trust him.

Tessa had tried her best to be patient with her brother, explaining to him that *she* liked Caleb. And enjoyed his company because he was the one person who wasn't always trying to convince her to accept that her husband was gone. In the end, Daniel had unhappily left them alone to go to work, with a thinly veiled threat to Caleb that she better be okay when he got back.

"He's trying to make up for lost time," she explained, and

pleased that so far her stomach was okay took another mouthful.

"He walked out on you when you were a kid right?"

Confused, "how did you know that?"

"Oh, uh, I think you said something the other day," he shot her a breezy smile.

Tessa didn't remember telling Caleb about Daniel, but then so much of the last few weeks was a fuzzy blur in her mind that she couldn't really be sure. "Yeah he left because of Emilie, our mother."

A dreamy look came over Caleb's face, "when I was little, on really cold stormy days my mom and I used to collect all the pillows and blankets in the house and pile them up on the den sofa. Then we'd go to the kitchen and mix up a big batch of cookie dough," chuckling softly at the memory, "my mom and I loved the dough, but my dad loved baked cookies. So we'd split the mixture in half and set the cookies in the oven then we'd take the rest to the sofa. We'd curl up under a sea of blankets, with rain pounding down and the wind howling outside, put on a movie and eat the dough."

Catching on to a thread of memory, "I thought you said your dad wasn't around when you were growing up?" Tessa asked.

"Oh," his eyes roamed the room as he seemed to search for an answer, "he was around for a little while before he left."

Sensing something was up, Tessa continued innocently, "how old were you when he left?"

Hesitating, "um, five I think."

Knowing she was onto something, any child who'd had a parent walk out on them knew exactly when it happened. She remembered vividly the day Patrick had walked out. It had been a mild fall day, they were all seated in the formal dining room eating breakfast, when Patrick announced he was leaving to marry his mistress. In the middle of the screaming match that ensued, a seven months pregnant Bridgette, now Patrick's wife and the mother of his two younger children Patrick Junior and Serena, had shown up to see what was holding up her soon to be available lover. Emilie had gone berserk, hurling cups and cutlery at Bridgette, while ten-year-old Tessa and sixteen-year-old Daniel had sat quietly at the table taking in the unfolding events that they both knew had been destined to happen.

"You don't remember?"

"It was a long time ago," Caleb replied defensively.

"I remember the day my father walked out."

"I guess I don't like to think about it, it was too painful," Caleb said darkly before drifting into silence.

Tessa wondered why he was acting so strangely. Thinking of Skylar's suspicions, and her own initial distrust of a man who had mysteriously appeared just days after her husband had disappeared. She was about to ask him what was going on when he suddenly brightened.

"I'll make us some tea," he announced, springing from the table and hurrying to the counter.

"I'll help," Tessa stood to follow but Caleb spun back to face her.

"No, no, you just wait there. I know you're feeling better this morning, but you don't want to push yourself."

Examining Caleb as he set about making the tea, Tessa realized how little she knew about him. Sure, she'd done a background check on him, but she knew from experience how easy it was to create a new identity. As Caleb returned to the table with the drinks she shot him her sweetest smile and begun her interrogation, "tell me more about your family, your mom seems like she was nice."

A sad smile settling on his lips, "yeah she was the best . . ."

Sipping on her tea as she listened to Caleb rattle on and on about what a saint his mother was, Tessa found herself pondering just what might have happened to make him so overly complimentary about her. She must have zoned out for a few minutes because when she blinked her eyes, Caleb's face was hovering just inches from her own.

"I never noticed that before," he smiled.

"Noticed what?"

"Your eyelashes are black."

Knitting her brow in confusion, "what?"

"All the rest of your hair is so blonde, but your eyelashes are black." He was staring at her longingly, "you're so beautiful."

Caleb's eyes were glittering with lust and as she found herself staring back at him, Tessa could feel her mind growing sluggish again.

All her niggling doubts and the questions she wanted to ask melted away.

* * * * *

10:48 A.M.

"You're really beautiful."

Caleb thought he'd gotten to her in time. The research he'd done on Parker's wife had told him that she had an IQ of 178, so it wasn't surprising that she was starting to catch on. He'd almost blown it earlier by accidentally letting on that he knew more about the rift between her and her brother than he was supposed to. He was going to have to be more careful in the future, make sure that he kept track of exactly what she'd told him and not confuse it with the other details that he knew.

He was also going to have to be careful not to give her too many sedatives. It had been unavoidable just now. The whole plan would be ruined if Tessa figured him out. However, if he wasn't careful and drugged her too much, then she would be too out of it for the two of them to properly bond. At first, Caleb had just wanted to take Tessa from Parker to punish him, but now he was starting to dream about his own happy life with Tessa and her child. A family of his own, a replacement for the one that had been ripped away from him when he was only seven years old.

Matilda Bell might have pulled the trigger but Parker was equally to blame. Lachlan Mountain Senior was a hero. A dedicated social worker who had helped improve the lives of hundreds of neglected children. A devoted husband and father, who would have given his life for his family, or for any of the children under his care. And give his life he had. Because of Matilda and Parker Bell.

They had single-handedly destroyed his family. After his father's murder his mother had fallen apart, hadn't been able to face life without her beloved husband. Theresa Mountain had spent most of the last twenty-one years sitting in a chair staring blankly at the blinking television in a near catatonic state. Little Lachlan had done the best he could to support his mother and take his father, his namesakes, place as the head of the family, but it had done no good. He couldn't save his father. He couldn't save his mother. And he couldn't save little Lachlan. Lachlan Mountain Junior was gone now, he was one hundred percent Caleb Brighton, and he was going to get everything he wanted.

"I'm sorry," Caleb painted a strained and embarrassed smile on his face as he apologized, "I'm making you feel uncomfortable." He was struggling to concentrate. He kept getting distracted by the white tank top that clung to Tessa's thin frame and the short denim shorts that showed off her legs.

"It's okay," Tessa mumbled, as she pressed the heel of her hand against her eyes, the drugs already taking effect.

"Are you okay?" he asked with mock concern. "You just went white as a ghost."

"I'm fine," she told him with a watery smile. "I just need a glass of water."

As she stood she swayed, just as Caleb had known she would, and he jumped to her side in time to wrap an arm around her waist before she hit the floor. "Whoa, hey, you doing alright?"

"Dizzy again. It keeps coming and going."

Tessa was leaning heavily against him and Caleb enjoyed the feel of her tiny body in his arms. Wondering what it would feel like to be inside her, to have his lips against her skin, and for a second he was tempted to take her right there and then. He could if he wanted, he had enough drugs in his pocket to knock her out, and before he knew what he was doing, he was reaching for them. Stopping himself at the last second, he wanted Tessa, but not like this. It would be so much better when she wanted him just as much as he wanted her.

"Come on," he started half supporting, half carrying Tessa towards the den, "come and lie down." Helping her get settled on the sofa, cradling her head in his hand as he slipped a pillow beneath it, spreading a throw rug over her. "I'll just get the rest of your tea." When he returned Tessa's eyes were closed and he thought she had drifted off. "I'm going to take care of you," Caleb whispered as he knelt beside her and softly ran a hand through her thick hair.

At his touch her eyes fluttered open, and she gave him a sleepy smile. "Hey."

"Hey yourself." Stroking her forehead, "feeling any better?"

"Not so dizzy when I'm lying down," she replied, letting her eyes fall closed. "Thanks, Caleb, you've been really wonderful. Wyatt, Casey, J.J., Marty, Maisy, Daniel, Matilda, Winter. All the people who Parker loved and trusted. All the people who are supposed to care about him, they all turned their back on him, on me, if it wasn't for you I'd have no one. I'd be all alone."

"I'm in love with you." The words tumbled out in a rush before he could stop them.

The look she gave him indicated that she wasn't shocked by his revelation. "I'm sorry, Caleb, but no matter what happens I still love my husband," she lifted a weak hand to squeeze his apologetically.

"I know," he squeezed back. "I'm sorry, I can't help how I feel, but I know that you love Parker." At least for now, he thought to himself as he held the cup of tea to her lips. But soon you'll forget all about that husband of yours and then it'll be just me, you, and your baby. A happy family. A perfect family.

"I'm really glad you're here though," Tessa murmured before passing out.

Keenly aware that Parker was watching his every move, he bent over Tessa and pressed his lips against hers, enjoying the sweet taste of her mouth even if she couldn't kiss him back. Running his hand up under her tank top and cupping her breast, dreaming about the day Tessa gave him permission to run his hands over every inch of her body.

Lifting Tessa carefully, so as not to disturb her, Caleb stretched out on the deep sofa and rested Tessa on top of him. She uttered a small sigh and snuggled closer against his chest, nuzzling into his neck. Unable to resist he tilted Tessa's head back and hungrily brought his mouth to hers once again. Weakly she briefly responded, then went still, Caleb didn't care he just enjoyed the pleasure of having a woman in his arms, something he wasn't accustomed too. He'd never had a real girlfriend, he'd had flings, and one-night stands, and a couple of affairs with married women, but never anything meaningful. Tessa was his chance to change all of that.

For Parker's benefit, and because he had gone to all the trouble to turn the sound on in the basement so that his prisoner could keep more abreast of the happenings at the house, he looked straight at the camera, "I'm going to have her, Parker, and there's nothing you can do about it."

* * * * *

11:03 P.M.

A clunk jarred him awake.

In the dim light he could make out his meal on a tray just

inside the cage, and Parker realized he must have fallen asleep and missed Lachlan's visit.

Wringing his hands together since it was the closet thing he could do right now to wringing his captor's neck. Lachlan was not going to get away with what he was doing to Tessa. Quite simply Parker wouldn't allow it.

Earlier he had gone ballistic when Lachlan had taken advantage of Tessa, kissing her and touching her while she lay unconscious in his arms. Parker had ripped and bruised his hands as he'd torn at the metal bars of his cage, his gaze drawn to the screen almost against his will. Unsure of how far Lachlan was going to take things with Tessa, but knowing then and there that if Lachlan raped his wife then he would kill the man without a second thought. In the end, Lachlan had stopped after running his hands up under Tessa's top, but it had been enough to set Parker's blood boiling. The tender way Lachlan had clasped Tessa so possessively against his body had almost been harder to watch.

Once again, Lachlan had had to resort to drugs in order to keep to his plan, because Tessa was starting to catch on to him, starting to realize that he wasn't what he appeared to be. Parker had seen it in her eyes, heard it in her voice when she was talking to him in the kitchen. For a little while he had seen the old spark reignite in her eyes, and he knew that something had happened to make her begin to doubt Lachlan, or Caleb as he was going by now.

The panic had also been evident in Lachlan's face when Tessa had started peppering him with questions about his past. Obviously he had tripped up in his story about his childhood. Parker hadn't heard everything he'd said, but most of what he had heard was untrue. Tessa was smart, brilliant really, and would normally have had no trouble figuring Lachlan out. But between his own disappearance, what she felt was betrayal by all her friends, and Lachlan feeding her sedatives she didn't have much of a hope.

Parker knew that it was now or never. If he didn't come up with a plan of attack soon then both he and Tessa were going to wind up dead. Lachlan was unstable, Parker could see it in his eyes, and when he finally realized that drugged or not, Tessa was never going to fall in love with him then he would kill her. Once Tessa was dead, then there was nothing left for Lachlan to torture him with, and therefore no reason to keep him alive.

Lachlan Mountain Junior might think that he was in control but he was wrong. He was never going to get Tessa because Parker would do whatever it took to prevent it from happening.

JUNE 28TH

11:23 A.M.

"Everything ready?"

His niece looked over at him with shining black eyes. "Almost."

The day of Winter's sweet sixteenth had finally arrived and guests were due to start arriving at any minute. Daniel couldn't believe just how grown up Winter looked. In the end, she'd decided against the mauve dress and gone with a knee length lemon halter neck dress instead. The color blended well with her straight black hair, which she had twisted up on the top of her head, and her milky white skin, adding a bright splash of color.

Despite Tessa's, and his own, trepidation, Winter had insisted that they hold her party at Tessa's estate. The mansion held a lot of bad memories for both of him and his sister, but the enormous stone house was spectacular. When Winter had announced that she wanted to hold her sweet sixteenth here both he and Tessa had voted against it. When Winter pressed the issue Tessa had quickly given in, shocking Daniel, since she was the one who had almost lost her life in this house.

Tessa, Matilda and Casey had spent the day decorating the ballroom in a pink, yellow and orange theme, and the whole place had a festive air about it. Hundreds of balloons floated by the ceiling with the aid of helium, streamers crisscrossed the room, and vividly colored lights shaped as ducks, Winter's favorite animal, shone brightly against the walls.

"You look amazing," Daniel told her.

Blushing, "thank you," Winter mumbled refusing to meet his eye. Daniel knew that due to her upbringing she had serious self-confidence issues.

"Where's everyone else?" he asked scanning the empty room.

"Matilda had to pop out to get some more drinks, Casey had to go home to watch the kids till the babysitter gets there, and Wyatt's upstairs with Tessa."

At the mention of his sister, Daniel felt another icy twinge of worry. Worrying about Tessa was like a full time job. She seemed to have an uncanny ability to attract the vilest examples of humankind.

She had picked up a little the last few days, but she'd still been tired, pale, hardly eating, and she'd almost fainted in his arms last night. She'd also been working hard at shutting him out. Immediately following the discovery of Parker's car, she'd clung to him desperately, constantly needing his presence to keep her panicked hysteria at bay. But something had changed. She'd grown distant and withdrawn. She'd barely said two words to him.

But she had no problem chatting away with her new best friend Caleb Brighton.

Wyatt was extremely worked up about the guy and didn't want him around Tessa when she was in such an emotionally volatile state. Daniel was concerned enough about his sister to go along with Wyatt's theory, but when he had tried to voice his objections to Tessa, when Caleb had shown up yet again yesterday, she had become instantly defensive.

"Everything okay?" Winter asked, her pretty face creased with concern.

Shooting her a bright smile, he didn't want to ruin her day with his concerns about Tessa, "fine, just thinking how amazing you are." Daniel would never have thought that after everything his niece had been through in the last six months, she would be as calm and settled and at peace.

"You don't have to hover constantly at my side, Wyatt," Tessa snapped coming through the doors. "I'm not going to break if you're more than an inch away."

"I'm aware of that, Tessa," Wyatt replied patiently as he trailed her into the room.

Ignoring him, Tessa focused her attention on Winter, "I think I heard a car pull up."

Practically bursting with excitement Winter hurried from the room. Daniel opened his mouth to ask if his sister was okay, but she shot him an icy glare. "What?" he asked innocently instead.

Choosing to ignore that too, "is Caleb here?"

Chewing on his lip to keep from blurting out an unpleasant comment about Caleb Brighton, a glance at Wyatt confirmed he was doing the same thing. "No, not yet." They'd argued about it last night when Tessa had announced she had invited Caleb to drop by the party if he was able to.

Before any more could be said, Winter returned with a couple of her friends, and for the next half an hour they were too busy greeting guests to argue further. Throughout the meal, the speeches, the gifts, the dancing, Daniel kept a watchful eye on his sister. Noting the way her eyes darted around the crowd, searching for what she saw as her one ally.

Deciding that if someone who irrationally believed that something bad had happened to Parker was what Tessa needed, then he would give it to her. Going along with her theory was infinitely preferable to having this stranger as her confidant. Before he had a chance to go and check up on her, Matilda came over to announce that it was time to cut the cake.

Distracted by the celebrations Daniel didn't spot Tessa again until the end of the party. She was over in a corner deep in conversation with Caleb, who seemed to be hovering in the shadows, his eyes darting nervously about, as though afraid that if he came out into the light he might burn up. Since all the guests had gone save for one or two of Winter's closet friends, Daniel sidled up to them, Caleb immediately shooting him a disgruntled frown.

"I don't need a babysitter, Daniel," Tessa snapped, her own

frown screaming irritated.

"I know that, Tessie," he smiled sweetly, and then focused his gaze squarely on Caleb. "You showed up late," he commented mildly, in fact he'd actually turned up after the official end of the party, after Matilda and the Wyatt's had already left to take Winter's friends home.

"I got held up," Caleb answered carelessly, but simmering in his bright blue eyes was pure annoyance that his private time with Tessa had been interrupted.

Hiding a smile, "oh," Daniel nodded sympathetically, "that's too bad, it was a really beautiful party, Tessie did a great job."

"Of course she did," Caleb's face softened as he smiled at Tessa, and Daniel wondered whether the man had genuine feelings for Tess.

About to push this line of questioning further when his cell phone chirped in his pocket, pulling it out he saw Matilda's name on the display and felt his body start to react. "Hey you," he said as he answered.

"Hey yourself," her voice innocently seductive. "I'm out front, could you come and help me bring some stuff in from the car?"

Goosebumps prickling his skin at the sound of her voice, "no problem." Daniel didn't elaborate. Since Winter's birthday was actually tomorrow they had a special surprise party planned. Tessa didn't know about it either, and Daniel didn't want her catching on and inviting Caleb. He wanted to break off contact between his sister and this man as quickly as possible. Popping his phone back in his pocket, "Matilda's back, she just needs some help bringing some things in," he explained.

Tessa nodded absently, "sure," her unreadable eyes fixed on Caleb, who suddenly appeared to be even jumpier.

Wondering what was going on with Caleb and whether Wyatt might be right, and he might know more about Parker's disappearance than he was letting on. As he skipped down the front steps and caught sight of Matilda, dressed in a bright red sleeveless top showing off slender shoulders, black pants clinging to her long legs, everything else flew from his mind.

When she turned to face him, he saw her eyes light with desire, and Daniel decided that maybe happy endings were possible after all.

* * * * *

5:42 P.M.

"I better be going," Caleb told her, pulling on his mask of disappointment.

Playing along, "oh that's too bad."

"Yeah, I'll call you later, okay?" Caleb was already heading for the back door.

"We can go out the front," Tessa smiled sweetly.

"No that's okay," Caleb jumped in quickly. "My car's round the side anyway, so it's closer to the back door."

Almost running to keep up with Caleb's long strides as they wound through the corridors and out the mansion's backdoor. Tessa followed him to his car, getting a chill, despite the overbearing heat, when he turned and quickly pecked her on the cheek. In his face Tessa could see that he wanted her, badly, it was a look she was used to seeing in men.

"I'll call you," he called over his shoulder as he practically threw himself inside his car.

"I'll be waiting," she called back, smiling to herself and waving as he sped down the driveway as fast as he could without being too obvious. She was on to Caleb, he wasn't what he pretended to be, and she was going to get to the bottom of exactly what it was he was hiding.

When his car was out of sight, she climbed quickly into her own gold Mercedes and followed him down the long, tree-lined driveway. Pleased that she'd managed to occupy both Daniel and

Skylar, so that she could do what she needed to without a barrage of questions from her bodyguards.

Catching up to Caleb quickly, but taking care to stay well back on the quiet country roads. She'd been following him for maybe ten minutes when her cell phone chirped, knowing immediately who it was, she kept one hand on the steering wheel and answered with her other.

"What did you find?"

Almost swerving into a tree when she heard the answer.

Positive that she must have heard wrong, "what?"

The repeated answer was exactly what she had heard the first time.

"How many?"

Twirling a curl around her finger as she listened.

"Where?"

The answer this time made her shiver in fear and repulsion.

"Did you do the test?"

Affirmative.

"And?"

Not at all shocked when she heard the reply, but plenty mad.

"Alright I have to go . . . no I don't need help. I can handle things from here . . . no I won't forget . . . thank you," with that she hung up, and then in anger threw the disposable cell onto the passenger side floor. Glad at least that she'd gone with her instincts and agreed to let Winter have her birthday party at the mansion to free up her and Parker's house.

Caleb was not going to get away with what he had done to her. Tessa didn't know who he really was or exactly how he was involved, but she knew that he had lied to her about his past, and she knew that he had been drugging her. Probably had been from the day he'd brought the photos, he'd been alone in her kitchen for an indeterminable amount of time while she had been throwing up in the bathroom.

At first she'd thought it was just more morning sickness. But after they had found Parker's car and Elisabeth had given her a sedative, she'd known that something else was up. Ever since Emilie had drugged her and tried to drown her in the bathtub, Tessa had avoided medications whenever she could. The feeling she got when she took them was something she always recognized, and that was the feeling she started getting after one of Caleb's visits.

When Caleb had visited her the other day and she had started questioning him, he had drugged her tea. Tessa had known it from the second he rushed to make it, but had drunk it anyway because it was the only way she could get the proof she needed.

And now she had it.

Breaking out of her reverie, she realized that she's lost sight of Caleb. Making a snap decision, she swung the car in the opposite direction, floored the gas and prayed that her hunch would work.

* * * * *

6:14 P.M.

She knew.

He wasn't sure how much, but she knew.

Caleb was panicking. Everything was falling apart. Tessa knew he'd lied, maybe knew that he'd been drugging her, maybe even knew about the cameras in her house.

It was her brother Daniel's fault.

He'd come over during his talk with Tessa to stir up trouble and doubt, going on about how Caleb had arrived late at the party. It hadn't been his fault that he'd been late. When he had arrived, he'd seen Matilda heading up the marble steps that led to a wide veranda on the largest house he had ever seen. There were at least twenty windows blinking out of the front of the house, over which vines and ivy were rampant, making the mansion feel like something out of an old movie. A little put off at first by just how wealthy Tessa actually was, but that quickly turned to anger that even after everything Parker Bell had done to his family, he had ended up with all of this.

Seeing Matilda, he had known that if she caught sight of him she would recognize him instantly, they would put the pieces together about Parker's disappearance, and his whole plan would be finished. Therefore, he had been forced to hide out in his car until he saw her leave with a car full of teenagers before heading indoors. His hasty getaway upon hearing that Matilda was returning had sparked suspicions from both Daniel and Tessa. Caleb hadn't been far from the estate when he had spotted Tessa's car behind him. At first, he'd hoped he was mistaken, but after veering around winding roads the constant presence of the gold car told him he was being followed. At last he seemed to lose her, but he wasn't quite ready to head home in case Tessa was just hanging back waiting for an opportunity to pounce.

Unsure what to do Caleb decided to head out to the location where he had abducted Parker, try to relive the memory, settle his racing mind, and refocus himself. Caleb had to admit he was pretty proud of his scheme. Picking the exact route Parker would use to get home, lying on the side of the road, managing to remain still while the do-gooder cop had checked him out, timing it perfectly to knock Parker unconscious.

Arriving at the place where he had put stage one of his plan into action, he saw that he was not alone. Getting closer he saw who his unexpected visitor was, and realized that it was over. But maybe, just maybe, not too late to still get what he wanted.

Approaching quietly, hoping to maintain the element of surprise, but . . .

"I've been waiting for you."

Caleb had to know, "how did you figure it out?"

She turned to face him and smiled sadly, "you slipped up with your story."

Nodding ruefully, "I thought I did."

Tessa's eyes shooting angry sparks, "you drugged me," she accused.

"I had to, or you would have figured things out," he pleaded by way of an apology. He desperately wanted, needed, Tessa's approval.

Narrowing her eyes at him, "you took Parker, I know it, I just don't know why."

Mind clicking through possibilities, settling on the one he thought would be most productive. Dropping his gaze to the ground, "I'm sorry. I'm sorry I hurt you, I never meant to . . ." looking up at her imploringly, sincerely meaning every word he spoke, even if he had ulterior motives. "I didn't think I'd really fall in love with you, I only wanted to hurt Parker," taking a tentative step towards her. "I really am in love with you, Tessa, I want to spend the rest of my life with you, you and your baby. Parker would never have made you happy but I can, if you just give us a chance then we can be the perfect family . . ." entering striking distance Caleb swung the butt of his gun around and slammed it into her temple. Tessa dropped instantly, crumpling into a tiny ball on the ground.

Crouching beside her he brushed at the trickle of blood already flowing from the wound on her head. "I'm sorry, Tessa, but this is the only way we can be together, the only way we can be happy," kissing her softly, she would be his, all his.

As he scooped her into his arms and laid her out on the backseat of his car, Caleb decided it was time for a little reunion.

JUNE 29TH

4:17 A.M.

"Something has happened to her," Daniel insisted. "What are you doing to find her?"

"Try to calm down," Wyatt soothed, attempting to hide his own panic and unnerved by the memory of Tessa saying those exact same words to him just days ago. "We don't know anything yet, maybe she just needed some time to herself."

Daniel frowned at him, "Tessa wouldn't go off without telling me."

"She did that just a few days ago," Wyatt reminded him patiently.

"That was a tantrum," Daniel countered.

"We'll find her," Matilda ran her hand reassuringly up and down Daniel's arm.

"Caleb did something to her," Daniel continued to fret, wringing his hands and pacing, as though trying to escape the fear that was swelling inside him.

"When was the last time you saw her?" Wyatt asked, trying to regain some control over the situation and ease his own anxiety.

"At Winter's party. Matilda called and asked me to carry some stuff inside for today so I went outside, when I came back, Tessa was gone. I checked the whole place for her, and then assumed she must have come home, but she wasn't here. I kept calling her but she didn't answer, so then I called you," Daniel looked at him helplessly.

The third time in a matter of weeks he'd been awakened from sleep by the shrill ringing of the phone. The second he heard that Tessa was now missing too, he had thrown on the first clothes he

267

could grab, jumped in his car, and sped all the way here to be greeted by a highly strung Daniel, who was convinced that something sinister had happened to his sister.

Wyatt on the other hand wasn't so sure. Tessa had been so erratic lately, that the possibility that she might have harmed herself haunted him. He wasn't about to float this possibility with Daniel just yet though. "I'm going to take a look around, see if anything's out of place."

"I'll help," Daniel volunteered immediately, obviously needing something to do.

Nodding his assent, "you do down here, I'll do upstairs."

Parting ways, Wyatt heard Daniel and Matilda dividing the rooms between them, as he leapt up the stairs. Scanning the hallway quickly, then heading straight for the master bedroom. Nothing appeared to be disturbed, but not put off Wyatt began a sweep of the room. He hadn't gone far when something partially obscured underneath the rocking chair caught his eye. Bending down he ran his hand along and scooped up the tiny object. Lifting it up he recognized it immediately, and instantly knew that Tessa had been right all along. Someone *had* done something to Parker, and now that same person probably had Tessa too.

Sprinting down the stairs, "Daniel! Matilda!"

Both Matilda and Daniel met him at the bottom of the stairs, panic written all over their faces.

"What?" Matilda asked.

"I found this in Tessa's room," holding up the tiny camera. "They're probably all over the house."

Daniel turned white. So white that Wyatt reached out a hand to steady him in case he fainted. "Someone's been watching her?"

"She was right. Someone did take Parker, and I think it's Caleb . . ."

Face shifting to bright red in a second, "I knew there was something strange about that guy, but Tessa wouldn't listen, she never listens . . ."

"Daniel, Daniel," Wyatt tried to calm him down, they didn't have time for hysteria right now. "We need to focus if we're going to find them." Leading Daniel and Matilda into the living room, "we need to figure out who Caleb Brighton really is."

Shrugging fitfully, "he told Tessa he was an old friend of Parker's, from when they were in foster care together . . ."

Knitting her brow, "the Caleb Brighton that we knew in foster care died when he was fourteen," Matilda explained. "I know because we were best friends."

"It has something to do with your past . . ." Wyatt started.

"And he knows that Matilda will recognize him because whenever he thinks Matilda is coming he leaves, like at the party yesterday," Daniel filled in.

"Describe him to me."

"He has sandy blonde hair, the bluest eyes I've ever seen, masses of freckles . . . whoa," Daniel grabbed Matilda as she swayed and lowered her down to the sofa, crouching in front of her. "Do you know him?"

Matilda didn't answer.

Shaking her, "Matilda, do you know him?" Daniel repeated sharply.

"Take it easy," Wyatt cautioned with a hand on Daniel's shoulder, then knelt down and gently turned Matilda's face so that she was looking at him, "Mattie, who is it?"

Blinking, the motion making a sea of tears well up in her eyes, "it sounds like Lachlan."

Trying to place the name, "Lachlan?"

"Lachlan Mountain Junior."

The name finally clicking, "the son of the man who you . . ."

She nodded, "the son of the man who I killed," she finished, the tears breaking through and beginning to tumble out.

"So he's planning on getting revenge on you by hurting Tessa," Daniel said, probably a little more vehemently than he intended.

"I'm sorry," Matilda cried immediately.

"It's not your fault," Wyatt told her, looking to Daniel and waiting for him to confirm this.

"It's not your fault, Matilda," Daniel echoed, somewhat half-heartedly.

"Do you know where he could be?" Wyatt asked, needing to keep them focused.

Dragging in a shaky breath, "I know where he used to live. When we were kids Parker and I used to talk about Lachlan Junior all the time, wonder how he was coping without his father. After we were adopted we went to his house a couple of times, never to talk to him always just to watch. He was a kid, like us, and we always felt sorry for him, I always felt so bad about what I did to him, to his father, to his family . . ." throwing herself against Daniel's chest she began to weep.

"I should have listened to her, Wyatt," Daniel whispered mournfully, seemingly oblivious to the sobbing woman he held in his arms.

"We all should have," he tried to console, but feeling every bit as guilty as Daniel did.

"Yeah but I'm her big brother," absently rubbing circles on Matilda's back.

"Matilda, I need the address." Glancing up at him she took the piece of paper he handed her and jotted down an address that was at least an hour's drive away. "Alright I'm gonna call for back up and head out there . . ."

"I'm coming with you," Daniel practically shouted.

"Me too," Matilda put in, brushing away teardrops.

"Uh uh, no way," Wyatt told them firmly as he stood and started for the door. "I have enough to worry about with your brother, and your sister, I don't need to be worrying about you two as well."

With that he jumped into his car and sped off down the road, praying ceaselessly that he wasn't already too late.

* * * * *

4:42 A.M.

"Tessa! Tess, come on. Wake up. You're scaring me. Come on, sweetheart, wake up now . . ."

The voice slowly cut through the fog. Latching onto it, she let it slowly pull her out.

"Come on, honey, wake up for me . . ."

Groaning she tried to lift open heavy eyelids.

"Tess?" excitement pushing away the fear in his voice. "Tessa, can you hear me?"

Managing a small moan in answer, her head felt like it was full of burning coals.

"Baby, open your eyes for me," the insistent command finally spurred her into action.

Lifting her head, the first thing she saw was her husband's beaming face. "Parker," mustering up a smile for him. Taking in his thin face, covered with a scrappy beard and moustache, his wavy black hair longer and wilder than usual, she felt tears welling up, "I'm sorry."

At the same time Parker uttered the same words, "I'm sorry."

"I should have told you about the baby as soon as I found out, but I was scared, I didn't know how I felt about it," she explained.

"And I should have told you that I knew, but I freaked out too." Grin growing wider, "you are a sight for sore eyes." His gaze shifting slightly to her temple, "are you okay?"

Wincing as she became more aware of the slicing pain in her head, "I'm okay. Now I'll have matching scars," she joked, referring to the scar on her other temple from a previous encounter with a maniac. "Maybe letting him knock me out wasn't the smartest move, but it was the only way I could think of to get him to bring me here." For the first time she actually took in her surroundings. They appeared to be in a cellar or basement, there were no windows, one wall was covered with TV screens and Tessa remembered the camera's that had been found in her and Parker's home. Turning worried eyes to Parker, "are *you* okay?"

"I'm fine, better now that you're here." His gold eyes growing fierce, "did Lachlan hurt you?"

Knowing instinctively what he was asking about, she shook her head, "he didn't rape me, but he had cameras all over the house." Unable to meet her husband's eye, "even in the bathroom."

"I know," Parker nodded with tightly controlled rage.

"Wait," steadying the tremble in her voice as she realized what he'd said before, "Lachlan?"

"Lachlan Mountain Junior, a.k.a Caleb Brighton, the son of the man that Matilda accidentally shot when we were kids," Parker filled her in. "Can you get free?"

When Caleb, Lachlan apparently, had brought her in here he had tied her to a chair, her ankles were bound to the front legs, her wrists behind her back tied together palms facing outwards. Smiling at Parker, "you know one of the benefits of being paranoid is that you're always prepared for the worst."

Focusing all her attention on twisting her hands around so that her palms were now facing together, ignoring how the rope ripped and tore at her flesh. Aware of Parker intently watching her slow progress, "got it," she announced triumphantly, managing to free the tiny metal blade from the band of her watch. Then with her thin fingers she began to saw at her bonds, oblivious to the little cuts that began to dot her hands each time the razor slipped.

Finally the ropes came away, "I'm free," she told Parker, almost giddy with relief, but when she brought her hands around and saw the blood smeared on them she felt her heart clench. The walls began to close in on her, the room seemed to drain of oxygen, she couldn't breathe, couldn't think, couldn't move . . .

"Tessa, Tess, it's okay. Honey, it's alright. Don't look at it, just look at me, just focus on me . . ."

Once again Parker's calm voice cut through her terror fuelled haze, and she held onto it, letting it slowly guide her out. As soon as she had regained some composure, she opened her eyes and raised her head, meeting Parker's eye.

"You okay?"

She nodded, not quite trusting herself to speak yet, then went to work untying her ankles. Her shaking, bloody fingers made for slow progress, but at last the ropes fell away and she stood on wobbly legs. Tessa had to clutch the back of the chair in order to remain upright as wave after wave of dizziness buffeted her. Taking a tentative step towards the cage where Parker was imprisoned, when her legs held she quickly crossed to her husband, who reached his arms between the bars and pulled her closer.

"I love you, you know that right?" he queried anxiously, brushing her hair away from the blood that she could feel caked to her face.

"I know you love me, I never doubted it. I knew you would never leave me intentionally," she assured him, and reached through the bars to pull his face down to hers, kissing him deeply, not wanting to break contact with him.

Pulling back, "what I said to you that night, I didn't mean it. I was scared and confused and I took it out on you. I regretted the words the second I said them," his eyes were imploring, begging for forgiveness.

"I know you didn't mean to hurt me . . ."

"But I did," he insisted, "and I'm sorry."

"Let's just forget all about everything that happened and just focus on getting out of here. Do you know where the keys are?"

"Lachlan keeps a set by the door," Parker gestured over to a key ring containing three old fashioned round keys.

Releasing Parker's hand, she hurried over to them and was reaching out to lift them off the hook, when the basement door swung open.

"I don't think so," Lachlan smiled at them.

The three of them stood staring at one another, then Tessa decided to risk it. If she could get Parker out then they had a chance of getting out of here. Lunging for the key ring, she was about to launch it across the room, but before she could, Lachlan was tackling her to the ground, the keys sliding along the floor and coming to rest, uselessly, in the middle of the room.

"It's over, Lachlan," she told him, as he wrapped an arm across her chest and yanked her to her feet.

"I see your husband filled you in on our history," Lachlan stated conversationally.

"Let her go, Lachlan, this has nothing to do with her and you'll still have me," Parker bargained.

"It doesn't matter anyway, Skylar should be on his way here by now," Tessa goaded confidently.

"He has no idea where we are, or that I'm even involved, in fact he has no reason to think of me at all," Lachlan shot back.

Shaking her head with mock sadness, "you don't know me at all, Lachlan."

"Tessa always has a plan," Parker added.

"When I didn't get home last night my brother would have called Skylar, who would have rushed right over. At first, he would have thought I'd hurt myself, but guilt would have made him check the house over anyway. He would have found one of the cameras you hid all over my home, I made sure one was left behind for him to stumble upon. He would have known that something happened to me, he already doesn't like or trust you, he would have spoken with Matilda and they would have put it all together," she finished smugly. "It's over."

Pausing for a beat, "you're right," Lachlan agreed, "it is over. I had hoped to keep Parker alive a little longer, but it seems I might have to move up that stage of my plan. I'll just get you out of the way for the moment," Lachlan started to drag her back towards the chair, "and then I'll finish off your husband. Still allergic to penicillin, Parker?" he asked patting his pocket.

Lachlan almost had her to the chair when she managed to twist free from his grasp, making a dive for the keys. Unfortunately Lachlan recovered quickly, grabbed her arm and swung her around, slamming a fist into her stomach. The force of the blow sent her sprawling to the ground, her already aching head smacking against the concrete floor, and she literally saw stars. Great big colorful stars that danced around her head before they burst into confetti and disappeared.

"Tessa!" Parker screamed her name.

She wanted to answer but her vision went blurry, white spots replacing the stars, bouncing merrily in front of her eyes, making her nauseous. Cramping pains, emanating from her stomach, stretched out tentacles to every corner of her body. She was vaguely aware of someone lifting her, carrying her, of someone screaming and another voice mockingly calm, and then everything was gone.

* * * * *

7:12 A.M.

"If you lay a hand on her . . ."

That was Parker's voice, and Wyatt thanked God that his friend was still alive.

"Lay a hand on her?" another voice, presumably Lachlan Mountain, asked incredulously. "I'm going to lay my hands all over her. Don't you get it yet? After I kill you, Tessa and I are going to have the family that you ripped away from me. Tessa is going to be my wife and we are going to be together forever."

Hovering at the door, waiting to time his entry perfectly, Wyatt heard a clunk and then metal scraping against metal, and brought his hand to the door handle.

"Time to say goodbye, Parker, it's a pity your wife isn't able to watch you die. Never mind I can give her the play by play later, when we're alone together."

Knowing it was now or never, Wyatt leveled his gun in front of him and swung open the door, "police. Freeze, Lachlan."

Both Lachlan's and Parker's heads swiveled around to face him. Wyatt quickly surveyed his surroundings, the poorly lit room, the row of monitors, the metal cage with a thin mattress on the floor. Tessa tied to a chair her head drooping down against her chest, and Lachlan who maneuvered Parker in front of him like a human shield and held a syringe to his neck.

"It's over, Lachlan," Wyatt said calmly, making sure not to meet Parker's eye because he needed to keep a level head and his emotions in check. "This place is going to be swarming with cops any second now."

Looking back at him with equal calm, "move an inch and he's dead," wiggling the syringe.

Wyatt didn't know what was in it, but even an empty syringe could cause a potentially fatal air embolism. Taking a cautious step forward, "let them go, Lachlan, it's not too late to end this positively, and we can get you the help that you need."

Laughing merrily, "I've already got all the help I need. All those years I dreamed about revenge, and it was just as sweet as I imagined. Making Matilda suffer, making her think she'd lost the one person she loved. Watching Parker squirm as I got closer and closer to his wife, it was all magical . . ."

While Lachlan babbled on Wyatt inched closer, aware of the silent presence behind him. "The only way you're walking out of here alive, Lachlan, is if you let Parker go," he reasoned.

"I'm never going to let him go," came the heated reply.

"You don't have the guts to kill me," Parker spoke up. "You go on and on about how Matilda killed your father, but you have no idea what it did to her, what taking a life, even in self defense, did to her. The nightmares, the flashbacks, the overwhelming guilt that prevented her from loving anyone because she didn't think she deserved to be happy. I've taken a life before, Lachlan, it haunts you, you never forget it, you don't have the guts to kill me, if you did you would have done it already."

With an angry snarl, Lachlan plunged the syringe into Parker's shoulder.

Wyatt fired off a shot, and both Lachlan and Parker dropped to the floor, neither of them moved. "He's down," he called over his shoulder, as the room suddenly filled with people. A couple of officers went to secure Lachlan, EMT's behind them to check over Parker. Wyatt headed straight for Tessa, dropping down at her side, "Tessa? It's Wyatt. You with me?"

"Skylar?" she asked weakly

Tilting up her face and examining the gash on her head, "it's me, I'm here, you're safe now, you're going to be fine." Releasing her to begin work on the ropes that bound her to the chair, pausing when the second lot of medics bounded down the stairs.

"Over here," the officer keeping pressure on Lachlan's chest wound called.

"Hey," he yelled, "Tessa needs help."

"He's bleeding to death, Wyatt," one of the other officers reminded him gently.

"He's a scumbag," he countered disbelievingly. "He kidnapped two people and tried to kill Parker. Tessa's a victim."

"That's not how it works, Wyatt, you know that."

"Another ambulance should be here any minute," the older of the EMT's consoled sympathetically.

With a scowl he twisted back to Tessa who was staring at him, her eyes clouded with shock and pain. "Everything's going to be okay," he assured her, somehow managing to keep his voice gentle despite his wildly pounding heart and overwhelming guilt.

"Penicillin," she mumbled back softly.

Puzzled, "what?"

"Parker, he's allergic," she elaborated.

"The syringe?" when she nodded he yelled over his shoulder to the paramedics, "Lachlan gave Parker a shot of penicillin, he's allergic." Attention returning to Tessa, who had closed her eyes, "you still with me, Tess?" he checked as he continued with the knots. She moaned quietly, but didn't seem to have the strength to answer further. As the last knot slid undone and the ropes fell away, he moved to pick her up but froze when he saw the blood. "Tessa, you're bleeding," Wyatt grabbed her chin and shook gently till she opened her eyes and looked at him. "You're bleeding," he repeated.

"The baby," she whispered. "I think I'm losing the baby."

Springing into action, "hold on, just stay with me," he urged, as he swung Tessa into his arms and rushed up the stairs.

"Parker . . ."

"Don't try to talk, just rest," he cautioned. "Parker will be fine, I'll stay with him."

"I can't lose him, Skylar," she implored, her hands folding themselves into his jacket.

"You won't lose him," he reassured with more confidence than he felt.

"Wyatt!" J.J. met them at the top of the first flight of stairs, eyeing Tessa worriedly, "is she okay?"

"Miscarriage. Head injury."

"Parker?"

"Anaphylaxis," he answered quickly, anxious to get Tessa to the hospital and to check on his friend.

J.J.'s gaze moved to something behind him, and moments later a pair of medics carrying Lachlan Mountain Junior came barreling past. "He going to make it?"

Shrugging, "fifty, fifty," the EMT answered as they continued by.

"Take her upstairs, another ambulance should be here any second," Wyatt handed Tessa to J.J. but she kept her hands twisted in his shirt.

"I need to see Parker," she pleaded.

Gently uncurling her bloody fingers, "you need to go to the hospital, honey." Watching her sink down into J.J.'s arms as though she were a hot water bottle that someone had let the water out of. "J.J. will stay with you and I'll stay with Parker, I promise," tenderly stroking her hair, and wondering how he was going to make up for not believing her.

Nodding to J.J., who cast him a last worried look, before dashing up the rest of the stairs and disappearing from view. Back in the basement, Wyatt almost collided with the EMT's who had an unconscious Parker in tow. His eyes were closed, a tube down his throat that one of the medics was using to bag him.

"It's just a precaution," the closer medic explained, "he went into anaphylactic shock, we gave him a shot of adrenalin, he's stable for now but we need to get moving."

Stepping out of their way, Wyatt's gaze drifted to Tessa's bloody handprints on his shirt, and then fell to the huge dark puddle on the floor. Parker's words echoing in his head, taking a life left you haunted. He knew it was true, but this time he wished that the bullet he'd fired *had* ended Lachlan Mountain Junior's life.

Deliberately turning his back, remembering what he'd told Lila Abbott, the only way to let go of the past was to focus on the future, he was going to follow the ambulance to the hospital and do just that.

JUNE 30TH

12:29 P.M.

"I don't see why *I* had to spend the night here," Tessa whined as she curled up on the hospital bed beside him.

"Because your system was pumped full of drugs, you have a concussion, and . . ." he paused and pulled his wife closer against him, then continued gently, "and you had a miscarriage." Feeling Tessa stiffen, Parker didn't know how to help her deal with what had happened, wasn't even sure how he felt about it yet. He wasn't happy that their child was dead, but he did know that he and Tessa weren't ready to be parents. "Do you want to talk about it?"

Her head bobbed back and forth against his shoulder. "I'm fine," she gave him her usual answer but without her usual vigor.

Leaving her be for the moment, Parker knew from experience that Tessa wouldn't deal with anything she wasn't ready to. They'd already had a barrage of visitors this morning. Every one of them had spent the majority of the time profusely apologizing for believing that he had walked out on them. He had to admit he had been hurt that all his friends and family had thought the worst of him. But given his behavior before his abduction he couldn't blame them, and after almost dying, he didn't want to waste time on anger. He just wanted to enjoy being back with the people he loved. Now all he longed for was to go home, unwind under a steaming shower, and fall into his own bed with his wife in his arms.

"Wyatt's coming to pick us up soon," he commented to Tessa. Enjoying the feel of her hair in his fingers, her body melded closely against his, for a while he had been convinced he would

281

never hold her again.

"I wish he'd killed Lachlan," Tessa stated vehemently.

Tightening his grip on her trembling form and lifting a hand to trace the old scar on her temple. The usual ripple of anger and fear in his stomach when he thought of the man who wanted Tessa dead so badly he would attempt to burn her alive.

"The same way I wish *he* was dead." She went completely still in his arms, barely breathing. "You went to him didn't you? To help you find me?" Mildly surprised when instead of shrinking away from him, as she usually did, she burrowed closer into him, grabbing his hand and wrapping his arms even tighter around her. "What did you give him in return?" he pressed. But Tessa was saved from having to produce a reply when a knock sounded on the door. Kissing the top of Tessa's head Parker felt her relax into him, balancing on his elbows, "come in," he called to whoever was at the door.

It swung slowly open and Lila Abbott peeked nervously around. "Detective Bell," she smiled at him.

Smiling back, noting the light that now shone in her eyes, she looked a lot more alive than the last time he'd seen her. "Call me Parker."

She nodded, "and you must be Tessa." Lila tried to hide her flinch as she took in Tessa's battered face, her hand raising subconsciously to brush her own head, no doubt remembering the attack that had left her in the hospital and her son dead. Parker may have been the one who almost died at Lachlan's hands, but Tessa was the one who had come out of it all looking the worse for wear, with an ugly black bruise covering most of one side of her face, the neatly stitched gash standing out across her temple.

Tessa sat slowly, still dizzy from the blow to her head that had left her with a concussion, and gave Lila a warm smile, "and I'm guessing you're Lila Abbott."

Lila ventured a few more steps into the room. "Sorry to

intrude, but I heard what happened and I just wanted to come and see that you were both okay. I also heard . . ." pausing and shifting uncomfortably from foot to foot, "about your baby. I'm sorry."

Wrapping a comforting arm around Tessa's shoulders when she shrunk into him. "Thanks, we appreciate that."

Coming the rest of the way into the room and taking the chair beside the bed. "I just wanted to come and say thank you, for everything that you did for my family," Lila's face grew serious.

Rising the rest of the way up and swinging his legs over the side of the bed. Tessa moved with him, climbing into his lap and entwining his arms tightly around her, and Parker realized just how much things had changed while he was gone. Tessa never voluntarily came to him for comfort, sometimes even refused it when he offered it since she was so used to dealing with things on her own. Now she was terrified to be away from him in case he disappeared again.

"I didn't really do anything," Parker focused back on Lila, "it was Wyatt who found your daughter and brought her home to you."

"You did a lot," Lila contradicted fiercely. "You tried to save Joey. You did everything you could to find Molly. And you . . ." looking shyly away, "you made me feel like there was a part of Joey still alive."

"You look like you're doing a lot better," he encouraged.

"I talked to Wyatt, he told me about his daughter, about what it was like after she died," she explained.

"It helps to talk about things," Parker agreed, as much for his wife's benefit as Lila Abbott's.

"Things aren't perfect yet, but at least I feel like there's light at the end of the tunnel." She gave a wan smile, "I don't want to wake up one day and realize that I've lost Eric and Molly too, that I'm all alone."

"Knock, knock," Eric Abbott pushed open the door. "I

wondered where you'd gotten to," he crossed to Lila and kissed her cheek, for a moment she stiffened but then she relaxed into him.

"I came to say thank you to Detective Bell, for everything he did for us," Lila told her husband.

Vigorously nodding his agreement, "you gave Lila comfort when she needed it the most, and for that I'll always be grateful. I don't know how I'll ever be able to repay you."

Eric teared up, and for a minute Parker thought he was going to cry. Tightening his hold on Tessa, "we're even," he told the doctor, "since you took such wonderful care of my wife yesterday." When he and Tessa had been brought to the hospital yesterday morning it had been Eric Abbott who had ended up treating Tessa.

Controlling his emotions, Dr Abbott turned to Tessa, "Lila wasn't the only one I lost, how about we go and give you a last check over before I officially give you permission to go home. Oh, Detective Bell, I think Dr Marco is on his way in to give you the once over before he lets you out of here too."

"It was nice to meet you, Lila. When everything settles down you'll have to come over and have dinner with me and Parker one day," Tessa smiled at Lila.

"I'd like that," Lila smiled back.

As Tessa stood, both he and Eric Abbott watched her warily in case she swayed. This earned them both a frustrated scowl, "you know I have been walking since I was nine months old," Tess snapped.

Eric gave an easy chuckle and took Tessa's arm regardless, "you know it looks bad for me if my patients faint while I'm right by their side."

Parker grinned and ruffled Tessa's hair, "I'll meet you downstairs, okay?"

Relenting with a huff, Tessa allowed Eric to help her to the door. "Lila, you coming?" Eric paused.

"Actually," Parker jumped in, "I just wanted to talk to her for a moment."

Dr Abbott shrugged, "Molly's with Teya when you're ready," he told her before leading Tessa from the room.

Once they were alone Parker stood and faced Lila Abbott, "I need to thank you too."

"Me?" Lila blinked in surprise. "What did I do for you?"

"When I was thinking of throwing my life away, you made me realize how important family is."

Beaming with pride, but a little doubtful, "I really helped you?" she asked as though she didn't think that was possible.

"Yeah you really did."

"I better go get Molly, it's time for a feed," Lila gave him another shy smile, before skittering to the door. "It's like we both got a second chance. I have Eric and Molly, you have Tessa, even after all we lost we still have a chance at having everything we dreamed of."

As he lay back down in bed while Dr Marco gave him a final examination, he thought of the words that Tessa had spoken to him six months ago. When he had been pressuring her to deal with her past, she had told him that if she focused all her energy on the past, then it would end up destroying her. Instead, she had told him, she wanted to focus on the future. Lila was right, they *had* all been given a second chance and he intended to make the most of it.

JULY 4TH

11:56 P.M.

They lay side by side on the soft grass on the back lawn of the estate she had inherited from her grandparents, watching the last of the fireworks. The oppressive heat had finally cracked and the sky was quickly filling with dark thunderclouds, a storm was on the way. Tessa entwined her fingers with Parker's and wiggled closer, she pressed her ear to his shoulder and curled her body as close as she could to his.

"I'm right here, baby," Parker whispered soothingly in her ear, his voice a deep rumble in his chest. "I'm not going anywhere."

Tessa couldn't prevent a shiver rocketing through her as she remembered seeing her husband in the hospital after Lachlan had sent him into anaphylactic shock. For a second she had been convinced that she was going to lose him and it had felt like a trapdoor had opened beneath her and she was plummeting down into a bottomless pit.

She didn't realize she was whimpering until Parker's arms encompassed her. Whispering in her ear once again, "shh, it's okay, sweetheart, everything's going to be okay. I promise."

She wanted to believe that.

Wanted desperately to believe his promises that everything would be okay.

But when they first started dating Parker had promised her he wouldn't ever leave her, and he had.

Tessa knew she was being unfair, irrational even. Parker hadn't left her of his own accord. But right now she didn't care if it was logical or not, because just like everyone else in her life he *had* left, and now for the first time in a lot of years she found herself petrified. She'd been scared before, but usually she just painted over it with another emotion, usually anger. This time however she seemed unable to come up with anything other that terror.

When she and Parker had first gotten together the thing that she had been the most worried about was that she would become too dependent on him, and in the last few days she found herself freaking out whenever he left her sight. The day after they came home from the hospital she had urged Parker to go back to work, knowing that it was important for him to continue on with things as normal. For the first hour or two she had held it together But then the pressure of being alone in her home, her home which had been invaded by Lachlan Mountain Junior and his cameras, had become overwhelming. Daniel had found her cowering in a corner of the bedroom, about an inch away from a full-blown panic attack. Parker had come straight home and hadn't left her side ever since.

Still the panic continued to pound down on her. Whenever her husband wasn't directly in her sight, whenever she thought about how close she had come to losing him, whenever she thought about how easily something could happen to him in the future. Her sleep was plagued with nightmares where she kept losing Parker again and again, each time in a way more horrendous than the last.

Deliberately separating herself from her husband Tessa sat and crossed her legs. Focusing her attention on the dull light of the moon, as it slowly became covered by layer after layer of thick clouds.

Parker left her for a moment, and then moved behind her. "Talk to me, Tessa," he implored as he began to rub her shoulders.

Suppressing a sigh, Parker should know by now that she didn't talk about things, that the way she dealt with them was to concentrate all her energy onto pretending they never happened.

When she didn't respond he pressed further, "are you thinking about the baby?"

Shivering as she thought of the baby they had lost. Tessa wasn't quite sure how she felt about it, she knew that they weren't ready for a child just now, but she had become accustomed to the idea that there was another human being growing inside of her. At the time she had been too preoccupied with her missing husband to spend too much time thinking about being pregnant. However, now that the baby was gone she found herself missing it and realized that she had in fact become attached to it.

"We can get pregnant again," Parker continued. "If you want a baby now we can . . ."

"I don't think we're ready for a child," she interrupted, sensing the relief radiating off Parker. "Anyway I wasn't thinking about the baby." Debating how much to tell him, "I can't go back there," she found herself blurting out.

"Can't go back where?" Parker quizzed.

"To that house, to our house, I can't go back there after everything that happened."

"Okay," Parker agreed, "we'll look for a new house."

"I want to stay here." Tessa felt him freeze.

"You hate it here," he protested weakly. "This is where your mother almost killed you, this is where you nearly died in a fire."

"I can't go back to that house," she repeated firmly. Even the thought of being back inside the house where Lachlan had watched her every move with his myriad of hidden cameras made her feel nauseous.

"Alright," Parker relented, resuming massaging her shoulders. "We can stay here for a while."

The wind picked up as they both lapsed into silence, the heavy presence of rain in the air. Tessa was starting to doze off, the rhythmic rubbing on her back lulling her off to sleep, when an almighty crash ripped apart the night and a torrent of rain cascaded down from the black sky.

Parker sprung to his feet, bringing her with him, and began tugging her towards the cover of the trees. But Tessa wormed her way free and spread out her arms, tilting her face up so that it caught the full force of the rain. Soaked to the skin in seconds, the icy water refreshed her, making her feel alive, and she began to twirl around in circles drinking in as much of the rain as was possible

Parker laughed at her, but then came to join her, and they both spun and spun until they were so dizzy they collapsed in a heap on the wet grass. Parker rolled her on top of him and she tucked her head under his chin, relishing just being together.

Losing all track of time, they could have being lying there for minutes or hours, when the spell was broken by the trilling of her cell phone. Reluctantly sliding back down to the muddy ground, she wiggled it out from her pocket and her heart plummeted when she saw who the caller was.

It was time to face the music.

It had been inevitable from the moment she had sought him out for help. As she slid her finger along the iPhone's screen to answer, Tessa wondered just what the price of having her husband back would be.

Jane has loved reading and writing since she can remember. She writes dark and disturbing crime/mystery/suspense with some romance thrown in because, well, who doesn't love romance?! She has several series including the complete Detective Parker Bell series, the Count to Ten series, the Christmas Mysteries series, and the Flashes of Fate series of novelettes.

When she's not writing Jane loves to read, bake, go to the beach, ski, horse ride, and watch Disney movies. She has a black belt in Taekwondo, a 200+ collection of teddy bears, and her favorite color is pink. She has the world's two most sweet and pretty Dalmatians, Ivory and Pearl. Oh, and she also enjoys spending time with family and friends!

For more information please visit any of the following –

Amazon – http://www.amazon.com/author/janeblythe
BookBub – https://www.bookbub.com/authors/jane-blythe
Email – mailto:janeblytheauthor@gmail.com
Facebook – http://www.facebook.com/janeblytheauthor
Goodreads – http://www.goodreads.com/author/show/6574160.Jane_Blythe
Reader Group – http://www.facebook.com/groups/janeskillersweethearts
Twitter – http://www.twitter.com/jblytheauthor
Website – http://www.janeblythe.com.au

sic enim dilexit Deus mundum ut Filium suum unigenitum daret ut omnis qui credit in eum habeat vitam aeternam